MECHANICS OF LIFE

E. G. GADDESS

This is a work of fiction.

Names, characters, businesses, places, events, or incidents are either the products of the author's imagination or used in a fictitious manner. Any resemblance to actual person, living or dead, or actual events is purely coincidental.

The Mechanics of Life

Cover art from iStock: © Irina Braga

Cover design by: portfolio.mo
(http://www.portfolimo.com/)

This book uses OpenDyslexic font from www.opendyslexic.org

ISBN 13: 978-1-938215-89-6 (OpenDyslexic)
ISBN 13: 978-1-938215-90-2 (Déjà vu)
ISBN 13: 978-1-938215-91-9 (Mobipocket)
ISBN 13: 978-1-938215-92-6 (EPub)

Quillian's log

Surgery was brutal today.

A young man of eighteen who'd lost his leg somehow (I didn't quite make out his story - seemed a bit patchy to me) arrived just before midnight. His leg was gone, half-way up his thigh, and he needed a temporary prosthetic leg put on while Dr. M made up a mechanical one that would fit. He was scrawny, with ragged clothes, smelling like he worked at the docks.

I guess the docks and piers are a rough place. We've seen a lot coming in from there lately. Most of them dirty and skinny and raggedy.

This bloke's stump was still bloody, the skin hanging in thready bits around the meat and bone. Maybe he fought back.

I got to do a bit of the attaching this go round. I think Dr. M might even let me do some of the mechanical leg when he comes back for that.

1

In the cramped attic bedroom stuck under the rafters, the pendulum ticked its final countdown and the clock's hammer tapped the small brass bell five times. Quillian groaned and turned away, covering her ears with her goose-feather pillow. Gusting out a sigh, she sat up, reaching out to the clock, pushing in the lever that would stop the alarm.

"Hey, Patch." The calico cat purred somewhere among the folds atop her bed. The quilt was old, its edges soft and feathered, the teal and brown and gold squares faded. Quillian's feet stuck out from the bottom if she stretched, so she slept curled in a ball—except in the heat and humidity of a deep Norfolk summer, when the quilt stayed in a neat square at the foot of her bed.

Patch was an amalgamation of white, black-tabby and marmalade, with what looked like a seam running the length of his back and down his tail, broken only by the brass buckle and leather strap that kept his mechanical back legs in place.

Quillian shifted and the cat rolled with her, the windup that worked its rear prosthetic whirring down. She wormed her hand beneath the blanket and found the cat, scratching it softly behind the ears before gently rewinding its key. Patch purred and slitted her yellow-green eyes, moving her head in an attempt to follow Quillian's hand.

"Watson!"

Jerking, her fingers gripped into the cat's fur; Quillian threw the pillow aside and kicked her quilt down. "Coming!"

Patch hissed and jumped to the foot of the bed, curling the front of its body around the near-straight mechanicals of its back end. She laid her tail straight out, only the tip flicking up and down, like a fisherman jerking a lure through the water.

"I'm sorry, Patch. You know how it is." Quillian rammed one leg then the other into the skirt of her stained tan cotton dress, pulling it up over the corset and slip she'd dropped to bed in, exhausted, in the wee hours of the morning. The dress smelled of blood and bleach. She wished she had time to bathe, even to wash her face, but she'd been summoned. She shoved her feet into her brown leather work boots, not bothering with the buckles, grabbing her dirty apron from the back of a wobbly, slat-backed chair.

"Watson!"

Groaning, yawning behind one slim freckled hand, Quillian ran down the polished oak stairs, tripping when she nearly lost a boot half-way down. She caught herself on the white-painted banister and shoved her foot back in. She skipped the last three risers and spun to run down the hall, boots clomping with every step.

"Watson! Where the devil are you?"

Panting, Quillian opened the surgery door. "Right here, sir."

"Ah." Dr. M looked up from the gleaming surgery table he was examining, his thin, whiskered jowls quivering. He wore his white laboratory coat open over tweed pants and buttoned brown vest. His shirt was white, the top button undone, showing the barest wisp of gray chest hair.

Quillian suspected that he could no longer fasten the top button; he'd gained weight these last few months. It looked good on his normally rod-thin frame. She didn't dare mention such though; it was not the proper thing for an apprentice to notice.

Dr. M ran one hand over the surface of the shiny, but stained, steel. The metal had a couple of pock marks in its surface and long scratches ran its length. The veins on the back of Dr. M's hand stood stark blue against the transparent paleness of the skin that covered it. "I don't believe this table was properly cleaned last night."

"You said I could bleach it this morning, sir, after our emergency patient came in so late last evening." Quillian stood straight, knees and ankles together, hands tight fists at her sides. She blew at a stray more-blonde-than-red kink that fell in front of her face.

"Yes, I did," Dr. M stood, the magnifying monocle over his left eye enlarging it to the point that Quillian could see the fine blood vessels in the white of it, "and it is morning now."

"Only just past five, sir."

Dr. M looked at Quillian, blinking the one enlarged eye. The monocle highlighted the wrinkles in his face, making them deeper where the brass casing pressed against the skin. The leather strap that held it in place mussed his straight white hair, making it stand up with static at the back of his head.

Quillian wasn't sure how old Dr. M was, but she knew he was older than Huddy, and Huddy was old enough to have grandchildren Quillian's age—though she didn't—and Quillian knew better than to ever ask either of them for specifics.

"I'll get it bleached right away, sir."

"Very good." Dr. M nodded and strode through the door, letting the thick wood slam shut.

Groaning beneath her breath lest the doctor hear her, Quillian threw her dirty apron into a large brass barrel used for collecting them and pulled a pristine one from the mahogany cabinet next to it. Slipping it over her head, she tied it round her waist whilst yawning.

The odor of bacon and eggs and fresh-baked bread seeped through the thin opening at the bottom of the door. It came from the kitchens down the hall and made Quillian's stomach rumble. She knew, however, that she could not sate her hunger until the metal surgery table was better than spotless.

The heavy brass bucket clanged against the deep porcelain sink. Water rushed from the hot tap, the steam rising to curl the shorter tendrils of hair; the spirals of hair around her face were lighter than the pure copper-red of the ringlets in back. The steam caused her cheeks to pinken, temporarily camouflaging her freckles.

Cranking the valve to off, Quillian pulled the bleach pipe over the bucket and turned the spigot, allowing a good amount of bleach to mix with the water. When her nose hairs started to wither, she shut off the bleach.

She donned her thick rubber gloves and grabbed a hard-bristled brush, dunking the brush in the water and scrubbing at the metal slab. Blood had seeped into the tiny seams and scratches and dried, and Quillian needed a metal wire brush to get the worst of it out. She had to rinse twice to remove it completely.

Water splotched the wooden slats that formed the floor, beading on the thick layer of wax. It, too, showed the wear and tear of the years, stain and bleach lending it a mottled dappling of mahogany and tan.

When no trace of blood remained on the table, Quillian bent to examine it from an angle, checking for any stain that she might have missed. She saw nothing, but ran the wire brush once more over it, just to make certain. If Dr. M found anything amiss when he rechecked it later, she'd be done for.

Satisfied, she dropped the brushes in the bucket and set the bucket in the sink. The brushes could sit for a while; there was still enough bleach in there to sanitize them.

Breakfast was cold by the time Quillian got to eat, the eggs congealed and the bacon no longer crisp. Only the heels of the bread loaf remained. She didn't care. She was hungry enough to lick the grease from the bacon pan if that was all that was left.

Huddy offered Quillian a fresh pot of tea, though, and tisked over her, fussing a bit about her hair. The housekeeper ran her thin, brown fingers through the messy curls, smoothing them, only to have them pop back up. Huddy's own hair was curlier than Quillian's, but cut close to her head, more gray now than black.

"He really shouldn't work you so hard."

"'tis fine, Huddy. I like hard work. And he pays me. Most apprentices in the city don't, you know."

The housekeeper sniffed and spooned sugar into Quillian's teacup, refilling it to its gold-leaf brim. She pulled a rag from her apron pocket and wiped at the gleaming table, her lean arms on display in the short-sleeved, yellow-printed blouse, lean and strong from kitchen work. She performed the same, slanted inspection that Quillian had used in the surgery. "Didn't used to be like that. It's decent I suppose, but the hours..."

"There are worse places to work, Huddy, worse hours to work. Leave it be." Quillian slathered butter onto the last heel of bread. "I'll bring my dishes in when I'm done."

Huddy sighed. "I know there's worse, chile. That I do." She patted Quillian's hair one last time, trying to tuck an erstwhile kink under a pin, before disappearing into the kitchens to begin preparations for lunch.

From the journal of G. J. Holmes

I am settling nicely into my new room. Father and mother have no idea where I am, and according to Reginald, assistant to the family solicitor, I am not cut off from my allowance yet. The family solicitor, the honorable Mr. Whitley, wasn't impressed by our contract, but admitted it was sound.

I can trust Reggie with the transfer of my allowance to my own accounts...the last name Holmes would sour his reputation in a native drum beat if I took to the papers. And since he aspires to one day open his own accounting office, it behooves him to be honest.

And I know he won't tell father where I am staying for that very same reason. Accountants and solicitors that don't keep the secrets of their clients soon find themselves devoid of those same clients.

Because if father ever finds out where I'm staying, there will be worse than hell to pay.

2

A soft rapping drew Greyson from his slumber, and for a moment, he was disoriented in the narrow bed. It was far firmer than the one he was used to, and the rough wool blanket, though softened by many washings, was not the fine-spun silk coverlet his mother had bought when she'd refurbished his room on his eighteenth birthday. Blinking away the fog, memory returning, he scrambled for his spectacles, pushing them off the side table to the floor before getting his fingers wrapped around the stems.

"Dash it." He shoved the frames onto his face. It was probably one of Madame's maids, sent to wake him so he could perform an errand for his new employer. "Yes?"

"Mr. Holmes? Madame said to wake you for breakfast. I believe you will be going out this morning."

He was correct. Though he'd only been at the brothel less than a week, he'd already learned that the working girls were wont to open the door at his voice, and not continue the conversation through the thick wood. He kept the rough wool pulled high to his chest just in case this one decided his answer was permission to enter.

"Thank you. Please let Madame know I am up and on my way down."

"Of course."

Thankfully, the door stayed shut.

Stretching, Greyson took stock of his body. There were no stomach cramps, no debilitating muscles spasms, no fever induced by the intake of forbidden foods. For a change, he felt healthy. Perhaps even whole.

Pushing the blanket down, he swung his legs over the side of the narrow bed, resting bare feet on the cool floorboards. Though sparsely decorated, the room held all the essentials: an armoire of the plainest design, a table to be used as a makeshift desk, with a wooden chair, a short bureau with a cracked mirror, and a folding screen hiding a wash basin and towel. His heavy coat hung from a brass peg by the door, his cane propped against the wall next to it. The bath was down the hall, shared by the lesser staff.

Which now included him.

It was a strange thought, though one that held no animosity for the young man. Being part of anyone's staff meant he was out from under his father's thumb, away from his mother's constant nagging and whining—with the ability to follow his regimen without interference.

Being an errand-boy-cum-question-asker for a brothel-keeper was several rungs down society's ladder from his family's perch near the top, and might even be a layer in the dirt beneath, but Greyson was unconcerned with that. Freedom, no matter how grungy, tasted sweet.

Madame was well-known in Norfolk, owning and operating one of the finest establishments in town. Theirs was a chance meeting on a busy sidewalk—he'd stumbled into her companion in a bout of sickness after taking tea with his mother and a young woman whose name he could not remember—that had led him to this opportunity.

Taking a deep breath, Greyson stood, splashed cold water on his face and shrugged out of his sleep shirt, hanging it from a second peg. Efficiently, he dressed in gray slacks, white shirt, and gray jacket, not worrying about a complicated knot for his tie. In the role of errand boy, he was not to stand out from the crowd, but move discreetly, invisibly even, within it.

The halls were silent, save for the soft shush-shush of brooms and cloths being put to use by the small cleaning staff. Gas lamps lent a soft glow to the gleaming mahogany floors and felted wall papers. Madame's brothel, even here, on the floor for the staff, reminded Greyson of the fine homes his family's privilege had gained him access to.

On the narrow staircase, he hooked his cane over his arm and used the banister to keep himself steady. Though he felt of good health this morning, he did not entirely trust his body; it had failed him too often in the past.

One floor down, where the halls and stairs were wider, the bustle of daily chores was more evident. The odor of lemon oil scented the air, and a brigade of gray-clad maids scrubbed the floor, three abreast moving back with their buckets and brushes.

Their low chatter was inaudible, even to Greyson's fine hearing, so he continued down the stairs. If the maids knew where Madame was heading off to this morning, he would not be gleaning any insight from their gossip.

On the main floor, a maid stood waiting at the bottom. She dropped a shallow curtsey and nodded. "Madame is waiting in the small parlor with breakfast."

Greyson recognized the voice as the same maid that had woken him. "Thank you. That is at the end, on the left?" He pointed down the hall toward the double entry doors.

"Aye. Second from the end." She bobbed her head once more and spun off, her black shoes clacking a tattoo on the slate tiles. "Hurry. Madame doesn't like waiting."

Marching down the hall, his own hard soles marking his quick pace, Greyson wondered that so many here seemed wary of the brothel owner. At the door, he knocked, pausing to hear Madame's raspy "enter" before turning the knob.

"Good morning, Madame. Sorry to keep you waiting." Greyson strode to the table, placing his hat and cane next to his chair before sitting himself.

"Good morning, Mr. Holmes. You slept well?" Eyes half-closed, Madame sipped her coffee, the pungent brew a daily ritual for the older woman. A thin cigar rested in a shallow bowl near her hand, smoke furling from the lit tip.

"Indeed. I slept quite well." Greyson glanced at the lit cigar; though the smoke did not bother him, he wondered that Madame enjoyed them so early in the day. His father was wont to take one with his brandy in the evening. The thin wrap of leaves smelled different than those of his father; the scent of Madame's was pleasant, even uplifting.

"And your health is good this morning?" Madame nodded at the platters set on the table. The dishes at Greyson's end of the table held steaming barley cereal, a small ceramic pot of what looked like white butter, a glass cruet of a light, amber liquid, and an assortment of chopped berries.

"Very good this morning." Greyson spooned a generous helping of hot cereal into his bowl, dabbing a spoonful of coconut oil on top to melt, adding a generous amount of berries and a drizzle of agave nectar. He found himself anxious to eat.

This was a strange feeling for Greyson. For so many years, all that he could remember, he'd been afraid to eat. Eating had made him hurt.

But here, Madame allowed him his doctor's regimen. Something not even his parents had been willing to do.

"You don't mind if I...?" Madame waved at the dishes set near her plate, full of the reliable kippers, toast, and eggs.

"Of course not. I suffer no ill effects if you eat your breakfast."

They ate in silence, and Greyson found himself taking a second bowl of the cereal.

"The food is to your requirements?"

Greyson looked up from his meal, swallowing the large spoonful of barley mush he'd just put in his mouth, a dull flush covering his cheeks. "Indeed, yes. I must thank you again for making an allowance for my dietary peculiarities."

Madame laughed, the sound sharp and clear, so unlike her voice. "Ah, Mr. Holmes, you are so proper. I'll soon break you of that habit."

Taking up another mouthful of cereal, Greyson kept his eyes trained on the table. Madame was his employer, was it not expected that he speak to her in such a way?

Waving her cup, Madame caught his attention. "Let us discuss our morning, shall we?"

Nodding, Greyson wiped his mouth with his napkin and placed it on the table.

"You may continue eating your breakfast, Mr. Holmes. I did not mean to stop you."

Unsure of himself and his ability to hold a conversation while eating mush, Greyson shook his head. "I am quite full, thank you."

"Suit yourself." Madame nibbled on a piece of toast. "You have done an exceptional job making inquiries so far. Tracking down May-Ellen's client at his club so fast—and getting out of him just where the attack occurred—was efficient."

Greyson nodded. He understood the ramifications of confronting the man on the steps of his townhouse. His new wife would not take kindly to the embarrassment of her husband being questioned about his intimate liaisons in public.

Madame smiled. "I knew you were the right man for this job."

"Thank you." Greyson shifted in his chair. He felt there was a "but" coming along in this conversation.

"I've told you about Jezebelle, and what happened with her?"

"Yes."

"I have more to tell you. I am not certain what, if any, information you will obtain, so I do not want you to feel a failure if you come up with nothing."

Greyson raised a brow, his interest piqued by the fact that Madame thought he might fail already.

"Three girls have gone missing. I want you to find out what happened to them, if you can."

Taking a small pad of paper from his inside jacket pocket, Greyson flipped to a clean page. "Three are missing?"

"Yes. I have no issue with the girls leaving my employ—and so I am usually informed when they plan to leave. That is why I find this so unusual. That three would leave without telling me is unheard of."

"I see." Greyson scribbled a quick note. "This often happens elsewhere?"

"So, I understand. Many a working girl is on the lookout for a better situation."

Greyson tightened his fingers on his pencil. He knew so little about the world of Madame's girls. Was this why she did not think he would find them? "A better situation?"

Madame leaned back in her chair, studying Greyson a moment. "Usually more money for their services. Or a less, shall we say, physical job?"

"Ah." The flush returned to Greyson's cheeks.

"Their names are Elizabette, Moniqua, and Sussanah. All three were out and about with a client—an approved and trustworthy client, I assure you—when they did not return the next morning."

Scribbling the names in his book, Greyson considered his next question. Tapping the paper with the pencil, he frowned. "Approved and trustworthy?"

"I do not allow my girls to leave the brothel with just any client. They must be on an approved list, and the girl must agree to go."

Greyson knew so very little about the brothel business. "I see." But he didn't see. Why did it matter if the client was approved or not?

"You are confused, Mr. Holmes?" Madame set her cup on the table and rose, taking up her cane to lean heavily upon it.

"I am afraid, Madame, that I know very little about brothels." Greyson stood himself, pocketing the paper and pencil, tensing when his breakfast companion shifted and teetered.

"That is one of the reasons I hired you, Mr. Holmes."

Feeling no better about his lack of understanding, Greyson picked up his hat and cane. "I was informed we are going out this morning?"

"Yes. I thought I would show you where the police took May-Ellen after her attack. I find it odd that she was taken there and thought perhaps you could suss out something."

Nodding, Greyson extended his elbow, as any gentleman worth his pepper would, and once again felt a wave on uncertainty when Madame smiled and shook her head before accepting the proffered arm.

Quillian's log

I don't mind working here with Dr. M.

Most days, I learn something new. The hours are rough, but they could always be worse. I do get to sleep a few hours a night. Usually unencumbered, except for Patch.

And Sundays are my off day—and I can sleep in all I want. Or stay in bed and read. As long as there is no emergency—and there rarely is on a Sunday, since the law keeps most of downtown Norfolk shuttered on the seventh day of the week. They don't say it's because it's the Sabbath, but everyone knows that's why.

And the job is one I can live with. I feel like I'm contributing to the betterment of society. Like so many single young women with no family, I could have ended up a whore.

3

After her late breakfast and a couple hours of studying in the library, a rumbling stomach led Quillian toward the kitchens and the possibility of a warm biscuit snack.

"Best be quiet. Dr. M has visitors—up front." Huddy jerked her head toward the formal parlor, rushing past and nearly knocking Quillian into the Chinese vase. "Maisie, get the kettle on!"

The housekeeper bustled through the kitchen door, rattling off commands to the scullery maid, busy cleaning up after breakfast, barking at her to drop it and get the vats boiling.

It was odd for someone to visit the house, unless they were bringing a patient, but if that were the case, they wouldn't be in the front part of the house—they would be in the back, having come in the rear service entrance.

And she'd have been summoned to prep the surgery.

Quillian tip-toed forward, careful to not make a sound on the polished wood. The salon was at the front, across from the never-used drawing room. The surgery and Dr. M's study were near the back, closer to the kitchens and the laundry that housed the wide brass vats for sterilizing sheets.

Recognizing the female voice, Quillian took in a sharp breath: it was Madame. Had she come to take her back?

If the woman had not spoken, she would have recognized her from a single glance of the deep red hair and the elegant tilt of head on the long, slender neck, her thin, slightly arched nose and sharp chin just visible through the crack between the slightly open door and the jamb. Madame wore black, par usual—black dress and black leather corset. The blouse of the dress had a deep vee neck, with wide, lace-edged collars that showed her "assets" and the skirt, not quite covering a crimson petticoat, fell to the top of her knee-high laced boots. She held a lace fan in her hands, resting it on her lap. Her black, wide-brimmed hat, adorned with deep red roses, with a veil to drape in front of her face, rested on the floor next to her chair. Her cane, made of ebony with a silver tip and lioness head carved from ivory, leaned against her chair within easy fingers' reach.

Yes, Quillian would recognize Madame anywhere. Anyone would, after meeting her once. Quillian supposed that was the point of being Madame.

Now, the pale young man, made paler-looking by the gleaming jet of his hair, standing just behind Madame and to one side, she did not recognize. He had one hand resting on the back of Madame's chair, the other in his trousers' pocket. He wore spectacles, with silver frames that glinted under the golden light from the overhead gas lamps. He was quite tall— possibly taller than Dr. M—and incredibly slim, almost gaunt. His features were sharp enough that Quillian wondered if he had only recently recovered from an illness. He wore a fine coat though, in gray, and fine trousers a shade lighter, with black, glossy boots and a messy white ascot at his throat.

Watching from just behind the door, Quillian held her breath, keeping still; she did not want to enter the room, but she wanted to know why Madame was here.

She also wanted to learn about the young man. She'd never seen Madame out and about with such a young man. Her solicitor was an older man and her accountant was the lone female in the business in Norfolk. Was this young man some new employee—or something more?

"I am certain you understand why I am asking for this information, Doctor." Madame smiled and riffled the black lace of her fan with her fingers.

Quillian studied those fingers. The nails were long and tapered and painted to match her lips. Those nails could hurt you, make you bleed if Madame so chose.

Dr. M sat across from the red-haired woman, still wearing his white lab coat, the tea table between them brimming with cakes and a steaming teapot with matching cups. "Actually, no."

"I thought perhaps you would understand my concern?" Madame riffled her fingers through the lace of her fan again.

"Not quite." Dr. M took up a dainty cake and ate it in one bite, wiping powdered sugar from his fingers on his leather apron. "The girl is alive and has a new arm. There is no bill for you to pay."

Madame raised her chin and gripped her fan in white fingers. "I am glad she is alive. But I cannot help but wonder about the bill. I paid for May-Ellen."

"You sent May-Ellen to me. Constable Dumphries had some charitable organization take care of this girl's bill."

"Charitable organization?" Madame lowered her chin and tightened the grip on her fan.

"One of those organizations that help young women in trouble." Dr. M nodded and chose another cake, biting into this one and examining the contents. "Mmmm. Raspberry filling: my favorite."

"Most of those organizations help young women with a different type of trouble."

The young man behind Madame frowned. "What kind of trouble?"

Quillian bit back her snicker. This was certainly not a man of the world. What on earth was he doing with Madame?

"Pregnancy. They usually help young women who are unexpectantly pregnant." Madame sighed, a slight smile accompanying it.

"How can one be unexpectantly pregnant?"

Madame closed her eyes. "That is a conversation for another time, Mr. Holmes. Dr. M?" She opened her eyes and blinked at the doctor.

Quillian stared through the crack. Dr. M had saved one of Madame's girls? More than one from the sounds of it. Had she helped? She must have. She helped with all his surgeries of late.

Madame had brought her to Dr. M almost six years ago now, and she had become his apprentice. Quillian had never understood why she'd come here, or even why she'd been at the brothel. And in the interim, hadn't cared to ask. Though she had no real memory of her life before she came to Dr. M's home, she knew she'd lived at the brothel, and she'd been all too happy to be leaving the three-storied Victorian with the purple gingerbread trim.

If she had not had a talent for mechanics, she might be a whore by now. If she hadn't already been one; who knew, without a memory? After all, she had come from a brothel. It would make sense that she'd been working there.

She expected she much preferred her current occupation.

The young man shifted, and Quillian took the time to observe him even more closely. His suit had the look of high quality—like that of Dr. M's neighbor, Mr. Roundtree. Perhaps, he was a new solicitor?

The young man turned and revealed his eyes—such a brilliant blue. Entranced, it took Quillian a moment to realize that he was looking directly at her. She startled, embarrassed to be discovered and stepped back into the hall table, making it thump against the wall and the Oriental vase atop it to wobble.

She grabbed the large porcelain urn, resetting it carefully on the tabletop, her heart high enough in her throat to make her gag.

"Watson? Is that you?" Dr. M's voice was garbled by cake.

"Yes, sir." Quillian pushed the door open and took a step forward, but did not fully enter the room. She could smell Madame's perfume, redolent of roses and musk. It caught in her throat, clogging her lungs like when the steampipe burst in the back alley and the steam had crept through the back gate while she'd been sitting under the apple tree with Patch. She found it hard to take another breath.

"Do not be rude. Come in and greet my guests. Madame was inquiring as to your health and continued presence in my household."

Nodding in Madame's general direction, Quillian remained silent—and near the door. She did not look the woman in the eye. The rustle of skirts signaled that Madame shifted in her chair.

"Quillian, my dear. My, you are looking fit and healthy."

Nodding again, Quillian refused to raise her eyes.

"I see you have grown quite a lot since I last saw you. You are turning into quite the young lady."

Quillian did not nod, but glanced to the young man.

"I am Holmes, Greyson Holmes." The man with the blue eyes stepped forward, offering his hand in the matter of gentlemen.

Taking his hand in a tight grip, Quillian was surprised at both the firm grasp and cool fingers. She'd thought it would be a weak gesture from the looks of him. She gave it a quick jerk, squeezing his fingers enough to demonstrate her strength. "Sir."

"Are you enjoying your work here, Quillian?" Madame smiled, her voice soft. Quillian couldn't help but glance at the woman. She looked expectant, staring at Quillian.

"Yes, Madame." Quillian controlled a shiver. "Very much, ma'am."

"It cannot be easy work?" The older woman rubbed over her leg, massaging the lower thigh. Quillian thought Madame didn't realize what she was doing. The movement reminded her of when Dr. M would stare out the window after reading the morning's paper, stroking down a chin that no longer sported a long white goatee.

"No, Madame, it is not. But it is satisfying."

"Is it?" Madame raised one brow, the artificial mole painted above it, disappearing beneath the artfully arranged wave of hair over her forehead. "You are satisfied here?"

"Yes, Madame."

"Do not forget, Quillian. You are almost eighteen, nearly an adult. On your birthday, you will be able to come back to the brothel."

Mr. Holmes frowned at Madame, his eyes darting to Quillian to scan up and down her form. "What would she come back to the brothel to do?"

Madame directed narrowed eyes at the young man.

Quillian took a step back. Such a gaze turned on one of the brothel's 'gentlemen clients' was usually followed by a slap or punch—or worse. Most that knew Madame would cower at just the turn of her head.

"She would simply be coming back to the brothel to live."

"If she is the age of majority, she might go anywhere she pleases." Mr. Holmes stood with his hands clasped behind his back, looking remarkably undisturbed by Madame's ire.

"Indeed. She will be able to do as she pleases. I hope that she will decide to return to the brothel. It is her home."

"Hmm." Mr. Holmes pondered the far wall, rocking slightly on his heels. "Interesting."

"That is not why you are here, Mr. Holmes. Quillian is no concern of yours. You have been tasked with finding my missing girls." Madame's voice stabbed through the air.

Mr. Holmes nodded. "Yes, I am aware of that. However, since we are not yet discussing the missing girls, I have nothing else to engage my brain while I am here."

So, Quillian thought, some of Madame's working girls are missing. Escaped more like it, run away to another brothel that promised more money and fewer 'engagements'. The newspaper was filled with opinion columns about the brothels in Norfolk, how they should all be shut down and the women and girls working there turned to other jobs. Those articles were always refuted by another article, explaining that there were no other jobs for these girls, and that visitors, from both the United Briton States and Carolinia, were drawn to the brothels and gambling—there was a reason Norfolk was known as the 'tourist and business-man's' city.

"So, you have missing girls?" Dr. M poured himself a cup of tea; he did not offer a cup to anyone else.

Madame watched the cup rise to the doctor's lips. "Yes. Three. Not seen for a fortnight." She flipped the lace with her fingers again and stared at something in the carpet. "They left for the evening as usual—all arranged by the brothel, of course—and did not return by morning."

Flicking her gaze to the teapot and the empty cups, Madame pressed her lips into a tight line that made her lip-tint crease.

Quillian regarded the teapot. Should she offer to pour for Madame? How long had Madame and Mr. Holmes been in the house?

Keeping an arm's length between herself and the brothel-keeper, Quillian approached the tea table. In the same room with Madame's elegance and the obvious refinement of Mr.

Holmes, she was acutely aware of the brown cotton work dress and water-stained apron she wore, the clunky work boots still a size too large for her feet. She picked up the pot, steadying it with her other hand, and nodded toward the cups.

Madame smiled and spoke softly. "Thank you, Quillian, dear. I would love a cup of tea."

After pouring, Quillian looked at Mr. Holmes, who seemed surprised, then shook his head. "No, thank you."

Quillian set down the pot and poured milk into Madame's tea, stirring it thrice with the teaspoon, before carefully handing the saucer to Madame.

Madame smiled and took the cup. "Your talents are being wasted here, Quillian. Would you not prefer to be entertaining in a drawing room?"

Shaking her head, Quillian retreated to the door. "I quite enjoy working for Dr. M."

"Invaluable, she is. Invaluable." Dr. M nodded to Quillian, a rare smile gracing his features.

"Thank you, Doctor."

Dr. M took a deep breath and rushed it back out, setting his cup on the table. "Quillian, since Madame does not seem to want to continue our discussion in front of Mr. Holmes, perhaps you could provide him a tour of the surgery, answer any questions he may have about what I do here."

"Of course, Doctor." Quillian smiled and curtseyed. She would do anything to escape the presence of Madame. She nodded toward Mr. Holmes and then nodded toward the door.

Mr. Holmes bowed to Madame and Dr. M, and preceded Quillian out the door.

From the journal of G. J. Holmes

I am not overly fond of doctors, having spent an inordinate amount of time in their offices, being poked and prodded and applied with leeches. I think I still have scars.

At first, I thought of declining the invitation to visit Madame's doctor friend, but then she explained that he was not a regular doctor.

I attend an unusual physician now, that is where I got my regimen, and thought visiting yet another unusual doctor might be educational.

4

Chastised by Madame's brusque reminder, Greyson stalked ahead of Miss Watson, hands tightened into fists at his sides. He now understood why so many of Madame's staff were wary of her.

Dr. M's house was as grand as any in Ghent on the outside, but inside, Greyson noticed a tinge of shabby in the light dust that covered the painting frames and the worn edges of drapes and wall coverings.

"This way." The girl brushed past him, her head held up, her strides long and certain.

Blinking and taking a breath, Greyson followed. The burnished curls at the top of her head barely reached his chin, so he could see where they were going as well as she could. They veered right down a short hall, stopping before a large door.

"Oi! Who's dis?"

Spinning around, Greyson nearly lost his balance when his escort pushed past him once more.

A boy about the age of 10, at Greyson's best guess, wearing scruffy mismatched boots and stained trousers and shirt, stood at the end of the hall they'd just passed. Where had the child come from?

"This is Mr. Holmes, Ralph. He came with Dr. M's guest and I've been asked to show him the surgery." Miss Watson stood over the child, hands on her hips.

The child scratched his head, further mussing his dirty-blond hair. "Why's he want to see the surgery? Is he broke and need fixin'?"

"I don't know that he wants to see it, and he certainly doesn't look broken, but I've been told to show it. You've been warned about your impertinence, Ralph. Shall I tell Huddy so she can box your ears good?"

Greyson thought he detected a hint of laughter in the last bit, but the child hadn't. The poor lad's eyes got big and he swallowed hard enough to make his small Adam's apple bob. "Aw, Quillie, don do that. I jus' got beat for snicking a couple snap peas from her garden."

"Then why are you tempting me to tell her?"

"I ain't. I jus' wondered who the fancy bloke was."

"Hmm. Will Mr. Holmes need to double-check his pockets before he leaves?"

"No, Quillie. I ain't in that racket no more." The child backed away, shaking his head so that his hair flapped around his ears. "You know that."

"I suspect as much, but I've yet to see the proof." She waved a hand in the general direction behind the boy. "Get back to your chores before Huddy finds you here in the hall where proper guests can see you."

With an audible gulp, the boy turned and dashed back up the hall, ducking through the bottom of a split door.

"Sorry about that. Ralph is new to the house and its routine. Huddy's been teaching him, but he's resistant and difficult. Dr. M thinks it's because he's been alone on the streets too long; Huddy says it's just because he's ornery like the doctor."

Briskly, the girl wiped her hands on her faded skirts and turned back to Greyson. The green of her eyes sparkled in the lamp light. She was close enough he could see the ring of tawny brown next to the pupil, and the thin spokes of gold that shot out from it.

"Does Dr. M usually hire his help directly from the streets?" His father, Sir Stanley, always used an agency, claiming he was too busy to check references and work history himself.

"Yes." The girl walked by, and the faint scent of lavender accosted his nose.

Sneezing, Greyson fumbled for his handkerchief, wiping at nothing on his nose out of politeness.

"Gesundheit." The girl nodded and patted him on the arm. "Allergies?"

"I sneeze at the scent of flowers." Greyson refolded the linen cloth and returned it to his jacket pocket.

"Allergies." Miss Watson nodded and patted his arm again. "Huddy probably has something for that if you want."

"Please, no. I have a doctor."

Miss Watson dropped her hand and narrowed her eyes. "I see. Come this way."

Her icy tone made him shiver.

The large door moved smoothly on brass hinges, which surprised Greyson. He'd expected them to protest movement, much like the rest of the doors in the home.

Glancing past his hostess, the surgery behind the door showed no signs of neglect or dinge. Inside the surgery, everything gleamed and shone.

Aha. So, this was where Dr. M spent his money.

Quillian's log

I had a dream about Madame again last night. Same as always, I was lost in the dark. It was the brothel by the sounds coming from the rooms and the paneling and colored walls. It could not have been Dr M's residence; his house is all mahogany and white paint.

I was running from something, or someone. I could hear it behind me. Getting closer and closer, its hot breath at my nape.

When I found Madame, I ran to her and she hugged me and held me and I felt safe.

Funny, when I think about my time at the brothel, I don't remember feeling safe.

Oh, and stranger yet, in my dream, Madame didn't limp.

5

"How long have you worked for Dr. M?" Mr. Holmes looked down his nose at Quillian, blinking behind the clear lenses of his spectacles.

"Near on six years now." She looked about the room a moment before stepping through the door and allowing Mr. Holmes to enter. "This is the main surgery."

Mr. Holmes stood in the door opening, leaning forward at the waist to see into the room before taking a measured step inside.

At its center was a large steel table, long and wide enough to hold an exceptionally tall man—or an exceptionally wide one. Its six legs were also metal, but set in wooden cups at the floor. Three large light globes hung from the ceiling, the chemicals in their frosted orbs providing bright, consistent light for operations.

"Interesting lamps."

Quillian loved the light from the glowing globes. It reminded her of moonlight. "Dr. M purchased them from an alchemical engineer who made them especially for the surgery. He discovered that certain gases glow, but do not burn, when they are agitated, and provide a sharper light than the gas ones purchased for general use. They are cleaner, too. No smoke or soot. Which is essential for a surgery."

She continued the tour, pointing to a wheeled tray that waited in the corner, Dr. M's instruments placed neat on its surface and covered by a sheer cloth to help keep the dust off.

"May I?" Mr. Holmes stepped forward to lift the cloth.

"Please, no. I will have to resterilize them if you touch them." Quillian reached out a hand and grabbed his arm, instantly releasing it when the impropriety of the action hit her. The steam sterilizer was the only piece of equipment she had trouble operating or fixing. Recent steam burns and several blemishes on her arms attested to her clumsiness with it.

Mr. Holmes glanced at the arm she'd touched, then stepped away from the cart and paced around the table, hands still clasped behind his back. He bent to look into a glass jar on the far shelf. "Do you know why Madame owes a debt to Dr. M?"

"No."

Mr. Holmes turned his head only and looked up at her, his gaze meeting hers over the rims of his glasses. "You do not know, or you will not tell me?"

"I do not know."

"How are you involved?"

"I am apprenticed to Dr. M until I turn eighteen."

"When will you be eighteen?"

"In two months." Two months, one week, and three days. But who was counting?

Mr. Holmes went back to perusing the jars. "What is in these jars?"

Quillian shrugged. "Various mixtures to put one to sleep, to dull pain, and to disinfect an area of the body." She breathed out a bit of the pent-up breath she hadn't realized she was keeping in her lungs. It was much preferable to speak of the surgery than her place in Dr. M's home.

"Dr. M has a lot of patients?"

"He has enough. Not every day. But with the violence of late, he is getting more."

"Violence?"

Quillian shrugged. "Constable Dumphries is always bringing in some victim of hooligans who's lost an arm or a leg or a foot. Cut clean off most times." She rounded on the young man, making him take a step back, and jabbed a finger at his face. "Once, someone had his eye poked clean out."

The man veered back, watching her finger behind the clear lenses. "His eye?"

Nodding, Quillian dropped her hand and cocked her head, her eyes closed. She remembered the young man lying on the table, blood pooling beneath his head. "Yes. The left one."

"How did Dr. M manage to fix that?" Straightening, Mr. Holmes peered with seeming fascination into a large glass jar filled with writhing leeches. His reflection undulated on its surface, like something was wriggling beneath his skin. The young man shivered.

Quillian rolled her eyes; she was becoming far too fanciful. She sighed, hard, an explosion from her lungs. The case of the man with the missing eye had been vexing from the start.

"He couldn't. All he could do was pack the cavity and seal up the hole." Quillian nodded toward a work bench along the wall. "I'm working on something, but I've not been successful yet. Dr. M. has the man's address so we can contact him when I figure something out. If I'm not too late."

"Too late?"

"If the whole thing heals up before I can make something. It would be risky to open the whole thing up again."

"I see."

But Quillian did not think he truly did. She walked to the bench and picked up the brass round, fitted inside with concave glass, a small aperture set behind it. She held up the contraption. "I'm trying to work it like a camera's lens, but I cannot make it small enough."

Quillian turned, contraption in hand, and nearly collided with the man, making him jump back. "Oh."

"My apologies, Miss Watson." Mr. Holmes bowed from the waist.

"Of course. Think nothing of it." Quillian wondered at the fast beat of her heart. Had he frightened her that much?

Mr. Holmes cleared his throat. "May I?" He nodded toward the eye mechanism.

"Please." Quillian held it out, backing away once it was in his hands. "It is still too large to fit inside the eye socket. I'm not worried about resterilization right now."

"Perhaps, you should make it more like a monocle. To fit over the eye area?" Mr. Holmes removed his own round lenses and placed the brass ring over his eye and blinked at her through the open aperture. "Such as the one Dr. M wears?"

"Perhaps..." Quillian did not want to admit that the simple solution had never occurred to her. She took the contraption from him and turned it in her hands. "If it was simply placed over the eye socket, the projection skin could be placed in the back of it and attached to the nerve, with only a small slit for the light to enter…"

Quillian set the contraption on her work surface and grabbed a piece of paper and stick of charcoal. She wrote something on the paper and sketched out the rough idea. When done, she held it up and nodded, smiling at Mr. Holmes. "Thank you. I think it might work."

Placing the paper on the work surface, she faced Mr. Holmes, bracing her hands on the counter behind her. "Why are you here? With Madame?"

Mr. Holmes sighed. "My brother was a one-time patron of Madame's establishment. He was a, shall we say, frequent visitor. He always had nice things to say about Madame, though our father hated those particular activities of his. De rigeur for Jacoby, I suppose. I met Madame in person one day—literally bumped into her—and sought refuge at the brothel when I had a falling out with my father. Madame offered me a job, of sorts—has asked me to look into some disturbing events of late."

"You're staying at the brothel? Like it's an inn?" Quillian blinked. She'd never heard of such a thing.

He ignored her question and resumed his perusal of the shelves.

Trying again, Quillian followed the young man. "Disturbing events?"

It seemed Mr. Holmes was much easier discussing the why of his visit to Dr. M. "Two of the young ladies brought to Dr. M's surgery with missing limbs—one missing a foot and the other an arm just above the elbow—were her girls, as well as the three that are missing. Madame brought one of the girl's here—May-Ellen was returned to the brothel—but the other was brought here by someone else, who then made certain the bill was paid."

Quillian blinked again and thought back. She remembered both cases: girls in fine dresses, though torn and dirty from the assault that took their limbs. She had thought them daughters of Norfolk's trade or industry barons, caught in the wrong place at the wrong time after being out to experience a thrill. They had come through surgery exceptionally well; they had both been of good health and had listened to Dr. M's instructions. "I did not recognize them."

"They were very young. I think they only began working for Madame in the last two years." Mr. Holmes frowned at a vile of liquid that bubbled like it was boiling without the apparent addition of heat.

"I see." Quillian turned back to the workbench and fiddled with the charcoal, smearing it along her fingertips. She could not deny that Madame took care of her girls. The older woman employed a doctor on her staff; the last one was a woman, the current one probably was, too. In her sketchy memories, an older woman in doctor's garb that was most likely the brothel's doctor had fixed many a scraped knee or bruise. She rubbed her temple when pain shot through it.

"And yes, I am renting a room at the brothel." Mr. Holmes looked down at Quillian over the rims of his lenses. "My father will never think to look for me there. I say, are you all right?"

Quillian nodded. "I'm fine." She dropped her hand from her forehead. "I see." But she didn't.

Mr. Holmes looked smug and rocked on his heels. "When I learned that Madame was upset, I offered my services. These girls are young and were attacked without provocation. From what Jezebelle remembers, the men that came upon her were all in black and had very sharp instruments. It was not a fight. It was not an accident. They grabbed the girl and sliced off the limb, leaving her to bleed on the street. According to Jezebelle, a brass chest on wheels was waiting nearby for the severed part."

"It was not an accident?" Quillian smeared charcoal across her palm. It was hard to fathom someone just slicing off another's arm or leg. What would one do with a lopped off limb?

"No. Definitely not an accident."

"What kind of services do you offer?" Quillian couldn't imagine what the young man could do about the hurt girls. Madame had a doctor, whom Quillian assumed was caring for them within the walls of the tall Victorian on Upper Granby.

"Investigation. I was studying law before the disagreement with my father."

"Interesting." Setting the charcoal down, Quillian walked to the deep sink, turning on the spigot for hot water and darting her hands under. She soaped up, then rinsed, removing all trace of black. What was there to investigate about the girls and their injuries? "The Constable explained that one girl had gotten caught in the middle of a fight, near the docks, where the workers are picketing for fair wages."

"That is hardly the case. May-Ellen was near Lafayette Park, close to the brothel, walking back with her gentleman after a night of gaming. Probably why she was brought back to the brothel after. Jezebelle was exiting her gentleman's apartment near The Hague. Neither had ventured anywhere near the docks, or any neighborhood where such violence is known to occur."

Quillian turned off the spigot and dried her hands. "You are certain?"

"Of course, I am certain. There is even a witness to Jezebelle's attack." Mr. Holmes crossed his arms and leaned against the counter. "And May-Ellen's gentleman carried her to the brothel, they were so close. I am nothing if not thorough in my investigations."

"You do this sort of thing often?"

Mr. Holmes raised his brows. "As I stated: I am trained in law."

"That is not the same as investigating."

He crossed his arms. "I made excellent marks in witness examination."

"I see. And how do you know the witness is telling the truth?"

Mr. Holmes frowned. "The witness lives in The Hague. He has the highest of reputations."

Quillian snorted and brushed past Mr. Holmes. She knew all about folks with 'high reputations.' "I should take you back to the front. Madame will not like to be kept waiting if she is ready to depart."

"How, exactly, do you know Madame?" Mr. Holmes stepped in front of Quillian, towered over her, looked down at her from behind his lenses, and squeezed her into the bench behind.

"I thought you would have figured that out by now. What with your 'investigational' abilities. I used to live at the brothel. I was raised there, until she gave me to Dr. M."

Using her shoulder to push him away, Quillian preceded Mr. Holmes through the door and stalked down the hall. "Follow me, please. You do not want to get lost in Dr. M's house. Many rooms have not been entered in years."

Quillian's Log

I've often wondered about the choices people make. Not about what they want for breakfast or where they want to buy their next pair of shoes, but what they want to DO.

I know that some folks don't really have a lot of choice, and sometimes it's between taking a job that you don't like and starving, but there is still a choice.

And sometimes, the options we have aren't so different as we think.

Is someone who sells their body for sex all that different from someone who sells their body for the mines or for labor on the docks?

6

Madame waited in the front hall, cloak already around her shoulders, cane braced between her feet, both hands clutching the lioness head. Quillian knew that meant she had been standing for too long.

"Quillian." Madame smiled at her. "You know you are welcome in my home whenever you choose."

"Yes, Madame." Quillian wasn't sure why was welcome. She would make a horrible prostitute: she was rude and inelegant—clumsy even, when in heels. And she couldn't stand being near the men that visited the establishment. What would she do if she had to go out with one of them? 'Perform' for one of them?

"Are you ready, Mr. Holmes? Taggage will be wondering what is taking us so long."

"Yes, of course, Madame." Frowning, Mr. Holmes bowed to Madame, then turned and did the same to Quillian. "Good day, Miss Watson."

"Good day, Mr. Holmes."

He tipped his hat on and inclined his head toward Dr. M. "It was interesting to meet you, sir."

"Likewise, Mr. Holmes." Dr. M tipped his lens a bit, examining the young man through the glass.

Quillian watched the pair leave, even standing, staring at the closed door when it had shut behind them.

"What did you think of that visit, Watson?" Dr. M stood next to her, hands clasped behind his back, staring at the door himself. His lab coat was still open, showing his brown vest and brass pocket watch.

"It was very odd." Quillian turned to Dr. M. "Were you aware that two of the young women we've done surgery on of late were from Madame's establishment?"

"So I gather from Madame. Brothel business must be going downhill, heh? Not surprising in this economy. Too many without jobs or with low wages. We'll be having riots everywhere, soon enough; perhaps we already are, what with all these injuries. It won't be safe to walk out one's front door to buy bread for one's supper."

"The Constable said they'd been by the docks and gotten caught in a fight?"

"Hmm? Oh, yes, yes. Frightful place to be. That's where most of our patients have been from of late. Surprised to find out that Madame's girls are hanging out there." Dr. M discovered a spot of jam on his coat lapel and dampened a finger to wipe it off.

"But they weren't. Not according to Mr. Holmes, anyway. And I can't imagine any reason for him to lie to me. He didn't know we'd been told a story about the docks. He said one was attacked at Lafayette Park, the other in The Hague." Quillian leaned close to the doctor, trying to catch the attention of the eye behind the lens. "And there wasn't a fight."

"No?" Dr. M frowned, pausing with one hand clutching the dirty lapel. His distorted eye blinked and refocused.

"No. The men just appeared and cut off the limb of their victim and stuck it in a brass box." Now that she had his attention, she leaned closer, thrusting with her hands to emphasize her words. "I guess it was lucky for the girls that a policeman was nearby in each case, to rush them here."

"Constable Dumphries. Always Constable Dumphries." Dr. M spoke low, his voice directed away, like he was simply thinking aloud and not to Quillian.

"Dr. M?" She lost contact with his eye.

"Hmm? What?" The doctor stared at Quillian. Blinking, with his white hair standing on end, still uncombed, he looked like a startled owl, its feathers raised in alarm.

"What do you mean about Constable Dumphries?" Quillian watched the doctor's face from behind tilted lashes.

"What? Oh, nothing, nothing at all." Dr. M waved her away, swiping at the raspberry spot once more. "Go on about your duties. Is the surgery clean? It needs to be in case there is another emergency."

"On Sunday?" Quillian blinked; had he forgotten the day? "Yes, sir. I'll go make certain that Mr. Holmes didn't touch anything he shouldn't have."

The surgery was immaculate; she'd made double-sure their guest hadn't touched anything sterile. She would, however, still check that nothing was amiss after Mr. Holmes' perusal, put a quick eye on Ralph to make sure he wasn't getting into too much trouble, and then take a quick walk in the back garden before lunch.

She had some things to consider.

From the journal of G. J. Holmes

Madame is a very strange woman. She is a brothel keeper, and I would have thought that she'd worked her way up through the ranks.

But speaking to her, she is knowledgeable about many things and shows a keen intellect. I cannot help but wonder what brought her to this. By all measures, she is a successful businesswoman and looks to live quite well. There was no mention of the extra cost for the food items needed for my regimen—and I know some of them bare a hefty expense.

My father had balked at the price.

7

Madame sat quietly in her carriage pulled by two silver-plated automaton horses, her gaze directed out the curtained window at the street outside. Carriages passed, most with mechanical horses, though none so fine as Madame's.

Hers bore none of the loud whirring, as with cheaper models, or those poorly maintained. Madame's horses moved smooth, with only the steady clop of hooves announcing their movement.

These horses were even better than those of Sir Stanley Holmes.

Silent, Greyson watched his companion. He had thought Madame to be close to his mother's age, but upon closer inspection, now thought her to be younger. The lines around the woman's gray eyes were faint and thin, and there was no hint of crêpey skin about her jowls.

"What did you think of Quillian?"

"What?" Greyson blinked. What kind of question was that? They'd been there to get information about the girls the doctor had treated. He hadn't noticed Madame train her gaze on him and was taken aback by her piercing gaze and question.

"Miss Watson. What was your impression of her?"

Swallowing, Greyson searched for an answer. "I'm not altogether certain I understand what you are asking of me."

Madame tapped the end of her cane on the seat cushion next to him. "I want to know if you find Miss Watson attractive."

Greyson took in a sharp, unexpected breath and choked on the air. "Attractive?"

"Yes. Do you think she's pretty?"

"Well, yes. I suppose. I didn't really notice." But he remembered the glint of red-gold in her hair and the tawny and green mix of her iris, and thought he might be lying.

"I see." Madame frowned at him. "You do like girls, yes?"

"What? Of course, I like girls!" Greyson shifted where he sat, glaring at the woman across from him.

"Just checking. I'd have nothing against you if you didn't. In fact, I might use you to help me find young men in need of employment." Madame turned her gaze back to the window and set her cane tip back on the floor of the conveyance.

Greyson turned his own eyes to the opposite window, flicking aside the swaying curtain so he could see outside. What impertinence would she ask him about next?

"There are brothels that employ men, you know. It is not unheard of."

Glancing back to the woman, Greyson found her focus still on the outside world. "As I explained this morning, I am not all that familiar with the business of brothels."

"Your father invests in several downtown."

"What?" Greyson dropped the curtain and whipped his head around.

"Indeed. I believe he and some friends are the main investors in the newest one. What is it called?" Madame snapped the fingers on one hand in the air between them, the red lacquered tips long and sharp. "Pretty Bird Revue or some such nonsensical name?"

"I'm sorry. I have no knowledge of my father's investments." His voice was high and cracked, so he swallowed and cleared his throat.

Madame snickered. "I have my doubts that your father does, either. Henri von Canters solicited the investments for an 'entertainment venue for men'."

"What is that?" Greyson's stomach churned.

"I believe the girls put on a show first—dressed as tropical birds, so the rumors go—then the audience may partake in intimate pleasures upstairs."

"Why are you telling me this?"

"You said you had no knowledge of the business of brothels. I thought I should take to instruct you."

"By telling me about my father's investments in them?"

"Many men invest in brothels, Mr. Holmes. You would be surprised at how many wives are buying their furs and silks from money made on the backs of young girls plying their bodies for the chance at table scraps. Not that much better than what goes on in Carolinia, if you ask me."

Her scathing tone surprised Greyson; after all, wasn't Madame's income based on that same premise? "How many invest in your brothel, Madame?"

"None. Mine is the only privately held brothel left in Norfolk."

"You sound proud of that."

"I am. My profits are my own, and I share the wealth. My girls earn enough to put money away for the future."

"For the future?" Greyson shifted on his cushion, his hands tightening on his own cane.

"Men don't like old women—that's why they look for ever younger ones, no matter how wrinkled their cock. These girls won't stay young forever. They need to plan for that."

Uncomfortable, Greyson remembered his father coming home late from his club, his mother sitting at home eating her chocolates and drinking spiked tea, waiting. Had his father been at a club or elsewhere?

Jacoby—god rest his pox-tortured soul—and Wilroy, his older brothers, had frequented brothels, though Greyson was not certain of Wilroy's current activities. Since Jacoby's death from 'that filthy female disease', he was keeping such visits from their mother's knowledge.

Which was why the idea that his father had an investment in a brothel was enough to make Greyson's stomach churn.

Quillian's Log

There are times when I wish most fervently that Huddy was my mother, but for some reason it makes me feel disloyal. And that makes no sense. I don't know who my real mother is, so how can I feel disloyal to her?

8

Quillian's walk in the garden was pleasant—though her dark thoughts courted a headache—and she had not had to save any birds from Patch. Stomach grumbling, she thought to see if there were any scones left over. Huddy always had a pot of jam on the cupboard, waiting.

"Huddy—" Quillian stood in the kitchen doorway, but did not enter. The big brass vats were full of steamy water, blood-soaked sheets inside boiling away the stains. "What's happened?"

"Dr. M is in the surgery, with a Dr. Bergeron. I think they went to school together or some such. The patient is a young man, I think. 'bout the same age as the one last night. I'm not sure it's going well." Huddy swiped the sweat from her brow, the deep-hued skin there looking darker with the wet and wrinkles. She wiped her hands over her closely shorn gray curls. "Best not to disturb him."

"Oh, but shouldn't I-"

"Nay, chile. Not today. They's both doctors. No need of your help."

"Okay." Though something seemed not quite right, Quillian backed out. "I'll be in the library if anyone needs me."

"Yes, chile."

Quillian looked down at Patch in her arms; the cat's eyes mere slits and its pink nose a little wet. "We'll see if we can't find you a mouse to catch, eh? They like living amongst the books, nibbling at the bindings. I think the kitchen is a little too busy for us to find a snack right now."

Patch purred and rubbed its soft forehead along her bicep.

"Good," Quillian snickered softly, "you agree with me."

Once in the library, Quillian set the cat down and it raced off, under the large table in the center of the room, the pat-pat-kerplunk of its normal and mechanical legs joined by the scurry of mouse feet. Quillian had to smile. Poor Patch was not likely to catch a mouse any more than she would a bird; the sound of the metal legs was better than a bell on its collar.

The library was dim, the curtains pulled tight against the outside light. Pulling the drapes back, dust settled over Quillian's hair and shoulders, and she coughed. It had been a while since she'd been able to visit with her books.

She pulled a favorite from a shelf and settled onto a window seat to read, but the letters scampered across the page, not letting her catch their meaning.

Who was Dr. Bergeron? And why was he here? Why had he not gone to the hospital? Who was the patient? Why hadn't she been called in to assist?

Resting the book in her lap, Quillian leaned back against the window frame, looking out the window at the cedar shakes on the wall of the house next door. There was only enough room to walk two abreast between the houses, so she could see the wood texture in the shingles.

The house next door belonged to Mr. Roundtree, an older, rotund banker. He was rarely home, what with the economic crisis Neo-Virginia had found itself in. He was under a lot of stress, and Quillian often heard him muttering odd things on the infrequent days he was home and in his garden.

Huddy had told Quillian many times that she shouldn't eavesdrop, but she couldn't help it when she was alone in their garden with Patch, and Mr. Roundtree was pacing about next door.

Had the curtains been open, Quillian might have been able to see right into Mr. Roundtree's house. She wondered what room was directly across from her now. Was it a library? The houses looked similar in style and architecture. Were they as alike inside as they were out?

Sighing, Quillian stood and placed the book back on the shelf, walking the perimeter of the book-lined room, trailing her fingers over the leather and canvas spines.

The visit from Madame and Mr. Holmes bothered Quillian, as well as the story of what had happened to two of Madame's girls—and the others that had visited the surgery of late. Why would someone want to take pieces of them? And what about the girls who were missing? Were all these patients connected?

Had the missing girls had something fatal taken and that was why they had not returned to Madame's brothel? Quillian's stomach churned at the thought. After seeing some of the patients Dr. M had worked on, she thought no one deserved to die under such horrible circumstances.

Quillian's thoughts turned to the ongoing surgery. Who was in there now? What had happened? And were they, somehow, connected to what had happened in the surgery last evening?

It was a jump in logic, to be sure, but according to Huddy, it was another young man. And though Huddy said she wasn't sure, Quillian thought Huddy knew more than most about what happened in Dr. M's home—perhaps even more than Dr. M himself.

Why hadn't Dr. M called for her? If it was a mechanical application, wouldn't he need her to help? Or was this Dr. Bergeron another human mechanist? She'd thought Dr. M was one of the only ones in Norfolk.

What was going on?

Feeling guilty that Mr. Holmes' words were making her wonder about such things, Quillian huffed and crossed her arms, frowning at the dusty spines. Dr. M's mutterings in the hall at Madame's departure didn't help, either. What did it matter if it was Constable Dumphries that brought the patients? Madame had brought one girl, so why wasn't she under suspicion?

Quillian shuddered. The thought of Madame being responsible for these horrible injuries bothered her. It bothered her more so than the thought that Dr. M might play a role in these attacks, though how he could be involved she couldn't fathom.

She needed more information. She'd just have to see what she could get out of Dr. M at dinner.

Quillian's log

All that thinking stirred memories about the brothel. One night, a gentleman had come in and chosen a young girl and decided to take a service room there at the brothel.

I remember the girl's screams.

Madame ran from the room where she'd been giving me reading lessons, yelling for the footmen to break in the door.

The man was thrown out and the girl brought down to the small infirmary that Madame keeps on the first floor. I remember one of the footmen carrying her down the stair, blood dripping from her nose where the gentleman had hit her, her face bruised, her arm dangling at an odd angle.

It seemed, he liked to hit girls when he, well, did what gentlemen do with young girls behind closed doors.

9

Greyson walked Madame up the back steps to the brothel and through the servant and delivery entrance.

"Are you coming inside?" Madame turned in the doorway. "I am sorry if my choice of conversation made you uncomfortable."

Looking at his employer, Greyson saw no sign of remorse, and thought she'd chosen that conversation on purpose, but said nothing. "No, I thought I would go visit the locations where May-Ellen and Jezebelle were attacked. See if there is any evidence left."

"The police already checked both places. Quite thoroughly if I am to believe the young copper that came to follow-up with me."

"And you trust they told you everything they found?" He wanted to add 'since you are a brothel-keeper after all' but knew better. "I found some particulars from May-Ellen's client that you hadn't gotten from the police."

"I suppose. Though I did request one of our clients to obtain a copy of the filed report."

"You did not tell me you had such a report."

"I do not have it yet. I have only requested it. We will see if he brings it. He has not patronized these halls since I made the request."

Sighing, Greyson shook his head. Sometimes he wondered at Madame. "I wish to make my own observations."

"Very well. Will I see you at dinner?"

"Yes."

"I will ask cook to make certain you are offered a plate conforming to your regimen."

"Thank you." Greyson offered a short bow and Madame swept into the house, closing the door behind her with a soft echoing click.

Lafayette Park was an easy stroll up the street, though the looming houses built close to the thoroughfare spread long shadows across the street and sidewalk. Greyson pondered the differences in the structures. Though Madame's was not the only brothel in Riverview, it was the most well-kept. While Madame's house displayed neat shutters and maintained shingles, others showed peeling paint, hanging gutters and mismatched, or even missing, trim.

At the other brothels, girls showing ample bosom and long expanses of leg sat on front verandas, splayed on mismatched wicker furniture or hanging over rickety railings. They cat-called to him, giggling when he ignored their lewd banter.

He sped his gait, anxious to pass by them and reach his destination. Once the brothels were behind him, he'd be able to relax and breathe. Closer to the park, the houses transitioned to regular boarding houses, and then apartments for the working classes. Farther down, the houses were single family, though several generations might live under their roofs.

The wide expanse of tree-lined grass that was the park led right to the river, a small exotic-animal menagerie occupied one corner and a rose garden donated by a now-deceased patron of the city encroached another. Standing at the wide walkway that cut through the manicured lawn, Greyson watched couples walk among the trees, families picnic on the grass, and a group of young men play pick-me-up rugby in the field.

He wondered if these people knew that a young woman had almost lost her life here, or if they just did not care.

The papers had reported the news, though the article had been small and lodged on the rear pages, next to the sparse employment listings. If it had been someone from the elite, it would have been front-page news.

Grass dampened his trouser hems, but Greyson took no notice. He headed toward the rose gardens, where May-Ellen's client said the attack took place. Vintage slate stones, first laid over a century ago, created a smooth path between rows of rose bushes, their blooms heavy and fragrant.

Greyson sneezed and retrieved his handkerchief from his inner pocket. One stone was stained a rusty red: Blood.

Standing on that stone, Greyson looked around. The rose bushes grew as high as his shoulders, layered thick between him and the road. Though lamps dotted the garden, they were distant, there to create a romantic ambiance, not a well-lit throughway.

It would be easy for someone to hide in wait and spring themselves upon an unsuspecting couple.

But how would they know someone would be here at night? The park sign proclaimed that it closed at dusk and opened at sunrise. All Norfolk parks bore such warnings, but Greyson wasn't sure how hard they were enforced. Especially in a place where the lamps would only need to be lit at dusk.

May-Ellen's client hadn't been worried about being picked up by the law. Perhaps his status held enough weight that he would have gotten off.

But maybe not.

There had been no other witnesses and May-Ellen had fainted in the attack. Lucky for her; she hadn't known what was happening to her.

Greyson investigated farther down the path. He did not know from which direction the couple had been walking. If they had been entering, as he had just done, the lamp would have been behind them, illuminating the path ahead, and the gentleman should have seen something.

He spun on his heel, marching back the way he'd come. If they had been exiting—Greyson held one hand up to shield his eyes—the lamp would have been in front, and it would be understandable for the man to have been blinded.

Turning once more, Greyson walked amongst the rose bushes, looking for more evidence. He checked the ever-dampening line on his trouser hems, and decided he could assume most visitors would stay on the path, but someone in hiding would have to get into the bushes. He examined the ground beneath them.

There had been very little rain since the attack, and the spring mists they'd been getting on a regular schedule wouldn't have done much to wet the protected soil beneath the roses.

Yes, right there: Footprints in the dirt.

Pulling a small folding ruler from his pocket, Greyson measured the footprints and recorded his findings in his notepad. From the measurements, he determined that there were three separate sets of footprints, though they all bore the same shape and sole tread.

It seems the attackers had been wearing uniforms. These weren't just goons. This attack had been more orchestrated than he could ever have suspected.

Though he did not run, per se, Greyson walked in a most unseemly manner back to the main road and hailed a steamtaxi.

"The Hague, please." He leaned forward and handed a few notes to the driver. He knew the fare from here to The Hague. His parents lived there, though that was not where he was going now. "Keep the change. If anyone asks, you picked me up downtown."

"Yes, sir." The driver pulled a lever and steam shushed through pipes and the vehicle surged forward, merging into traffic. "Bit early to be heading home from the brothels. Course, you're a young man. Not likely a wife at home worrying, eh?"

"No." Greyson looked out a window and the driver didn't try to maintain the conversation.

The stone houses of The Hague fronted a concrete-enhanced curve of the river, the cobbled street protected by a boardwalk and short wall. Swans and geese paddled in the brown water and a young maid in gray pushed a pram along the wall while a toddler in short pants and sailor hat walked beside.

It was a scene well-known to Greyson, and it made his stomach clench.

"Here is fine."

The driver stopped along the house side of the arched drive, setting the vehicle in idle while Greyson debarked. Curtains fluttered in various windows, and Greyson recognized some of the faces that peered out.

His mother might know he was here before he had the opportunity to leave.

"How much to wait for me?"

"Ten quid." The driver had placed his hand on the drive lever, but rested it back on the seat.

Greyson passed another piece of paper over the back of the seat. "I won't be that long."

On the sidewalk, he stared at the numbers. He knew his old neighbors were as elderly as his parents, and neither fit the description of the young man that had been Jezebelle's client. It was frustrating that Madame wanted him to investigate, but was unwilling to provide client names or addresses. She said she had to maintain her level of confidentiality, especially since he'd not been a regular, but if he could convince her that information was relevant, he believed she'd give it to him.

He'd been unsuccessful in that regard so far.

The maid with the pram disappeared down a narrow lane between the houses, the clackety-click of its wheels on the uneven stones replaced by another set of wheels, this time of a wheelchair.

A young man in a light brown morning suit pushed a woman in a wheeled chair along the boardwalk. They were laughing, the woman pointing at the swans and tossing breadcrumbs in their direction.

Greyson watched the couple, making mental note of the gentleman's stature and hair color as he didn't dare pull out his notebook. He didn't think he needed it though. It was damn close to the description of Jezebelle's client the night she'd been attacked.

The woman's right leg was raised and set on a large pillow, like she'd recently had surgery.

And it was Jezebelle's right leg that had been hacked off in the back alley.

Hurrying back to the steamtaxi, stomach roiling like it was trying to erupt, Greyson fumbled in his pocket for his notebook, scratching notes on the paper. "Back to Granby, please."

"Back there?" The driver turned in his seat, brows raised.

"Yes, back there." He didn't bother to look up, but kept scribbling, trying to capture all that he had seen, ensnare the tumbling thoughts tripping through his brain. When he was done, he leaned back in the seat, watching the passing houses, panting.

"Everything all right?"

"It will be."

But really, if what he suspected was true, nothing might ever be right again.

From the journal of G. J. Holmes

I didn't believe Madame at first, that there was something fishy about the attacks on her girls. I mean, as far as I know, such attacks are frequent in the lower classes: domestic abuse, child abuse, thieving, and assault.

But this is different. My gut is telling me so.

And now, seeing that couple, knowing the gentleman was with Jezebelle just before the attack that took her leg, and discovering his wife has had some type of surgery on her leg...

My gut is screaming.

10

Quillian ate her breakfast of kippers and toast alone while Huddy bustled around the room, checking the state of the silver and the cleanliness of the best China on display. Dinner last evening had been a bust. The surgery had kept Dr. M and his friend busy into the wee hours of the night, long after Huddy had hustled Quillian off to bed and turned off all the lamps.

She hoped to interrogate him this morning.

"Dr. M isn't yet awake?" Quillian spoke around a bit of fish. She would not have dared do so had Dr. M been at the table; the doctor was big on manners, even though his own sorely lacked. She was eating a hot breakfast, making the most of the opportunity to take her time, plying herself with kippers, steaming eggs, crispy hash potatoes, and two still-warm biscuits with butter. Still, a sense of duty had made her check about Dr. M's whereabouts before fully indulging.

"He left early this morning. Had only a quick bite of toast before hurrying off to do some business." Huddy refilled Quillian's teacup.

"Business where?" It was rare indeed for Dr. M to conduct business outside of the house so early, even rarer for him to have nothing but toast for breakfast. The man liked his eggs and kippers. And how had he been up and about so early after working so late? Quillian had to wonder at the doctor's departure from his normal routine. "Nothing in downtown would be open this early."

"He mentioned something about Dr. Bergeron. I assume his business is with him. Or p'raps at the hospital. The patient and Dr. Bergeron left in a hospital steam-wagon after midnight. Man was fussing how as the patient would be upset. Can't imagine the patient would care who did the surgery, so longs he was alive at the end. Must have been something else. Man was wailing and sobbing like a baby."

Quillian took another bit of kipper, enjoying the treat of eating all she wanted. The questions about the hush-hush patient were piling up.

"More tea, Quillian?" Huddy stood at the ready, steaming pot in hand.

"Oh, yes please, Huddy." Quillian tipped her cup toward the pot. "Thank you."

"There's more eggs and scones if ye want 'em. Dr. M don't like 'em warmed up, so eat yer fill."

"Yes, ma'am."

Quillian took another scone, splitting it down the middle and spreading Huddy's homemade lime curd on each piece. She took a bite and sighed, closing her eyes. The curd was tart and sweet at the same time—just as she liked it.

"Missus Huddy?" It was the footman, a young black man just up from Carolinia. His ill-fitting uniform was wrinkled and he pulled at the buttoned collar. "There be a man at de door, fer to see Miss Watson, ma'am."

Huddy looked at Quillian, one brow arched to her hairline, a grin spreading across her face, big enough she showed her teeth. "A young man?"

"Yes'm."

"Show him in, then. Show him in. P'raps he'll like a spot of breakfast." Huddy snatched up one of the scones and thrust it toward the footman with a wink.

The footman offered a shallow bow and backed himself out, the scone clutched safe in his fist.

"You need to bend all the way at the waist, young man. And leave that collar alone." Sighing and shaking her head, Huddy rounded on Quillian, hands on her ample hips. "You be polite and lady-like now, ye hear?"

Quillian sighed resisted the urge to roll her eyes. "Huddy..."

"And no talking with yer mouth full." Huddy wagged a gnarled finger. "I said be lady-like."

Swallowing the too-large bit, she nodded. "Yes, ma'am." Sometimes, Huddy forgot that Quillian wasn't a lady. But Quillian knew better than to argue with the housekeeper— she'd lose the scones in half an automaton's hoofbeat.

Quillian took a sip of tea and perused her plate. She still had kippers and eggs on her plate, but not so much was left that one might think she ate too much. She shoved the rest of the ready scone in her mouth though, chewing and swallowing without tasting. Another wouldn't look unlady-like now.

"Missus Quillian?" It was the footman. "A Mista Holmes to see you, missus."

She looked past the footman's shoulder to the thin, spectacled man behind him. "Good morning, sir. Do come in. I'm in the midst of breakfast. Would you care to join me?"

Mr. Holmes doffed his hat and offered it, his cane, and his overcoat to the waiting footman, who stared a moment before scrabbling the lot to his chest and spinning to rush out of the room. "I have already broken my fast, Miss Watson, but I have no issue with you finishing yours whilst we speak."

Quillian nodded and took a scone from the tray. "Please, have a seat, sir." There was no reason to impress her guest. She could eat all she wanted—as long as Huddy didn't see.

Pulling out the chair across from her, Mr. Holmes settled like he intended to stay a spell. "I do hope you don't mind me disturbing you so early in the morning."

"Of course not. I am sorry that Dr. M is not at home to speak with you, as well." She busied herself buttering her scone.

The young man dropped his eyes to the table and fingered an empty teacup, his brows knitted about those brilliant blue eyes. "Yes, that is too bad."

Quillian watched him from beneath her lashes. She thought that perhaps Mr. Holmes had already known that Dr. M was out. She took a bite of scone and chewed.

Mr. Holmes gathered a breath and leaned his elbows on the table, twining his fingers together. "I was hoping to determine more about how Madame's girls were brought to Dr. M's surgery."

Swallowing yet another unchewed bit of scone, Quillian sipped her tea, swishing it about her mouth before swallowing. She set the cup in the saucer before taking a breath and answering. "It would be best to ask that of Dr. M. I am afraid I know nothing of the circumstances of how they arrived, only that they did, and their state upon arrival."

"You told me it was a constable that brought them?"

"Yes, Constable Dumphries."

"For both?"

"Aye. And most others as far as I can recall." Quillian frowned, sorting through her memories. "Constable Dumphries must work the roughest route in the city. He keeps mentioning the docks—like I told you before. He's forever bringing us thugs and ruffians of the poorest sort, and their poor victims. I wonder how Dr. M makes back what he puts out for them; they have no money to pay for his services. Constable Dumphries keeps talking about some charity that pays the bill."

Mr. Holmes frowned. "Dr. M is always paid by a charity?"

Quillian put a bite of kipper in her mouth and watched Mr. Holmes while she chewed. The young man drummed his fingers along the table and stared into the mirror above the steam radiator.

She swallowed. "I don't know how Dr. M gets paid all the time. I've seen the constable offer an envelope. Even you mentioned a charity paid for one of Madame's girls, and Madame paid for the other."

Mr. Holmes raised his brows. "You don't have anything to do with his accounting books?"

Shaking her head, Quillian ate the last of her egg, frowning when she realized her breakfast was cold. "No. Why would I? I'm not good with currency calculations."

"Dash it all to Hades. Does the housekeeper keep the books?"

Quillian shook her head. "You'd have to ask Huddy, but I think she only handles the household finances. The surgery is kept separate. Business, you see. Though, I doubt she'd tell you if you asked." The housekeeper's loyalty to Dr. M was legendary among the maids and footmen that worked for Dr. M, as well as the neighbors.

"I suppose not. She's worked for Dr. M a long time, hasn't she?"

Neatly placing her fork along the top edge of her plate, Quillian placed her hands in her lap. "Yes. And very loyal. He saved her life, a long time ago."

"So, she owes him a debt?"

"I don't know that he considers it a debt. Or her, for that matter. I've never heard it spoken of in such terms. Why are you fixated on everything being a debt? I thought you studied law?"

Mr. Holmes leaned back in his chair, silent for the moment. "Did Dr. M perform surgery on Madame's leg? And on Huddy?"

Quillian remained silent. She had nothing to say about Madame's debt. She knew nothing about that, whereas she had oft heard Huddy's story of flying to Neo-Virginia from the wilds of Carolinia, meeting the handsome Dumaka and marrying him, and the two of them living and working for Dr. M. "No. I think it was for something else."

"Do you intend to go back to the brothel?"

Quillian raised her chin. "Oh, hell, no."

"Madame thinks you will. She seems to think it is inevitable. That you belong there." Mr. Holmes frowned at her, a pink flush spreading along the height of his cheekbones.

She raised a brow. "Madame told you I owe her no debt. I can do as I please when I turn eighteen." Perhaps Mr. Holmes needed further instruction in listening.

"I am under the impression, however, that there is more to your story." Mr. Holmes' directed gaze made Quillian suspected he knew exactly what Madame had said, and had chosen his words to make her say more than she should. Perhaps he was better at investigating than she gave him credit for.

"Then you are mistaken. My story is simple. I was brought here to train as an apprentice to Dr. M, and I intend to continue doing so even after I am of age."

Mr. Holmes stared at Quillian, those bright blue eyes sparkling behind the clear round lenses. "I see."

Quillian didn't think he did; even if he did wear spectacles.

E. G. Gaddess

From the journal of G. J. Holmes

Miss Watson is quite the intriguing young lady, over and above the interest spurred by Madame's interest in the well being of the chit.

She seems quite intelligent - much like Madame in that respect.

I had hoped she might be the kind of girl one could persuade with flowers and chocolates to spill everything they know, but I suspect that will not be the case here.

Which is probably for the best. I'm not the sort of gentleman to offer chocolates, since they can give me hives, and flowers make me sneeze.

11

"So, you have nothing else you can tell me?" Greyson sat across the table, fingers laced, his hands resting atop the table.

"Nothing about me or Madame. Or this charity that paid for that girl's surgery." Quillian set the last bit of biscuit in her mouth and wiped over her mouth with a napkin.

"Have you remembered anything else about Dr. M's other patients?"

"No. Nothing."

Greyson sighed and rubbed his hands over his face. "I feel as if I will get nowhere with this."

"Why are you investigating for Madame?" The young woman set her napkin down and stared across the table.

"She is allowing me to stay at her home. In a way, I suppose it in an attempt to repay a debt of my own."

He'd used that word again: debt. Why did he think of everything in terms of a debt? His father was constantly repaying a debt to friends or earning one that they could repay him in the future. It seemed the nature of business in the elite circles of Norfolk. Did all men think in such terms? He could never remember his mother speaking of debts between friends.

No wait—she and her friends did *favors* for each other. Perhaps it was only a difference in terminology. He would have to investigate this in the future, when he had time.

"But you are paying for your room. You said you were renting."

Blinking, he returned to the conversation. "Yes." Greyson stood and pushed his chair in to the table, aligning the back precisely with the edge of the polished wood top. "The debt I am repaying is that she is keeping the knowledge that I am staying there private."

"You are hiding?" Miss Watson stood as well, too quickly, since she had to catch her chair to keep it from slamming to the floor and alerting Huddy.

Greyson was startled to find that he thought the flush that started over her cheeks quite becoming on the girl. He scuttled that thought and concentrated on the matter as hand.

"In a way, I suppose. I don't particularly want my father to know where I am at the moment. I believe I mentioned that in our last conversation."

"Oh."

Mr. Holmes offered a curt nod and moved to the door. The girl followed him.

"Where are you off to now?"

"I thought to go back to the dock area, ask a few more questions."

"Dock area? You said Madame's girls weren't assaulted at the docks."

Mr. Holmes nodded and glanced into the hall. "True. But you said the constable told Dr. M that they had, as well as that other patients came from that area of the city."

"Yes." The girl looked out the door herself.

"I wish to discern if that is true, or if the constable lied about those other patients, as well."

Miss Watson cocked her head at the young man. "Perhaps I can come along?"

Greyson reared back. "You want to come along?"

"Yes, perhaps I can get information that you can't." The girl had the audacity to put her hands on her hips, like she was his nanny and he'd been a naughty boy.

"How would you propose to do that?" Greyson mirrored her stance and stared down at her, hands upon his own hips.

"I don't look like a nob sticking his cane where it doesn't belong." Miss Watson stuck her nose in the air and raised her brows. "If you ask the folks at the docks your questions in the same manner you asked them of me, they'll likely punch you."

"Well, I never-"

She shook her head, canting it ever-so-slightly to the side. "No, I suppose you haven't."

Ralph came out of the kitchens, a half-eaten peach in his hand. The boy's eyes grew wide when he spotted Miss Watson.

Shaking her head at the peach, Miss Watson nodded to the cloak closet when Greyson's hat, cane, and coat had been set. He'd have to check his pockets to make sure the urchin hadn't taken anything.

Nodding, Ralph set the peach—pit side up—on a hall table, scrubbed his juice-laden palms down his trouser front, and scrambled to retrieve the items.

Smothering her laugh behind closed lips, Miss Watson turned back to Greyson, and he thought he'd caught the sparkle in her green eyes that somehow danced along the nerves of his spine. The reaction was so startling, he forgot all about worrying about his pockets.

"I see." Greyson frowned at Ralph, trying to remember why he'd been peeved at the child. The boy's face and clothes were cleaner than the last time he'd seen him, and he hadn't sassed at Miss Watson, or asked about her visitor in the rude fashion of the poor. "Very well. Come along. It certainly can't hurt anything."

Miss Watson jumped and clapped her hands. "Just let me tell Huddy that I'm off with you so she'll know where I am."

Quillian's Log

I don't know what to think of Mr. Holmes. He is quite striking, though rather pale and skinny for my tastes.

Though, maybe, I am not as attuned with my tastes as I thought, since I have found myself thinking of him on a regular basis since we met. I do think there might be more to this brothel business than he lets on.

12

In the kitchen, Huddy stood at the counter, arms buried in bread dough. The aroma of the first batch, already risen and baking in the oven, was almost enough to make Quillian reconsider the outing.

"Yer goin' out with that young man, Mr. Holmes?"

"Yes. We're going for a walk." Quillian kept her voice even. One little crack, and Huddy would know she was fibbing.

"A walk? A walk where?" Huddy stopped kneading and looked askance at her.

"Oh, just around." Quillian waved a hand. "I won't let him take me anywhere dangerous."

Huddy snorted and began pulling the batter up from the bowl, only to let it drop back again. "This got anything to do with those missing girls he and Madame were on about?"

Quillian blinked and straightened. "Of course not."

Focusing a sharp gaze on her, Huddy pounded her fists into the bread dough, the scent of yeast strengthening with each blow. "Just be careful. And don't be gone too long, chile; I don't know when Dr. M will be back, and he might need you if a patient comes in."

"Yes, Ma'am." Quillian backed out of the kitchen, grabbing a brown knitted cap and shawl from a peg in passing.

Once in the hall, she paused before venturing to the landing where Mr. Holmes waited. It would be so much easier to ask questions if they had names. Dr. M's study might provide them with something of a trail. She considered only for a moment before deciding to invade his office. Though the door was kept locked, Quillian knew where the key was kept hidden.

Creeping along, she stopped next to the large fig tree in the koi pot. The tree was in the corner, and actually bore small fruit when properly watered.

But Quillian knew it wasn't there for the fruit or for decoration. Stooping in front of the pot, she reached around to a small crack in the bottom and closed two fingers around a toothy bit of metal.

Glancing up the hall, she set the key in the lock and turned it, slipping into the darkened room. She had been inside before, so the looming, jagged shadows were familiar. Making her way to the desk, careful not to disturb anything, she turned on the globe lamp hanging over the desk and spied Dr. M's open datebook.

In his shaky scrawl were the names of every patient brought to him by Constable Dumphries, along with the dates they were brought in.

He'd been thinking about those patients last night.

Running a finger down the list, Quillian spied the names of two men identified as coming from the docks: Wilbur Dawes and Antonio Guerrera. From the notes accompanying the list, Mr. Guerrera had been the young man with the leg cut off from a few nights ago. Mr. Dawes had been older and lost an arm just above the elbow.

At a creak from the hall, she whipped her head up, freezing her fingers on the paper, listening. She didn't have time to write them down, she'd just have to remember them. Dousing the globe, she backtracked to the door, tip-toeing once again—though she paused to listen before pulling the door shut behind her. Taking the key, she slid it back to its hiding place and took a deep, steadying breath.

Spinning, she rushed up the hall, letting her footsteps click on the tile once she was in the clear.

Mr. Holmes waited at the door, his hat and cane in his hands, his jacket over one arm, one foot tapping the floor. He glanced at her shawl and cap and sighed. "Are you ready?"

"Yes." Quillian rammed the cap over her errant curls and swung the shawl about her shoulders, tying it in front.

Mr. Holmes doffed his own bowler, pressing it onto his head until his ear tips curled. "Let us be off then."

He held the door open for her, stepping back for her to move through.

Quillian held in her snicker. She'd never had anyone hold a door open for her before, or at least not since she was a child and too small to open the door herself.

The sun was out, spreading early spring warmth over the earth. Mist rose from the rapidly heating ground, forming a gauzy curtain at street level.

"Do you mind the walk?" Mr. Holmes set out at a brisk pace, calling over his shoulder, "At least until we reach the main road and can grab a public steamtram?"

"No, I rather enjoy the exercise." She caught up in a few strides.

"Good."

Trotting every so often to keep up with the longer strides of her companion, Quillian watched him on the sly. He didn't seem to notice his unseemly pace. She didn't say anything. If she was too much a bother, he might send her back.

The main street was busy, filled with a dense smog that could catch in your lungs if you weren't careful. Automaton horses pulled fancy carriages, while steamcars wound amongst them, anxious to go faster than the speed they were built for. Here, the steampipes ran underground, only the hot mist rising from the grates in the sidewalk evidence that they even existed.

The pair strolled past the courthouse, as well as the customs building and the head offices of His Majesty's Bank of Neo-Virginia—an odd name, since the King no longer had anything to do with the country.

"Here." Mr. Holmes stood next to the placard that reserved the sidewalk for those waiting for the steamtram. "There should be one along any moment. Our system is the best in Neo-Virginia."

"How do you know that?"

Mr. Holmes looked down at her, a faint smirk marking his lips. "My father told me so when he decided to invest in the upgrade a few years ago."

Quillian couldn't tell if he was serious or not, so she remained silent, on the lookout for the steamtram. "Ooh, there it is."

The steamtram was a long vehicle with open sides, the wood a polished oak, the metal painted crimson and orange, the front reminiscent of a ship, what would be the prow adorned with a mermaid—the symbol of the city. This particular mermaid was covered in a seashell motif with seaweed covering her breasts and steam blowing out her mouth in little puffs.

Passengers embarked at the front, putting their coin in a wide jar next to the driver, and debarked at the rear, where a footman waited to assist the ladies in their skirts and to keep jumpers, those who wanted to ride, but not pay, from getting their intended free ride.

The vehicle stopped before them, a burst of hissing heat emanating from the bulky engine at the front, the little puffs from the mermaid's mouth turning into a steady stream. Mr. Holmes stepped on first, sliding two coins into the slot for the meter. "For the lady."

The driver nodded and tipped his hat, first at Mr. Holmes, then at Quillian.

Quillian climbed up after, smiling at the driver before following Mr. Holmes to a seat. The benches were wooden, but gleaming. Gas globes hung in each corner, but were unlit since it was daytime.

"Have you ridden a steamtram before?" Mr. Holmes rested his cane tip on the floor in front of him and folded his hands over the plain brass knob at the top.

"No." Quillian leaned forward to look out the side beyond her companion. They moved quickly down the street, jerking to avoid carriages and pedestrians. "Not very smooth, eh?"

"Not in the height of traffic, no." Mr. Holmes regarded her with half-closed eyes. "It is still faster than walking, and far less tiresome."

"You tire easily?"

"Only when I am feeling unwell."

"Do you often feel unwell?" Quillian squinted at his pale face, wondering once again at the young man's pallor and slender build.

"Not since moving out of my father's townhouse."

Quillian frowned. "Your father made you unwell?"

"No, his food made me unwell."

"How could his food make you unwell?" Food was the source of nutrition and energy. Quillian couldn't imagine any of Huddy's fabulous meals making anyone sick. Had his father employed an incompetent cook?

Mr. Holmes sighed and looked out the side at the passing carriages. "It is a rather detailed story."

"I have nothing better to listen to at the moment. We still have a bit to go before we reach the docks."

"Indeed." The young man shifted in his seat and stared straight ahead, taking a single deep breath, holding it a moment before letting it out all at once. "I have several sensitivities to certain types of foods. I am unable to eat wheat flour, for instance. If I ingest too much, which is not much at all really, I am in excruciating pain."

"Oh, I'm sorry. What do you eat then?"

"There are other flours, such as barley flour, that does not cause me any discomfort. I eat foods made with those instead."

"Did your father not know this?"

"He does not believe in my condition. It was diagnosed by what he termed an unconventional doctor."

"Unconventional?"

"My doctor is of Indian descent."

"Oh. Huddy sees a Chinese herbalist for her female issues." Quillian nodded knowingly. "I have used some of his herbs on occasion myself."

"Female issues?" He blinked at her, his eyes large behind the lenses.

Quillian stared at Mr. Holmes. "Your mother does not have female issues?"

"Not that I am aware of." Quillian thought the young man might simply be avoiding a discussion of those issues, for a redness seeped up the back of his neck beneath his short collar.

"Oh." Considering that flush, Quillian felt silly. She had never considered that some folks might not discuss such things like Huddy did. For all Huddy treated her like a lady, and implored her to behave like one, Quillian had very little formal instruction on the notion.

They remained silent a few minutes, Quillian watching the buildings pass—there was the hospital, with its special children's ward and the Mariner's Union Headquarters—wincing at times when someone let loose a shrill whistle to force their way into the heavy traffic.

"It is time to debark. We can walk the rest of the way. It will be longer to continue by tram."

Quillian rose from her seat and stepped aside so Mr. Holmes could rise as well. She followed him to the rear of the tram and waited for it to stop.

```````

The docks held all manner of ship and boat, of both the steam and sail variety, as well as the occasional paddle wheel. The public docks housed the gambling boats that ran the river
```````

when not in use, the watertaxis that carted folks from the docks in Norfolk to the docks in Portsmouth, and the assorted cruise vessels for public entertainment.

Beside the public docks were rows and rows of private piers, where the nobs' sailing yachts and rowing shells were stored in the off season. Whereas the public docks were of gray, weathered timbers, some aslant, some broken, the private docks were housed behind tall wrought-iron fencing with brass finials, the docks themselves constructed of straight timbers, replaced on a regular schedule. A concrete bulkhead protected these docks from the waves and debris of the river proper.

Beyond the private docks, were the commerce docks, where trade ships came in, usually steam and usually large, delivering goods from all over the world, before taking on cargo for the return voyage. These were the dangerous docks, where hooligans and villains hung out, looking for odd jobs to pay for their myriad vices. Huddy was always warning Quillian to avoid these docks, for nothing good could come of a visit.

The Government docks, where the military ships moored and underwent repair, were beyond the commerce docks, but no one could access those except sailors, officers, and politicians. Guarded gates, with militia-men carrying hand cannons and attack dogs, kept everyone without proper paperwork out.

Quillian was quite happy that they would not have to pass the Government docks. She was not particularly fond of dogs.

Mr. Holmes set a brisk pace once more, and again, Quillian found herself forced to skip to keep up.

"Where exactly are we going?" Quillian was breathless; Mr. Holmes had set an even faster pace than earlier.

"Dr. M mentioned that Constable Dumphries indicated a couple of his other patients had been wounded near the commercial docks. I thought I might ask around to verify."

"He did? What, do you think Dr. M is lying?" Quillian stopped walking, grabbing for, but missing, her companion's arm.

"Not necessarily," Mr. Holmes stopped and pivoted to face her, "but someone lied, since neither of Madame's girls were anywhere near the docks when they were attacked, and yet Dr. M indicated that is what he was told."

Quillian dragged her heels to catch up. "How are you going to ask your questions?"

"What do you mean?"

"Do you have names?"

Mr. Holmes stopped and looked down at her, rolling his eyes. "You know I do not."

"I checked Dr. M's records. A Wilbur Dawes and Antonio Guerrera were brought in by Constable Dumphries from the docks." Quillian grinned up at him, raising on brow.

"I see." Clearing his throat, Mr. Holmes pulled out his notebook and flipped through the pages. "I think we can assume Mr. Dawes was a big man, probably worked in manual labor. Caucasian, red-haired, wore a long, braided beard."

"How so?" She hadn't said anything about the age of either man.

"That is the description Dr. M gave for one of the patients, and that doesn't sound like someone named Antonio Guerrera."

"I see. I think I remember him. He lost a foot, I believe." Quillian nodded but didn't look at Mr. Holmes.

"Yes, that is what Dr. M said." Mr. Holmes wrote in his notebook.

"So, you think he worked near the docks?" Quillian remembered a muscular man; at the time, she had been surprised that such a man could be injured in such a way. She'd thought he was rather the sort that would have more likely inflicted that type of injury.

"It is possible. There are a lot of manual laborers at the docks to move cargo on and off the ships." Mr. Holmes flipped his notebook closed and stuffed it back into an inside pocket.

"What about the other man?"

"He sounds like an immigrant. Dr. M indicated there was a patient that spoke little English. But, we will inquire about Mr. Dawes first, since we seem to know a little bit more about him."

Quillian tried to remember such a patient, but she could not remember anyone in the surgery who could not speak English. Of course, they were usually unconscious by the time she was called in to help. "He was recent, I believe. And lost a leg, above the knee."

Mr. Holmes raised a brow but said nothing, nor did he make a note.

The commerce docks smelled like dead fish and stale, oily steam. Men in dirty, well-worn dungarees stood in lines passing barrels and crates along in assembly-line fashion, from a large steam ship to a waiting steamwagon. The vehicle in question, was large with a long, open back, where the crates and barrels were stacked efficiently and strapped down.

The men in line watched the pair approach, but never stopped moving, never dropped a piece of cargo.

A tall broad-shouldered black man barked at the workers. "Keep yer eyes on the job!" The workers turned their eyes away, looking to the ground instead of at the approaching pair.

"Can I 'elp you?" The black man approached, pulling himself to his full height when he stopped in front of them, blocking their movement further down the wharf.

"Yes, good morning, sir. My name is Greyson Holmes, and I was hoping to ask some questions about a gentleman that may have worked here on the docks, but was injured." Mr. Holmes held out a hand, the other still holding his cane.

"Ain't had no on-the-job injuries here." The black foreman ignored the out-stretched hand.

"I don't believe he was injured while working." Mr. Holmes dropped his hand, patting at something in his jacket pocket.

Quillian watched the assembly of moving crates. A couple of the men were watching them again. She smiled; they sneered.

"Then I don't know nothin' about it."

"I thought someone might have seen something."

The man shrugged and turned back to the laborers. "Keep it movin'!"

"The man's name is Wilbur Dawes."

"Never 'eard of 'im." The black man did not bother looking at them, but kept his slitted eyes trained on the line of cargo.

"Are you certain?"

"You callin' me a liar?" The black man spun back and stomped forward, towering over even Mr. Holmes.

"Of course not, sir." Quillian spoke up and stepped around Mr. Holmes, wedging herself between the two men. "We simply thought you might not have remembered his name at first."

"You sayin' I gots a lousy mem'ry?"

"Granton! You're supposed to be watching the unloading." A suited gentleman, his brocade vest unbuttoned and flapping in his rush, approached from an office. He strode forward, frowning, his head bare so that the few strands of hair on his balding pate flickered in the breeze off the estuary.

"Yes, sir." The black man turned back to the line. "Careful with that barrel, Dobbs."

"Can I help you?" The man in the suit brushed his fly-away hair across his head, attempting to make it lay flat. He looked flustered, his cheeks flushed pink, a smear of mustard tinting his top lip yellow.

"Perhaps." Mr. Holmes held out a hand. "My name is Greyson Holmes and I am inquiring about an accident that injured a Mr. Wilson Dawes."

"I'm Philip Morton, owner of Morton Imports and Exports. We haven't had a work-related accident here for a long time." Mr. Morton also did not accept Mr. Holmes' hand, though he did look down at it.

"I don't believe this accident occurred while Mr. Dawes was working." Mr. Holmes dropped his hand, ignoring the slight.

"Then how would I know anything about it?" The man wiped his lips with the back of his hand.

"It has been related to me that the incident occurred near the docks, and I was hoping someone may have been a witness."

Mr. Morton stared a moment, looking up and down Mr. Holmes' figure. "Are you a lawyer?"

"No." Mr. Holmes grip on his cane tightened.

"An insurance dealer?"

Mr. Holmes' grip loosened, and he twisted the canes in his fists. "No. I am simply inquiring about the incident."

"Then I have no reason to answer your questions. It's best you leave and quit your inquiries." Mr. Morton spun on his heel and marched back to his office. He did not look back.

Sighing, Mr. Holmes spun his cane in a wide arc, looking around. "Let's try another dock, shall we?"

Quillian snorted and leaned close, whispering. "You're asking the wrong folks."

"What do you mean?" Mr. Holmes bent his head and kept his voice low to match hers.

"Follow me." Quillian strolled away from the working dock and headed back toward the street.

"Miss Watson, I really think-"

"Please, just let me try asking someone. If I get nothing, you can go back to asking your questions at the next business."

"Very well." Mr. Holmes tapped his cane on the ground.

Back at the street, curbside vendors sold meat pies, sausages, and hot tea to the workers. It was late morning, so they were setting up their drays and wheeled ovens, feeding coal into the bellies to keep them hot.

At the corner closest to the dock, an old woman and a young boy sat near a cart full of pies and chilled cider jugs. Quillian smiled and approached, looking over the pies.

"Ooh. These look delicious."

"Oh, they is." The old woman stood and smiled, showing the gaps in her teeth. Her thick dark hair was pulled back in a tight bun, a loose-knit shawl tied around her shoulders, barely covering her patched, flower-print dress and crackled leather corset. "Made 'em fresh this morning. I gots beef and turkey and egg."

The woman pointed to the pies. The aroma that drifted to Quillian's nose made her mouth water. "Which one should we get Mr. Holmes?"

"What? We're not getting any of them. I am unable to eat them."

Quillian sighed. "But I can and I'm hungry. Please purchase one for me. I think I shall take an egg." She smiled at the woman. "Are the egg ones sweet or savory?"

"Savory, with bits of potato and kale in 'em. Indian spices, too, to give 'em kick." The woman grinned and plucked a pie from the steaming oven.

"Miss Watson-"

"Mr. Holmes. Please. Purchase the pie."

He sighed and reached into his vest pocket. "How much for the pie?"

"Four."

"Four?"

The woman leaned forward, pie clasped in her hands. "Four."

Grimacing at Quillian, he handed over a fiver.

"Keep the change." Quillian winked at the old woman.

The woman grinned and handed over the hot pie wrapped in a sheet from yesterday's Norfolk-Portsmouth Gazette.

Quillian took a bite. Steam rolled out of the pastry. "Mmmm." She swallowed and licked her lips clean. "'tis a shame you have stomach troubles, Mr. Holmes."

"Stomach troubles?" The old woman looked up and down Mr. Holmes, one brow raised.

"Aye. He gets pains in his stomach if he eats wheat." Quillian took another bite, licking the crumbs from her lips.

"Miss Watson, I have no desire to tell the entire world of my frailties."

Snickering, Quillian took another bite of the pie. She would have to mention the egg pie to Huddy; perhaps the housekeeper had a similar recipe.

"'ere." The old woman pulled something from the back of the dray, wrapping it in newspaper. "Ain't no wheat in that. I make 'em for a Chinese feller what works the books for Morton."

Mr. Holmes stared at the paper, only taking what was offered when Quillian jabbed him with her elbow.

"Thank you." Quillian smiled at the old woman and shook her head at Mr. Holmes' lack of manners.

"The outside bread is made from rice flour and its jus' got veggies inside, with a little turmeric and garlic, the potatoes mashed up with a little vinegar to keep it together."

Mr. Holmes unwrapped the pale pie and sniffed before taking a bite. He swallowed and nodded. "It's quite good. Rice flour, you say?"

"Aye. There's a shop at the far corner what sells it." The woman pointed down the street.

Mr. Holmes looked to the indicated corned. "Thank you. I shall have to inquire about it."

The old woman stared a moment. "What you two be doin' 'ere? Ye look more like ye belong strolling around The Hague."

Quillian smiled at the woman's certain attempt at flattery. "We are looking for anyone who might have seen an attack near the docks about a month ago."

"An attack?" The woman busied herself with rearranging the pies, her eyes darting right and left.

"Aye. The victim was a man named Wilbur Dawes."

The woman continued playing with the pies. "Don't know no Wilbur Dawes. Don't remember no attack. And ye shouldn't be askin' questions 'bout it. Not 'round 'ere."

13

They were never going to find out what happened to the missing girls. The lower classes just wouldn't talk to the uppers.

Tightening his grip on this cane, Greyson glared back at the old woman and the pie-filled dray. Maybe he should listen to his father after all and take an apprenticeship at one of his lawyer friends' offices.

Spinning to head back up the street, loose cobbles clicking beneath his soles, Greyson considered what he might have to do if he couldn't fulfill Madame's requirements in an errand boy.

Not that he planned to stay at the brothel long-term, but for many businessmen in Norfolk, a reference from her would hold weight. He'd been rather banking on getting a good word from her when he moved on to his next position.

"Ahem."

Someone grabbed his arm, and he jerked it away, rounding on the person.

It was Miss Watson, staring up at him like she'd never seen him before. "Remind me never to piss you off."

"It's just frustrating is all." He straightened his jacket and huffed.

"You need to keep your temper. It won't help matters for you to storm off every time someone refuses to answer you. If you're going to ask questions like this on a regular basis, you need to build a reputation as someone to be trusted." She put her hands on her hips, glowering up at him with much the same expression she'd used on Ralph.

"A reputation? All I want is a couple of answers!" He threw his hands in the air, waving his cane enough that she swayed to avoid it making contact with her shoulder. He took a breath and set the cane to the ground. No need to take his temper out on the girl.

"Yes, but folks in the lower classes can get in trouble when they answer questions. It takes nothing but a complaint by someone in the uppers to get them picked up and thrown in gaol. They need to know you won't go telling their bosses what they're saying."

"And how do you know so much about the lower classes?"

Raising one brow, Miss Watson made a show of displaying her dress.

Greyson's stomach tightened. The dress was fashioned of basic brown cotton, stained and fraying at the hem, the corset laced up the front made of cheap leather, already cracking. He'd forgotten for a moment that Miss Watson, despite her learned speech and semi-refined manner, was not from the upper, or even the middle class.

"I, good sir," her voice dripped icicles and made Greyson squirm, "have been observing Dr. M for a long time. The lower classes trust him and bring their injured to him because they have learned that he will help them, no matter what. Nor does he go blabbing about whatever they've been to see him for to their employer. He keeps their business to himself, and so they trust him."

"And how am I supposed to let them know that they can trust me? I don't have years. I need answers now, before another girl goes missing—or someone else has a fatal accident under suspicious circumstances." He took another long breath and tapped the tip of his cane on the cobbles.

"First, by not flying off the handle when they won't answer your questions. And second, by taking a look around."

Greyson eyed the docks and the street. He could hear the mismatched clop of hooves echoed between the warehouses; live horses still had a place here, since they had no metal parts to rust, and so manure, fresh and weathered, littered the ground in places. Men hollered and whips cracked, and unlike the mechanical version, these horses shied and whinneyed in protest.

Barrels rolled, sounding like thunder on the ground. Men yelled direction to the steam-crane operator and something dropped heavy onto a wooden deck.

There were people everywhere.

"It's hard to imagine this place ever being quiet." Greyson winced at a less than pleasant curse someone shouted.

"It's probably very different at night and even busier at shift change in the evening and early morning."

Frowning, Greyson considered the possibilities. Though the docks were still inhabited at night, the gas lamps were few and far between. It would be easy for someone to hide in the dark. And, if timed with the bustling noise of a ship coming in and taking on cargo, the cries of a man being attacked could easily blend in and be ignored.

Maybe no one had an answer for him.

"This is very different from where the girls were attacked." It was more musing than comment.

"Where were they attacked?"

"What?" Greyson glanced down at Miss Watson. He'd almost forgotten she was with him.

"Where were they attacked? You want me to provide you information, but haven't shared anything with me at all." Miss Watson crossed her arms across her chest and cocked a hip. The stance emphasized her curves, and for just a moment, Greyson forgot what they were talking about. He blinked.

"If you give me a little bit of knowledge, I might better be able to answer you."

Greyson blinked again. What questions? What?

She stomped her foot, dropped her arms and making tight fists with her hands. "You aren't even listening to me, are you?"

"I'm sorry." Greyson scrambled to find something to say that wouldn't put him in an even worse light. "I was trying to compare the docks to the Lafayette Park."

"Lafayette Park?"

"That is where May-Ellen was attacked. One hooligan held her companion at bay while she was accosted. Once released, he carried her to the brothel, bleeding and all."

Miss Watson swallowed, her face pale. "Lafayette Park is only a few of blocks away from the brothel."

"Indeed. That is why she was carried there." Greyson spoke slowly, leaning down to make sure she heard his words.

"Rather bold, don't you think?"

"Yes. The most bold of all of them."

"Why were they in the park?"

"It seems her companion that evening wanted to take an evening stroll in the moonlight."

"Hmm." Miss Watson frowned and looked away. It seemed she was now the one not paying attention. "That's not a usual brothel activity."

"Hmph." Tapping his cane hard on the pavement, Greyson spun on his heel and marched up the street. "Nothing else to accomplish here. Might as well head back. Come along."

From the journal of G. J. Holmes

My investigation is not going as planned. At school, I took classes in interrogation. It seemed so easy then. Perhaps it was because I practiced on fellow students.

In real life, no one actually wants to answer my questions.

14

Quillian didn't try to keep up with Mr. Holmes' quick pace back to the main road and the steamtram pickup area. She was tired and he was angry enough she thought steam might just come out his ears.

It had been obvious to Quillian that the woman knew something, but just didn't want to say so right then. Who knew who had been involved? The old woman had a right to be scared, especially if someone was going around lopping off body parts.

"She's just being difficult. Wanted more money, I suppose." Mr. Holmes stalked towards the transit stop, his long strides eating the distance with ease, his cane tapping a rapid cadence on the sidewalk.

It was like their conversation had never happened. Maybe, he'd never been scared before. Maybe, he wasn't used to not paying for information.

Sighing, Quillian scuffed her boots along the paved walk. She admitted she was frustrated, too, but she would not be telling that to Mr. Holmes.

She heard running from behind and glanced back. A young boy, chased by a group of older boys and a couple of mutts, approached from behind. He was fast, but appeared to be running out of steam.

"Hey, you lot! What do you think you're doing?" Quillian rounded on the approaching boys, hands on hips, a scowl on her face.

The young boy darted behind her, clutching her skirts and peeking around at the rough-looking gang that now stood on the sidewalk, the fur-matted mutts circling and barking and whining.

"Well, well. What do you care 'bout what we be doin'?" The tallest boy, wild brown hair capping a dirty face, slowed but didn't stop.

"Stampeding down the sidewalk is likely to get someone hurt." Quillian decided tact might be the best course of action. The boy was almost as tall she was, and probably outweighed her by a stone, if not two.

"Oy, true. Might be you be the one getting' 'urt." Another boy, this one dark skinned but with unexpected slanted eyes, pushed through the short mob.

One of the dogs jumped on one of the boys and he staggered back. "Git down, Burt." He pushed the dog away.

"Shut up, Cam."

"You shut up."

The boys pushed at each other and the dogs barked louder, joining into the fray, jumping and running. Soon, the whole gang fought each other, ignoring Quillian and the small boy that still clutched at her skirt.

"Miss Watson? What are you about?"

Quillian twisted; the small boy rooted her to the ground so she couldn't turn to face him proper. Mr. Holmes marched back to her and the boy. "Nothing."

"What is that hanging off your skirts?"

"A boy."

"Why?"

She shrugged. "I'm pretty sure it's a Mendelianist decision. I'm sure you've heard of it."

He sighed and stared down at her, his lips pressed tight together. His nostrils flared and he took a deep breath. Once again, his fists clutched around his cane. "Indeed, I am quite read up of the subject."

Quillian smirked and raised a brow. She turned back to the fight. One boy was on the ground, two others pummeling at him. Another was trying to climb an iron fence to get away, but one of the dogs had a hold of his scruffy pants cuff. "If your question was directed at why he is using me as a shield that would be because a gang of older hooligans was chasing him."

The clutching boy smiled up at Quillian. "Thanks." He shoved something into her hand and ran off, back through the original chasers who were now oblivious to everything in lieu of their tumbling brawl.

"Let's be off before you decide to join them." Mr. Holmes grabbed her elbow and jerked her forward.

Quillian pulled her arm away. "No need to get rough. I'm coming."

She squeezed her fingers around the gift from the boy. It felt like paper, but she didn't want to look at it yet. She remembered the boy now; he'd been with the old woman at the pie dray. She glanced behind. The fighting mob had already dispersed, leaving no sign that anything untoward had happened there on the side of the street.

"Miss Watson, is it your desire to remain in this part of town?"

She spun back to face Mr. Holmes. They were at the steamtram station, her companion already aboard the waiting vehicle, the driver looking bored and the passengers disgruntled.

"Sorry." She climbed on, head down, following Mr. Holmes to a seat. The wad of paper, still tucked in her palm, an itch of skin urging her to take a look.

But she would wait. Mr. Holmes might not appreciate whatever the gift was.

She looked out the side, ignoring her seat mate. He spent the time sighing and shifting.

"What's wrong?" She rounded on her companion; she couldn't take his fidgeting anymore.

"Why on earth did you stop? Those hooligans could have done you harm." Mr. Holmes held his cane straight up, pushing it into the floor.

"They likely would have done harm to the boy if they'd caught him." Quillian watched the young man's face. He held his jaw clenched, and his nostrils flared when he exhaled.

"It was not your responsibility to help him." He spoke the words in measured steps.

"Then whose responsibility was it?"

"I don't know. His parents?" When Mr. Holmes looked at her, his blue eyes glinted, the black center dots tiny.

"I didn't see them anywhere near."

Mr. Holmes sighed again, long and heavy, and shook his head, looking out the other side of the steamtram.

"I wasn't raised to not help those who need it."

"I wasn't raised to put myself in unnecessary danger."

"I don't think I was in any danger. Those boys were just bluster." Quillian jutted her chin up.

"That's why the little one was running, eh?"

Quillian shrugged and decided to check the child's offering. She opened her hand, taking care not to drop the paper. It was yellowed, torn from a piece of old newspaper.

There was writing on it.

She spread the paper out on her lap, leaning forward to decipher the shakily written words.

"We need to go back."

"What?" Mr. Holmes swung his head back around.

Quillian sprang up from the seat and grabbed the cord that rang the bell that let the driver know someone needed to get off.

"But I've paid for us to get all the way back to Stockley Gardens."

"The old woman knows something. And why Stockley Gardens?"

"I already figured the old woman knows something. And Stockley Gardens because I want to drop in and speak to my doctor about rice flour."

"Well, the old woman wants to tell us. Just not out in the open where someone can see or hear. Your doctor works in a garden?"

"And just how do you know this woman wants to talk to us? No—my doctor doesn't work in a garden. Stockley Gardens is the closest stop to his office. And it isn't a real garden, not anymore anyway."

"Well, the boy being chased gave me a note from her."

The steamtram stopped and Quillian pushed on Mr. Holmes' shoulder, making him stagger into the aisle.

"Let's go."

"It might be a ruse." He straightened to frown down at her, adjusting the bowler that had slipped at her shove.

"It isn't." Quillian barreled past the young man and down the aisle to exit, ignoring the arm of the footman and leaping to the ground.

"I say, Miss Watson," Mr. Holmes stepped down behind her, cane out to block her wayward run down the road, "you really must learn to curb your enthusiasm." He rubbed his shoulder.

"Come on. She may not wait long." This time, Quillian set the pace, and Mr. Holmes had to keep up.

Quillian's Log

Mr. Holmes is a strange biscuit. He seems to have no clue about how the lowers operate. He may be smart and may have attended school to be a fancy-schmancy lawyer, but he has no people skills. I can't imagine him actually talking to someone he would have to defend in court.

Of course, maybe that's how it is with uppers. I have to remind myself not to compare him to Dr. M.

Dr. M turned his back on the elite a long time ago, and is now probably more like a lower than an upper.

15

"Here." Miss Watson stopped before a dark storefront and peered into the large, cracked window.

"Here?" Greyson looked up at the sign above the crumbling sidewalk: Lo Man's Market, with Asian characters set below the English words. He breathed in short, deep gasps.

"The note says here." His companion opened the door and stepped inside. She took a deep breath. "Mmm."

Cool air, fragrant with exotic spices, brushed against his run-flushed skin. Greyson bumped her from behind. "Get on with it then." He tapped his cane against the floor.

Miss Watson made a show of looking over the items on the shelves: dried herbs and vegetables in large glass jars, sacks and bins of the same for bulk purchases, copper and stone and ceramic cookware.

"May I assist you?" An older man of Asian descent bowed behind the counter. He wore a yellow silk tunic with a black-embroidered design of dragons and snakes.

"Yes, thank you." Miss Watson stepped forward, not even giving Greyson a chance to acknowledge the man, the note gripped tight in her fingers. "We are looking for rice flour."

"Rice flour?" Greyson thought she'd gone mad. They weren't looking for flour, rice or otherwise. "But I thought-"

The girl sighed and grabbed his arm, and he closed his mouth, exhaling in a rush out his nose.

"Indeed. Do you not recall? After you tried the pie for lunch? You said we should look into the purchase of some rice flour so Huddy can make you some pie at home."

"I did not."

"You implied it. I heard you."

"Miss Watson-"

"It is in the back room. Please, do follow me." The gentleman bowed again, deeper this time, showing a faint bald spot near the back of his head, his palms pressed together in front of his chest, and led the way into the back, past a curtain of beads and an incense burner.

Miss Watson followed, glancing back at Greyson over one shoulder, her sharp glare relaying the message to follow.

Nostrils flaring, Greyson rapped his cane against the floor thrice, but did as those green eyes had commanded, his footsteps heavy on the floor.

In the back room, the proprietor stopped before another door, this one of solid wood. He knocked twice, and someone from inside knocked twice in reply.

The door opened from within, and the man ushered the two of them inside.

"I'm not sure this is a good idea." Greyson didn't like the musty smell of incense. His nape-hair rose in alarm. His heartbeat quickened. The scent reminded him of one of his mother's séances.

"All will be fine." She threw the words over her shoulder, her voice low but sharp.

But would it? Why was Miss Watson so certain of the validity of the note? For all he knew, it was an elaborate ruse to jump them and make off with some of their most desired body parts and what little coin was left in his wallet.

The only light in the room spilled from a dusty oil lamp in one corner. The door closed and locked. A match flared and someone lit a stronger lamp.

"Ah. There ye are." It was the woman from the pie cart, sitting on a large pillow on the floor. "Sorry 'bout the secrecy. Gots to think 'bout me safety an' the grandboy."

Miss Watson nodded; Greyson didn't, but studied the room, absorbing every detail of his surroundings: Black drapes covered a single window, a long table before it littered with broken contraptions in various states of repair. A bookshelf lined one wall, only half-filled with books, scrolls stacked in the other half. Oddly, nothing that one would expect in a grocer's book rooms.

A young woman, who looked like she might be the daughter of the gentleman in yellow, stood next to the bright floor lamp she'd just lit. Cushions, in bright jewel colors, dotted the floor. Miss Watson chose one to sit on and nodded to one next to it for Greyson.

Greyson curled his lip but lowered himself to the pillow, grunting, sitting crossed-leg, his cane balanced across his knees, his hat resting on the floor beside him.

"Do you have information for us?" Miss Watson leaned forward on her cushion, bracing her elbows on her thighs.

Greyson had to wonder at her ease in this situation. Just how often had the girl met strangers in a dark, locked back room in the poorest part of town?

"Oh, indeed I do. I 'member the day Dawes got 'urt. Mr. Morton asked him to stay late and work and no one else were asked. Just 'im. Right strange it were, too. There were no cargo fer 'im to unload." The woman spoke in a whisper, eyes darting like they had earlier, even though they spoke in private.

"No cargo?" Greyson frowned, focusing on the old woman. "What was he asked to do?"

The woman shrugged. "Don' know. All I remember was the screamin' a bit later and a black steamcar racing by with smoke comin' out the back." The woman leaned back, nodding. "Police came and took Dawes away on a stretcher in a truck."

"Why were you still there?"

"Takes a while to pack me stuff up and I still 'ad pies to sell. Thought maybe Dawes'd buy one, seeing as 'e 'ad to stay late an' all."

"Does anyone know you saw anything?" Miss Watson looked worried for the woman's safety.

"Don' know. But that's why I wouldn't talk to ye earlier. I'll be leavin' 'ere with a big sack o' rice flour and me spices. You ought to take somethin', too."

Miss Watson nodded, straightening her spine like she was in charge. "We will. Likely the rice flour for wheat-free pies."

"Lo Quan will 'elp you with that. Might be some other stuff 'e 'as that ye can eat, too." The old woman nodded and flapped a hand at Mr. Holmes. She grabbed the edge of a side table and made to stand up.

"Wait." Greyson held up one hand; he needed to take control of the situation. The old woman froze, clutching the edge of the table. "Do you think Mr. Morton asked Mr. Dawes to stay after for a real task?"

"Wha' de ye mean?" The old woman looked ready to jump from her cushion and sprint for the door.

"Does Mr. Morton usually ask men to stay late and work?"

"Don' rightly know. 'e 'as in the past, I s'pose, but never jus' the one. Most usual when a ship arrives late and 'as to put out again early in the mornin'."

"So, it was odd?"

"That's wha' I just tol' you." The woman groaned and stood, curtseying, nearly falling over when she tipped her head, and left the room. The young woman followed, leaving the door open behind them. The sounds of commercial exchange drifted in from the front; the woman was haggling over the price of a bag of flour and a tin of spice.

"Well…" Greyson gripped his cane hard enough to turn his knuckles white.

Miss Watson sniffed and pivoted toward the door. "Do you think Mr. Morton knew what was going to happen?"

"Seems likely, Miss Watson, but the proof is not ours yet."

"You're lucky they spoke to you, you know."

Her sneer was surprisingly distressing and Grayson brushed the feeling aside. "What do you mean?"

She leveled another look at him and left, starting up an easy conversation with the grocer about some vegetables she wanted to purchase for Huddy.

Grayson suspected he'd be putting out the coin for them, but didn't really mind. The trip had turned fruitful after all.

And, reluctant as he was to admit it, he might have to give Miss Watson some credit. It seemed she would be coming in handy in his inquiries after all.

16

They departed the public steam tram in Stockley Gardens, as planned, though later than Mr. Holmes wanted judging by the way he kept frowning at his pocket watch. Quillian didn't care; they had more information. She was beginning to suspect there was a lot more to this business than anyone originally supposed.

Stockley Gardens was a different world. One etched in permanent, manicured splendor.

The rows of neat brick townhouses flanked a wide green garden for several blocks. Rose bushes bowed under the weight of their dense blooms, azaleas reached ever skyward, and the leaves of the Japanese maples fluttered in the breeze. Standing at the bottom, the muted stench of the Elizabeth River at her back, Quillian stared up the three blocks. "Was it always like this?"

Mr. Holmes stood next to her, resting, his cane propped over a shoulder. "As long as I can remember. My mother has a painting in her drawing room of it from at least fifty years ago, and it looks just like this."

"Huh." Quillian glanced over her shoulder at the river, the water calm in a slight inlet. "Even the river isn't so busy here."

Farther up, small ships would litter the Elizabeth, delivering goods, passenger ferries crossing back and forth between Norfolk and Portsmouth, dwarfed by the gambling boats with their huge churning paddles.

"Indeed. It is almost as calm here as in The Hague." Mr. Holmes swung his cane down to the cobbles at his feet and pivoted to watch the shoreline across the way. "My parents have one of the townhouses there. Inherited it from my grandfather."

"So, old money?"

He shrugged. "It started as old money. My father considers himself a bit of an investor and made a killing lending money to a couple of business buddies."

Quillian turned to stare at the far shore, too. Like Norfolk, Portsmouth's main hub was on the water, and many buildings extended into the water on piers so that boats could dock right outside their doors, barges docking beneath the larger ones so that their cargo could be hoisted straight up into the warehouse that sat on top. On the other edge of the waterway, Portsmouth's business district extended farther down than Norfolk's, trimmed at the end by the old Naval hospital that now served as the main treatment facility for the area. It was privately owned by a group of investors, and most local doctors paid a fee to operate out of their buildings. The only such facility that might be considered more important was the Children's hospital on the Norfolk shoreline, sitting on the water just up from where they stood. It was run by a charity, though children born into money were served in a separate wing than those from the indigent.

"Well, we'd best make tracks. It's getting late and my doctor doesn't keep his office open late." Mr. Holmes started off at a jaunty pace, swinging his cane at his side.

Trotting to catch up, Quillian smoothed the wrinkles in her plain cotton skirt and pulled her faded shawl up over her shoulders, sticking a finger under the edge of her leather corset to let air underneath. All this walking was making her sweat and the corset felt like it was tightening around her stomach.

Feeling shabby next to her companion, and decidedly dull in their surroundings, Quillian patted her hair back under her cap and raised her chin. Huddy said folks were more impressed by confidence than fashion, and Quillian was about to test that theory.

"Your doctor has an office in a residential neighborhood?"

"Yes. He works out of his home. That's one of the reasons he doesn't keep late hours. He doesn't have a medical degree or perform surgery, so he has no need of an agreement with the medical magnate. He is considered more consultant that anything else by most of the establishment."

"Oh." Quillian followed Mr. Holmes, letting herself fall back as they climbed the steady incline up the row-houses' sidewalk. Her corset was starting to cut in and she didn't want to chafe. There was no worry here of being left behind. This was a safe neighborhood, and though it would take her into the late evening, she could walk home if they got separated.

"Are you coming?" Mr. Holmes stopped at a corner, glancing first for traffic on the cross street, then back at Quillian.

"Go ahead. I am just enjoying the garden atmosphere." Birds whistled in the trees and squirrels chattered back.

"His house is half-way up the last block, on the right. Wait for me if I am inside when you get there." Mr. Holmes glanced right and left and crossed the street, whirling his cane once more.

"Okay." Quillian slowed her gait even more, even stopping to take in a cardinal darting among the greenery.

Ahead, Mr. Holmes reached his destination, and waved before trotting up to a door and lifting the knocker.

The road was quiet. No steamtram or automaton-led carriage clattered on the pavement. No children played in the street or swung from the center trees. Deserted except for the scant urban wildlife, it reminded Quillian of a still-life painting.

Crossing the last street, Quillian noticed a man watching her. Dressed in natty business attire—the same gray trousers, dark jacket and bowler as Mr. Holmes—he frowned at her from the top corner of the neighborhood.

Quillian ignored the stare and continued her wandering and waiting, keeping to the bottom of the block. Stopping, she watched a squirrel chase a pigeon, while yet another squirrel stole the first one's cache of tree nuts.

She didn't want to get too close to that man, but didn't want to get too far away from Mr. Holmes; he was close enough she could call out if she needed.

***

"Ah, Grayson. How are you, boy?" The man who had been watching Quillian stood at the bottom of the steps to the townhouse Mr. Holmes had just stepped out of to wait. Quillian thought the man spoke extra loud to make sure she could hear.

"Mr. Nichols, good to see you. How is Trent? Still at university?"

"Yes, yes. Finally abandoned his unfortunate dream of becoming an actor and has decided to study accounting, he has. What are you up to these days?"

"I've moved out from Mother and Father to make a stab at life on my own."

"Good, good." The man shifted closer, shooting an obvious look in Quillian's direction. "Best be careful there, son. Seems the vagrants have wandered in from who knows where."

"I beg your pardon?" To his credit, Mr. Holmes's reared away from the conspiratorial head tilt of Mr. Nichols.

The man looked down the street again, his gaze crashing into Quillian's. He jerked his head in her direction, grabbing Mr. Holmes by the arm and spinning him to face up the street. "There's one, right there."

"I assure you, Mr. Nichols, Miss Watson is not a threat to you, unless you first threaten her. Of course, if you were to threaten her, you would be dealing with me before you ever had to deal with her." Mr. Holmes jerked his arm from the grasp of the older gentleman and pivoted to stalk down the street.

"Do your mother and father know the kind of company you're keeping these days, Greyson?" Mr. Nichols voice dripped with scathing venom.

"Even you do not know the kind of company I am keeping, Mr. Nichols." Mr. Holmes did not turn back to the gentleman, but continued with slow, steady steps toward Quillian, stopping in front of her to tip his hat and offer his arm. "Miss Watson."

"Mr. Holmes." Quillian nodded and accepted the arm, resisting the urge to stick out her tongue at the rude gentleman.

"Your father would not be pleased, Greyson. Nor your mother." The man yelled after them, loud enough that a door opened across the street and a maid poked a head out to see what the fuss was about.

Mr. Holmes grinned. "You might be surprised, Mr. Nichols, to learn that I don't care to do anything that pleases them."

From the journal of G. J. Holmes

I'd been shocked when father first refused to support my regimen. I shouldn't have been. That is the way of things in the elite. Father had always been strict in how my brothers and I needed to act in public, but it was always more relaxed at home - though certainly more stifling than at the brothel. My parents tried their damndest to influence my circle, but didn't exactly choose it for me.

I grew up with the stories my friends told, of lessons and classes forced upon them to receive their allowance, parents choosing their friends and even their future spouse.

I have never understood it. Is it because they have miserable lives, and so feel their children should, as well?

17

They turned at the next street, cutting left through the next neighborhood, the newer brick row-houses just as quiet and looked just as deserted as the others. Here, the pavement was newer, the small, rounded river stones pressed into a thick layer of hot tar. There was no wide greenway down the middle, though the row-houses were lumped in groups of five with wide swathes of lawn running between them.

Greyson remained silent, his gait slow and controlled, his arm stiff beneath Miss Watson's hand. His cane provided an irritating tick of background cadence faster than his feet.

"You know that man?"

"He is a friend of my father's. I attended grade school with his son, Trent."

"The man said his son wanted to be an actor?" Miss Watson kept glancing at him out the corner of her eye. It made Greyson think she was looking for something? A reaction?

He took a breath and kept his gaze straight ahead, ignoring her little looks. "Aye. He was good at it. Shame his father bullied him into studying figures."

"Bullied?"

Greyson nodded, clenching and unclenching his jaw until his teeth hurt. He shouldn't be talking to her about this. "That is how fathers of the elite work. They bully their sons into conforming to their idea of what they are."

Miss Watson kept silent, and Greyson wished she would speak, change the topic of conversation. But she didn't, so he kept on, his words falling faster from his lips,

"They cannot accept their children as they are. They must badger them into being 'like their old man.' I suppose it might be even worse for the daughters. I'm certain they are forced to marry young men modeled in that image." Grayson's steps got faster the more he spoke, his swinging cane cutting through the air next to his head. He couldn't stop.

Miss Watson patted his arm beneath her hand, and the dabbing touch was a comfort that amazed Greyson. Surprising himself, he discovered he wanted to share more.

"Any child that balks at their parents' machinations are broken into submission, either physically or emotionally. I think I might rather the physical to the mental. My mother is an expert at growing guilt in the bosoms of her offspring."

When Miss Watson had to skip, the awkward hop pulling on his arm, Greyson finally realized the racing pace he set.

Clearing his throat, he slowed his stride. He was too abrupt in his manner, though, and Miss Watson almost tumbled to the cobbles. Greyson grabbed her other arm with his, steadying her, pulling her upright and closer.

He could smell her again: honeysuckle, with a hint of sweat. He swallowed and eased his grip. "My apologies, Miss Watson."

"Certainly, Mr. Holmes. You are unduly upset. I understand entirely."

"Do you? Did the good doctor bully you into becoming his apprentice?"

"What?" Miss Watson clutched at his arm with both hands and Greyson took a step back, surprised. "Oh, no. I want to become a human mechanist. I love being his apprentice."

"Truly?" Greyson stared down into her green eyes, surprised at the sensation of falling into the golden-brown centers for the first time. "You feel no pressure of his expectations?"

"Well..." Miss Watson looked away, her cheeks flushing. "His expectations are high, and there are times when I fall short, but that is something different in its entirety."

"Is it? How does he make you feel when you fall short?" Tucking his cane under his arm, Greyson shifted to hold her hands in his. For some reason, he wanted her to understand what he meant. To have experienced it so that she could understand him. "Does his disappointment make you feel ashamed?"

Miss Watson glanced off at the downtown skyline, misty in the smoggy distance, and Greyson admired her defiant profile. "Yes, but-" she tugged on her hands, but he would not let her pull them from his grasp, "if I make a mistake, someone could die, or be hurt more than they already are. I need to push to be better."

Greyson nodded, his brow furrowing. He resisted an impulse to grip her hands ever tighter. "I see your point. Imagine that feeling, that shame, over something as unimportant as whom you choose as a friend. You would not believe the lecture I receive from Sir Stanley about befriending Trent when he was still resisting the will of his father. Or what occupation you choose to pursue. Whether you prefer coffee to tea, or better yet, Orange Pekoe to Earl Grey."

"I'm sorry, Mr. Holmes. I've never experienced such." Her green gaze met his once more, the irises thinner now, concealing the golden middles.

Greyson dropped her hands, smiling so she wouldn't look so pitying. "Then you are very lucky, Miss Watson, and I envy you your ignorance." Tapping his cane to the cobbles, he indicated they should resume walking.

"I truly am sorry." Miss Watson grabbed one of his hands in both of hers, squeezing it. "You have siblings?"

He sighed and tapped his cane sharp against the ground. He did not want to talk about his brothers, but something about the earnest tug of her hand made him continue. "Yes. Two brothers, though one has passed, leading the life expected of an elite young man of leisure. Spent too much time in the cheaper brothels, picked up a couple of diseases. I was quite disgusted by the time and energy—and money—my father was willing to put into Jacoby's recovery, and yet he was completely unwilling to spend anything to combat my health issues."

"And your other brother?"

"Wilroy is following in Jacoby's footsteps. Though in a quieter manner, so as not to upset my mother." Greyson stopped, planting his cane to the pavement. "Shall we discuss something else?"

"I haven't asked about your mother, yet." Miss Watson tilted her chin at him, and Greyson was struck at the angularity of that feature. From this vantage, all daintiness disappeared.

"I have no desire to speak of my mother. I would like to talk about something more pleasant.

Greyson thought the flare of her nostrils cute and wondered at his odd thoughts about the young woman.

"Certainly." Miss Watson nodded and dipped her chin, looking down.

Grinning, Greyson took her arm again, tucking it at his elbow and beginning their stroll once more. "Why do you work for Dr. M?"

Pursing her lips, Miss Watson stared ahead, at the National Bank of Neo-Virginia's clock tower, the second hand still stuck at six o'clock. "You consider this a pleasant conversation?"

"Compared to the old one? Yes."

She snorted and shook her head. "I enjoy human mechanism theory."

"Did you enjoy it before you went to work for Dr. M?"

Opening her mouth, the girl paused, rolling her jaw to one side. Frowning, she swished her skirt, dislodging a roaming ladybug. "I am not sure I even knew what it was when I was placed under Dr. M's apprenticeship. I found it fascinating, however, and am getting quite good at it."

"Were you already able to read when you started at Dr. M's?" Greyson's curiosity about this girl expanded. There was no way her intellect had manifested itself but six years ago. To learn and comprehend such advanced subjects, she had to have had some schooling when she was young.

Rounding on him, she shot her answer at him. "Of course, I could read and write. I could do sums and higher calculations, as well, and I knew my history and basic science. That is one reason, I believe, that Dr. M agree to take me on."

"Who asked him to take you on?"

The girl frowned, like she was trying to remember.

"Hmm?" Greyson tapped her shoulder when she didn't answer right away. Surely it wasn't that hard a question.

"I'm not certain. I remember coming to Dr. M's in a fine carriage—not one that belonged to the brothel, though. And Madame was there. Huddy served us tea."

"You were twelve?" Most twelve-year olds, especially those with a better than rudimentary education, would remember such a life-changing event.

Miss Watson nodded. But she was pale, and dots of sweat beaded along her brow, trickling along her hairline to her neck. "I think Dr. M and Madame already knew each other, there were no introductions, just between me and the doctor."

"You say they already knew each other? Did they have a pleasant conversation, or was it strained?" Greyson worried about Miss Watson's state. Her face was beyond pale now and venturing into translucent.

Rubbing fingers over her wrinkled brow, Miss Watson took a deep breath, stopping their forward pace altogether. She placed the fingers of her free hand to her temple, rubbing there like it pained her.

"Miss Watson?" Greyson looked around for a tea or coffee shop, even a pub would do. It looked like Miss Watson was in dire need of a good chair and a steadying beverage.

But there was nothing but private residences.

Blinking, Miss Watson looked up into Greyson's concerned visage. "I think we need to make our way home. Suddenly, I am not feeling all that well." Her grip on his arm tightened, and she leaned into his side.

Holding her upright, Greyson marched her into the heart of downtown before seeing an available steamtaxi on the main street. People swelled in and out of buildings, darting around the automaton carriages and steamtaxis. The bombarding noise was enough to give even Greyson a headache; he could only imagine what it was doing to Miss Watson in the state she was in.

Whistling, he caught the attention of the nearest driver, and the man jumped from the front of his conveyance, opening the back door and bowing.

"Here. Climb in, Miss Watson." Greyson passed her into the seat, shifting her over so he could follow. Ducking into the open door of the steamtaxi, he barked the address to the driver, who ran around to his own door and climbed in.

At the push of a lever and the hiss of steam, the vehicle moved off down the street, jerking in the heavy traffic.

"We'll have you home soon, Miss Watson. Why don't you close your eyes and rest?" Greyson leaned over her, pushing the short damp tresses back from her face so he could study her face.

Her eyes were glassy, the lids fluttering over them, as if she were ready to swoon.

"Give it some speed man. Give it some speed." Sitting on the plush bench seat, Greyson let Miss Watson lean into him, let her head rest on his shoulder. Her breathing was rapid and shallow, and fear gripped him. What the devil was wrong with her?

Holding her close, he watched her face for further signs of distress, but saw none, and within a few blocks her breathing deepened. Greyson bent to listen closely and nodded. Ms. Watson appeared more asleep than in pain.

It was only when the conveyance halted in front of Dr. M's grand home that realization struck. Holding his breath, Greyson traced the line of her jaw and ran a finger up over the gentle swell of her cheek. Though the skin was freckled, and still displayed the roundness of youth, Miss Watson shared her profile with Madame.

Quillian's log

Mr. Holmes questions got me thinking about what I know about Madame – and my time at the brothel. I suppose, I might owe her something for taking me in to the brothel when I was a baby. I don't know my parents. I don't even really know how I came to be there in the first place. All I know is what little Taggage has told me on my forced monthly visits to the brothel.

She told me I was a bastard brat and that I ought to be grateful for whatever I got. If she'd had her way, I never would have been there.

I've never had the courage to ask Madame her opinion.

Maybe that needs to change.

18

Huddy set the flask of headache tonic on the breakfast table in front of Quillian. "Take a big spoonful, missy."

Grimacing, Quillian curled her nose. The tonic was bitter, like dandelion greens before they were stewed in vinegar and salt pork. But, she took her grits spoon and poured the thickish liquid into it, holding her nose to get the goop down.

"Argh!" Sputtering, Quillian grabbed up her cup of tea, spilling some of the precious liquid, gulping the hot brew to wash away the lingering taste of the tonic. "Can't you make it with honey or something?"

Snorting, Huddy took up the bottle, ramming the cork stopper into the top nice and tight. "If it's bitter, no one takes too much." Huddy wagged a finger and retreated to the kitchen.

Quillian smacked her lips, not daring to lick them lest she find a stray drop of the abhorrent medicine. The pain in her head eased, though, so she'd curb her complaining.

Sighing, she took up her fork, spearing the slices of boiled egg and grilled tomato on her plate. Toast with coconut oil to lend it a hint of sweet lay across the edge of her plate, the edges crisp, the centers soft and chewy.

Dr. M sat behind his copy of the Neo-Virginian News, chomping away at his kippers and fried potatoes. The Norfolk Gazette waited at his elbow.

"Doctor?" Did she dare actually ask him?

"Hmm?" Dr. M remained behind the paper barrier.

"What do you know of Madame? And how I came to be with her?" Quillian set her fork down, straightening in her chair.

The paper bent at the middle, Dr. M's shaking fingers holding the fold. "Why do you want to know about that?"

Shrugging, Quillian looked down at the still-full plate. "I was just wondering."

"Has Mr. Holmes been asking?" Dr. M creased the paper with neat strokes into a square and tucked it beneath his plate. He clasped his hands and leaned forward, training both eyes on Quillian.

"Well..." Should she tell him? If she said yes, Mr. Holmes might be refused future entry into the house, and for some reason, that possibility did not set well with Quillian. "He's asked questions about when Madame brought me here—in passing you realize, when he's been asking about your surgery—and made me realize that there is much I don't know. Things I may not remember."

Dr. M's magnified eye stared at her while the other blinked. "Why would you want to know about Madame?"

"I don't know that I want to *know*, but I want to *remember*. I don't remember much from before I came to live here."

Picking up his newspaper, Dr. M shook it back out, disappearing once more behind its thin sheaves. "Perhaps that is your subconscious telling you there is nothing good in remembering."

"But-"

"That is enough questions, Watson. Finish your breakfast and review your anatomy text. I think I shall administer a quiz this afternoon."

Pressing her lips together, her jaw clenched, Quillian glared at the columns of news. It wasn't fair. Why couldn't he give her some answers? A photograph above one article in Dr. M's paper caught her eye. She cocked her head and squinted, trying to get a better look, but the image was blurred and sketchy. Still, Quillian thought she recognized the face. She couldn't ask for the paper yet; not until Dr. M was finished.

Picking up her fork, she dug into her breakfast, eyes on the shifting column, trying to read the caption under the photo. She couldn't make out the letters, though; Dr. M kept moving the paper. Giving up, she concentrated on finishing her breakfast at the same pace as Dr. M. If they were done at the same time, there was a better chance she could get her hands on the paper before he threw it away.

Huddy was bringing the second pot of tea when Dr. M sighed and set the paper aside, patting his stomach. "Wonderful repast, Huddy. Just wonderful." The doctor smiled at the housekeeper.

"Thankee much, Doctor. Is there anything else you'd like afore I clear?"

Dr. M shook his head, stretching and yawning. "No, no, I'm good. Think I'll just pop into my study for a bit. See me this evening for your quiz, Watson." His pointer finger tapped the table next to her plate. Standing, he picked up the paper, rolling it into a tube and slapped it against the table.

Quillian watched the old man leave, paper in his hand. There would be no way to get her hands on that paper, unless...she'd be taking a quiz with him this evening. Might she be able to nab it then?

Watching Huddy clear the table, Quillian finished the last of her egg and toast, washing it down with fresh tea. "Huddy?"

"Yes, chile?"

"What do you know about Madame?"

"Madame?" Huddy straightened from the table, damp cloth in hand. "What ye want to know about her for? Has her visit put thoughts in your head?"

Taking care to rest her hands in her lap—Huddy would snap that cloth at her in a heartbeat if she dared rest her elbows on the table—Quillian tried to look unassuming. "I was just wondering about her. I don't remember much about my life before I came here."

"I should think you'd be happy about that, chile. Can't imagine it was a very good life in that there brothel."

"Have you ever been there?"

"What?" Huddy reared back, and Quillian thought she'd ruined her chance of getting any information from the housekeeper. "Why on earth would I go to a place like that?"

"I was just wondering. I have memories, or maybe dreams, and I think it might be the brothel, but I'm not unhappy in them, so I don't know for certain."

Sniffing, Huddy leaned back over the table, her hand making quick, vicious strokes over the oak table. "It's best leaving the past behind ye, chile. No sense digging up stuff others want buried."

Buried? Quillian thought about that word. It sounded like something really bad had happened, and Huddy knew about it. Probably Dr. M, too.

Why wouldn't they tell her?

From the journal of G. J. Holmes

I am nearly as intrigued by Miss Watson and Madame, and their relationship, as I am the investigation of the attacks.

I do not understand why Miss Watson does not remember living at the brothel. She was twelve when she left. What with the regular visits with Madame – the older woman has mentioned those to me several times - I am surprised that those years were never discussed.

And I am curious about where Dr. M fits into this. Had he been a client of Madame's? Or a friend?

Or something more?

19

Greyson stood outside the open breakfast room door, surveying the table laden with platters before venturing in. Madame sat at the head of the narrow expanse, sipping tea from a gold-rimmed china cup. The teapot sat at her elbow, steam curling from its spout.

"Good morning, Madame." Greyson sat to the woman's right, placing his cane and hat next to him on the floor.

"Is it?" Madame closed her eyes and took a long drag of hot tea. From where he sat, Greyson could smell the brandy that had been added. "Rather dismal if you ask me."

Outside the mahogany trimmed windows, rays of sunlight streaked down through the low-lying clouds. "It looks to be brightening."

Madame held her head and moaned. "Please, Mr. Holmes. Can you not be quite so cheerful?"

"My apologies, Madame." Greyson lowered his voice and helped himself to the carafe of coffee that sat to the left of his place setting, applying a liberal amount of cashew cream to the dark liquid before taking a sip and inspecting the platters and bowls. Much of it was from his dietary regimen.

"I thought to try your breakfast, Mr. Holmes, and instructed cook to only prepare your regimen this morning."

She poured another cup of heavily doctored tea. "Perhaps I was a bit too hasty last evening."

"Ah." Greyson ladled a large portion of steamy quinoa into his bowl, followed by some coconut cream and a spoonful of honey. "You have a hangover?"

"I have a headache, Mr. Holmes. I went teetotal yesterday."

"Perhaps my regimen is just the thing for you this morning, then. I am told by Dr. Bhatnagar that it contains a good many of the vitamins and minerals we need."

Madame glared at him over the rim of her cup. "Vitamins and minerals?"

"Indeed. They are the compounds that keep us hale and hearty." Greyson spooned cereal into his mouth, relishing the creamy sweetness. "Please, try some Madame. It cannot hurt your head."

The older woman eyed the concoction in his bowl. "What exactly did you put in there?"

"Shall I?" Greyson set down his spoon and scooped up a small amount of grain, poising it over her bowl.

Madame nodded and watched him create the same mixture in front of her, though in a smaller amount, and with more honey.

"Thank you, Mr. Holmes." Madame picked up her spoon and took a dainty mouthful, chewing and swallowing before raising a brow and nodding. She took another mouthful and continued eating, sipping at her special tea blend between every few bites.

Greyson finished his own breakfast in quick order. It was easy without conversation to distract him.

"Mr. Holmes. Have you found anything new?"

Setting his cup on the table, Greyson played with the handle before answering. "I'm not sure it's new information, but I have discovered that there were likely three men at the park when May-Ellen was attacked. I found three distinct sets of footprints in the dirt."

"Surely it would be too late to say for certain those prints were from the attackers?" Madame dished more quinoa into her bowl, adding fruit and honey, but omitting the coconut cream.

"There has been little rain to disturb them. And I doubt many visitors crouch beneath the rose bushes."

"There is that. Anything else?"

"I think they wore uniforms. The treads from the imprints were identical."

"Uniforms? You mean they weren't just thugs hired to make the attack?"

"Indeed." Greyson pushed his cup away. "I think I may have found a reason for you to tell me the name and address of Jezebelle's client from the night of her attack, although, I suspect I already have the address."

"Oh?" Madame sat back in her chair and set her spoon in her bowl, one brow arching to her hairline.

"Number 127, The Hague. Brick, three story, near the end of the arch."

"That is correct. The client's name was M'arcus Dolan."

"Mr. Dolan is married, yes?"

"Yes." Madame sighed and crossed her arms.

The move reminded Greyson of Quill- Miss Watson when she did much the same thing, and he covered his smile with a cough and a well-placed hand.

"His wife is one reason we must remain discrete."

"Well," Greyson leaned back in his chair and splayed his fingers on the table, "Mrs. Dolan looks like she has had recent surgery on her right leg."

Madame took a sharp intake of breath and paled, her arms dropping to her lap. "What?"

"I visited The Hague yesterday, after looking over the Rose Garden in Lafayette Park."

"And no one called the police to report someone lurking on the street?" Madame's laugh was short and explosive. Her face was still pale, though her arms were no longer limp. Like Greyson, she gripped the edge of the table.

"You forget, Madame, I used to live there. I am certain I was recognized. I was lucky to get away without my mother coming into the street and accosting me. Or rather, Wallace being sent outside to accost me in her stead."

"Yes, of course. I did forget that fact."

"In any case, I spied a gentleman pushing a young woman in a wheeled chaise, her right leg raised and sitting on a cushion."

"And you are certain this was Mr. Dolan?"

"Not then, though he fit your description of the client. They entered 127 The Hague, and you just confirmed the address for me."

Madame stood, scrambling for her cane to keep herself steady. She paced to the window and back, the cane bearing the weight when she stepped on her left leg. "It is my fault."

"Madame?" Greyson stood and walked to stand beside his hostess at the window.

"He was a new client. I checked my files. He'd been recommended by many reputable gentlemen that have frequented the brothel for years. I thought my system was foolproof."

"We cannot be certain he was in on the attack."

"No?" Madame rounded on him, and Greyson had to grab her arms to keep her from falling when she wobbled on her cane. "What does your gut say?"

"That my regimen is working."

"Not about your health, Mr. Holmes, but about this attack."

"I know what you meant, Madame. I am just unwilling to assume anything. I desire to gain further information about Mr. Dolan and his wife. If her surgery was performed before the attack, it would be hard pressed for me to think he was involved."

"Regardless, he will never cross the door to this establishment again."

"Madame?"

"I cannot believe he was not involved. Not after hearing this. Until you can convince me otherwise, he is barred from my girls."

"Will he not complain?"

"Why would I care? Let him complain." Her hands flew and Greyson had to duck to avoid being scratched by her nails.

"But..." Greyson let his confusion get the best of him and he could not put his question into words. He opened and closed his mouth like a guppy gulping water in a fish tank.

The woman laughed. "This brothel has plenty of clients, Mr. Holmes. More than it needs really. They understand how I do business. I make the rules, not them. If they refuse to follow those rules, they do not get to play." Madame stepped back, pulling her arms from Greyson's grip.

"Do not be too hasty, please. I have a plan to find out when his wife had her surgery."

Madame raised a brow. "Indeed?"

Greyson swallowed. Though it was a plan, it was not one he felt entirely comfortable executing. It meant going back. It meant..."I'm going to ask my mother to let me call on her for tea."

The woman relaxed and snickered. "I thought it was something dangerous, Mr. Holmes."

"It is." Greyson let his arms fall. "Madame? There is more. I also visited the docks, with Miss Watson."

"Quillian accompanied you? With Dr. M's permission?"

"Not exactly. He was not home when I called upon her, though I believe the housekeeper gave her consent."

"You have Huddy's favor?" Laughing, Madame shifted a curtain and looked out at the street and smiled, though Greyson thought it was not a happy one.

"She agreed to her coming with me."

"And what did you find out, Mr. Holmes?"

"That a couple of the patients did come from that area, but that not everything about those attacks has been reported truthfully."

Madame turned back to him, leaning a hip against the windowsill, arms crossed. "You thought it had?"

"I had no proof otherwise. Now I do."

Nodding, Madame narrowed her gaze and resumed perusing the scene outside the window. There were no carriages or automatons on the street, only a couple of ragged-looking children running up the side. "I sometimes wonder about you, Mr. Holmes."

Greyson frowned, but found he had nothing to say to the confusing comment. "Madame?"

"Yes?"

"How is your head?"

"Much better, actually. I shall ask cook to make your regimen for breakfast every morning in the future."

"Might I consider that you now owe me?"

Madame stiffened halfway to her chair, gripping the silver knob of her cane so that her knuckles turned white. "I owe you?"

"For the headache remedy."

"It could have been the brandy."

"Then why are you not thinking of asking cook for brandy every morning?"

The woman sighed and resumed making her way to her chair, sitting and picking up the teapot to pour another cup. "Point taken. Continue. I assume you are going to ask a favor of me."

There it was. A woman using the term 'favor' instead of debt. Greyson would have to keep note. Though the investigation would be anecdotal at best, it might be useful in the future.

"Yes, I would like you to answer a question for me."

"Very well, what is the question?"

"First, I would like your assurance that you are going to answer the question before I ask it."

Madame set the teapot on the table rather hard, the sharp clink of china on polished word echoing. "It is that bad a question?"

"It is a personal question."

The woman watched him from narrowed eyes, her chin rising. "Your question concerns Quillian?"

Greyson raised his brows, taking in his own quick inhale. Should he say yes? That might make her refuse to agree to answer. Perhaps he should ask something else, instead? What else might he ask that was personal in nature?

"Never mind answering, Mr. Holmes. I can tell it does." She sipped her tea and swallowed, licking her lips and sighing. "Yes, she is my daughter."

Quillian's Log

While I enjoy training to be a mechanist, I hate tests. And Dr. M loves them.

I remember my first test, after I first arrived. I was told to write an essay about the state of Neo-Virginia and Norfolk, in particular. I didn't know much about any of that and failed.

Dr. M gave me a second chance, though, and we had a discussion about it instead, where he described a situation from the newspaper and then I gave my opinion on a solution.

I'm not sure that I passed, because Dr. M disagreed with most of my solutions and shot cannon holes through them.

But he kept me on. And I guess that is what is important.

20

"Now then. Are you ready for your quiz?" Dr. M lounged behind his desk, hands clasped across his middle, elbows resting hard on the upholstered leather arms of his chair.

Sitting in the solitary wing chair before the desk, Quillian nodded. She had to be prepared; she'd been studying and reviewing the textbook since she'd woken from her nap after returning with Mr. Holmes. It had been an awkward arrival at the house; she'd been asleep, probably drooling, on the young man's shoulder.

She didn't want to remember how embarrassing that had been.

There was a lot at stake over this quiz. If she didn't answer enough of the questions correctly, her dinner would be sparse, and taken in the kitchen while reading and reviewing even more.

"What is the purpose of the sternum?"

"To hold together the ribs and protect the heart and other internal organs." Quillian blinked. That was a simple question.

Dr. M nodded. "What is the purpose of the spleen?"

"The spleen manufactures white blood cells, stores platelets, and acts as a filter for the lymph system." Quillian let out a slow breath and tightened her fingers, staring at a nick in the wooden panel at the front of the desk. That question had been harder. "Oh, and it recycles red blood cells, too."

"What are the main muscles in the foot?"

Quillian swallowed. "The anterior tibial, posterior tibial, peroneal tibial, the extensors, and the flexors."

"What else are in the foot that work to make it move?"

"Ligaments and tendons."

The doctor leaned back, raising one brow into his hairline.

Shaking, Quillian chased her thoughts. What had she forgotten?

Dr. M opened his mouth-

"Ooh. The metatarsal bones and, of course, the fibula—which is one of the leg bones."

Smiling, the doctor nodded. "And what is the strongest tendon in the foot?"

"The Achilles tendon, at the back."

"Name three other tendons in the foot."

Quillian shifted in her chair, struggling for a moment to remember. "The peroneus tetius, extensor halucis longus, and the peroneus brevis?"

"Is that a question or an answer?"

Choking, Quillian nodded then got out, "an answer."

Tapping his fingers together, Dr. M observed her for a silent moment. "Where is the subcutaneous layer?"

"Between the top and bottom layers of the skin?" Quillian frowned, trying to call to mind the illustration in her text book.

Dr. M shifted in his chair, his lips pressed tight together.

"Wait. No." Closing her eyes, Quillian concentrated, recreating the inked illustrations from the textbook in her mind. "It's the layer of fat between the muscles and the skin. It acts as an insulator and reduces frictions between the muscles and the skin."

Relaxing, Dr. M smiled. "Very good recovery."

"Thank you." Quillian's stomach tightened. There was no chance she'd earn a slice of blueberry pie after her pork and potato stew. She might not even get a dumpling in the stew.

"Explain to me what the pancreas does."

Quillian took a long, calming breath. She knew this. "The pancreas aids in digestion, producing insulin and enzymes. It is located near the liver."

"Good, good." Dr. M dropped his feet to the floor and leaned forward, the loud thump in the otherwise quiet made Quillian jump in her seat. "That will be all for now."

"That's all? I mean, sir, my quiz is complete?"

"Yes, yes." Dr. M waved a hand at the door. "Go on. Don't waste the evening away, you need to review the dermis layers and what they contain and protect, but I don't need to ask you any more questions right now."

Quillian stood, spying the folded newspaper on the edge of the console that stored his bourbon and brandy. "Might I read the Neo-Virginian News?"

"The paper?" The eye behind the enlarged monocle darted over her before sliding away to focus on the sheaves of creased paper. Dr. M frowned, his wrinkled brow shifting the monocle. "I don't see why not. Don't spend too much time on the gossip pages. Pay attention to the politics. What goes on in those social circles affects everyone more than anything else in there."

"Yes, sir." Bobbing a quick curtsey, Quillian grabbed the paper and dashed out the door, letting it drift closed behind her.

Huddy caught her in the hall. "Done already?" The housekeeper carried a basket of fresh greens in her hands, the rooted ends still dusted with damp black earth.

Quillian nodded, tucking the newspaper behind her back.

The older woman frowned, looking around her and down to the now-closed door to the private study. "Dr. M feeling okay?"

"As far as I can tell, he's fine. He just asked me a few quick questions and let me go."

"How did you do?" Huddy shifted the basket.

Tightening her fingers on the paper, Quillian shifted to one hip, fingering the bottom edge of her corset and tucking the end of the pamphlet under. She shifted straight again, letting the leather's hem hug the paper between it and her cotton dress.

"Let me take that basket, Huddy." Quillian held out her hands, smiling.

"Oh, thankee. I'm not getting any younger, ye know." Huddy spun around and led the way to the kitchen.

Letting out a stagnant breath, Quillian congratulated herself on keeping the paper away from Huddy's prying eyes. If the housekeeper determined that Quillian was getting involved in "something she shouldn't", she'd never get to help Mr. Holmes figure out this mess.

"Greens again?" Ralph stood at the sink, paring potatoes, an over-large apron wrapped twice around his waist.

"Yes'm. And an extra helping for you." Huddy swatted a towel at the boy's behind, but Ralph was too quick and swayed his hips away so the hit wasn't that hard.

"Oh, I love your greens, Huddy."

Huddy narrowed her eyes. "Then you can have three servings with your supper."

Ralph stared, forgetting to peel the potato in his hands.

The housekeeper pointed to a counter and Quillian set the basket atop it, starting the work on the tender young kale and collards.

"Ain't you supposed to be studying?" Huddy's voice sounded far away and echoed. Turning, Quillian found the woman with her head buried in the cold box, pulling out the pots of butter and lard.

"Well, yes." Quillian shuffled toward the door. "But I thought you might need some help."

"Off with ye, now. Git yer studying done. And no straining yer eyes on it." Huddy pulled her head out, her cheeks flushed from exertion. "I'll call ye down fer supper. I've got blueberry pie with lemon curd for dessert."

"Oh, yum!" Ralph jumped on the stool her stood on, the legs creaking at the unfair movement.

Huddy snorted and returned to the cold box. "You'll only be getting a slice if you finish them 'taters."

Grinning, the boy turned back to the sink, a renewed vigor in his paring fingers.

Quillian backed out the door before Huddy changed her mind. It looked like she'd get to read over the paper before dinner.

```
```

```
```

<div style="text-align:center">```</div>

Tucked under the eaves, her lamp lit and turned up high, Quillian spread the Neo-Virginian News over the neat blanket on her bed. She smoothed the folds, skimming the headlines: MAYOR SIGNS NEW ANTI-LOITERING LAW, GANG FIGHT NEAR THIRD DOCK RESULTS IN FIVE DEAD, DAUGHTERS OF THE KING HOLD MAJOR HOSPITAL FUNDRAISER, LOCAL BUSINESSMEN MAKE DEAL.

It was the photo below that last headline that caught her eye. It was black and white—though she'd heard rumors that New Briton State's capital, Boston, had colored photos in its newspaper, Global World News, she hadn't seen any of them yet—and held three men, all holding fat cigars aloft in a toast.

One man looked familiar, and she frowned down at the image. If he was a businessman, did he work at the docks? Perhaps she'd noticed him when she'd visited with Mr. Holmes. Or, had he been here, to consult with Dr. M?

She rubbed her temples and sighed. Where had she seen him before?

"Quillian! Dinner!"

Jerking, ripping the edge of the paper, Quillian cursed under her breath and refolded the leafs. How would she ever figure anything out if she kept getting interrupted?

From the journal of G. J. Holmes

The last time I had tea with mother was two days after Jacoby's funeral. Wilroy had been in attendance, as well, though Father was drinking alone in his study. Mother had been eating her chocolates, far more than usual, and I suspect they were the type that contained liqueur in the center.

My stomach had been cramping horribly. Not just from my ailment, I suspect, but also from the loss of Jacoby. I had been but fifteen at the time – too young for either of my parents to explain what had sickened my eldest brother and killed him.

Wilroy had no such qualms.

I admit, I had suffered from an extreme case of hero worship with Jacoby. I thought he could do anything.

That all ended that day with Wilroy's blunt explanation of Jacoby's penchant for whoring and the disease he'd contracted and died from.

Mother, bless her poor broken heart, had been too full of chocolate and cherry cordial to even notice.

21

The note from his mother was short.

Come at 3pm; your father will be home.

Greyson took a long sip of tea. He should have finished lunch before reading it; he'd lost his appetite.

"Is all well, Mr. Holmes?"

Madame sat at the head of the short table, the morning's Norfolk Gazette spread out before her, reading glasses perched precariously upon the tip of the nose.

"I have received confirmation that I may visit home this afternoon."

Madame raised her brows but said nothing.

Greyson sighed. "My mother is in the know on everything that happens in the neighborhood. She'll know when Mrs. Dolan last took a bath, let alone when she had the surgery that put her in that chair. She will likely know the full details of the procedure, possibly more than Mrs. Dolan knows. I also hope to speak with my father. One of his, suggestions if you will, for treatment of my malady leads me to suspect he might know something of this business, as well."

"Do you honestly think your father will talk to you?" Madame removed the glasses and set them on the newspaper. "I thought he's been refusing an audience with you?"

"I am not certain he is knowingly involved. With this limb business. I think, well I hope anyway, that someone was fishing for a patient, and only baited him. Indeed, he may not offer me anything, but I have no other place to begin my questioning. And my mother is making the arrangements. I am hoping to catch him by surprise."

Greyson sipped his tea again, resting his elbows on the table. "I think there are many others involved. Unless they, too, are caught, the business will continue. And I doubt that those near the bottom of the scheme are aware of who is ultimately in charge."

Madame sighed. "This is what I was afraid of."

"Hmm?" Greyson's mouth was full of tea.

"That it is bigger than just my girls." Madame sat back in her chair. "And I am afraid Quillian will want to be involved."

Quillian.

Greyson cleared his throat. "How is Miss Watson?" He was afraid to bring up the subject since the abrupt end of their conversation that morning after she'd answered his question regarding her relationship with the girl without him actually asking it. Madame was sharp, perhaps sharper than he, and he wondered why she was not out asking questions.

Madame shrugged. "Fine, as far as I know. I have not seen her since that morning when we questioned Dr. M. I do not actually see her on a regular basis Mr. Holmes. Had you not figured that out?" The auburn-haired woman stared into the unlit fireplace, a frown settling over her lips and brows.

Saying nothing, Greyson stared with her. He did not know the full story of Quillian's placement with Dr. M. Or why it was Madame who had placed her there. Or what the debt was that Madame owed to Dr. M. Or a lot of other information about Madame and Quillian and Dr. M, but that was not the intrigue he needed to investigate.

Right now, Greyson needed to concentrate on finding the mastermind behind what he suspected was limb stealing and reselling.

"When are you visiting?"

"Huh?" Greyson looked up from the fireplace. He blinked, retracing the conversation in his mind to interpret her question. "I'm sorry. When am I visiting my father? Mother said to come at three this afternoon."

Madame nodded. "So, you have plenty of time to run an errand for me before then?"

Greyson considered. He did not like being an errand boy for anyone, let alone a brothel-keeper, but it was part of his rental agreement, so there was not much he could complain about. "Of course, Madame."

Madame sat forward in her chair, placing her spectacles back on her nose. "I would like you to visit Quillian for me. I am not truly welcome at Dr. M.'s home. Although, I am sure you have already discerned that. I think you could visit without much scrutiny—you did so for breakfast that morning and I do believe Huddy quite welcomed you. You could even mention your suspicions regarding the scheme if Dr. M is about, gauge his reaction. He, too, may have some information."

"Do you think that wise? To mention my suspicions? What if Dr. M is the mastermind? He has, from what I understand, many connections to the elite."

Regarding Greyson over the golden rims of her spectacles, Madame flicked the edge of the newspaper once. "I will confirm that Dr. M was born into the elite. I think you have guessed that already." A second flick of the paper. "But he turned his back on them a long time ago—a lifetime ago to some. If he were part of any scheme concerning the elite, it would be to bring about their downfall, not to provide them with new body parts."

"But what if-"

"Mr. Holmes." Madame flicked the paper a final time and began perusing the pages, though Greyson suspected she was not seeing the words. "Trust me when I say that you have no reason to believe that Dr. M is involved in this scheme other than as an unwitting participant for providing the mechanical bits for the unfortunates who had limbs stolen from them."

"Yes, Madame."

Greyson sipped more tea and attempted to swallow more of his cucumber sandwich on rice-flour bread. When it threatened to forcibly remove itself from his stomach, he set it down.

It seemed that once this business with the limb stealing was done, he would have even more questions he wanted answered.

Now, he really wanted to know who Quillian's father was.

Quillian's Log

I am amazed sometimes by what we take for granted. Take food for instance. I have always eaten healthily, but enjoyed all of Huddy's treats whenever they were offered - either by Dr. M or by Huddy herself.

Poor Mr. Holmes, though, having to be careful of every tiny ingredient that goes into his mouth, or he is sick. I cannot imagine the very thing that sustains us causing so much pain.

I will never take my food for granted ever again.

22

Quillian chewed her fried egg and cheese sandwich, licking when the soft yolk ran out and down her palm. Spicy fried potatoes, made from leftovers from last night's dinner, sat on her plate. Cold limeade sweated in her glass.

Taking lunch alone in the dining room, the paper was spread out on the table, she focused on the grainy photo she'd spotted last evening. Though the face looked familiar, she now realized she'd never seen the man before.

He was older, with graying hair and muttonchop sideburns that needed a trim. A fat cigar was held up in one chubby hand, his other hand wedged between the neat buttons of the vest that strained over his rounded stomach.

The other men were equally well dressed, though thinner, but not skinny by any means.

Beneath the photo, the caption mentioned a celebration of the success of a new medical investment venture. There were no names; it was assumed the reader would recognize the men.

Which meant they were uppers. Not that she couldn't tell just by the clothing and manner and overt rotundness.

So there was no way he worked at the docks.

She skimmed the short article that accompanied the photo, gasping when she found the names of the men involved near the bottom of the column.

One was Sir Stanley Holmes of The Hague. Was that Mr. Holmes' father? Quillian examined the photo once more, holding it close to her face, and imagined the man younger, clean shaven and thinner. It must be.

Nodding, she took another bite of sandwich, chewing vigorously. She thought of how Mr. Holmes had described his father—though that had been more a description of his temperament than appearance—and she tried to assimilate Mr. Holmes' rancor with the jovial-looking man in the photo. She supposed that the face one showed in public might be very different than the one shown in private.

She thought about Huddy, and how the housekeeper snapped and nagged at Dr. M within the walls of the house, but once outside, was every inch the demure servant.

Shrugging those thoughts aside for later consideration, she skimmed the article for more information. The gentlemen were celebrating a successful investment in a company that provides risky transplant surgeries out of a private wing at the Portsmouth hospital. Was this where the senior Mr. Holmes had gotten the idea that his son would benefit from surgery? Had he thought to replace his faulty organs?

Sir Stanley was only an investor, part of an investing coalition that put money into several medical programs, and according to the article, this particular program was making substantial returns.

Quillian wiped a bit of runny yolk up with her finger, considering the article, following it with a still greasy-crisp potato. Would the reporter know anything more about the company? Might she or Mr. Holmes be able to arrange an interview? She wiped her fingers on a napkin and picked up the paper, flipping through the pages, looking for any similar articles—or ones about all the accidents and incidents of late.

Without thought, she forked potatoes into her mouth, swallowing before she even tasted what was one of her favorite foods.

But she found no mention of anyone losing limbs, whether at the docks or anywhere else. From its content, it seemed the elitist Neo-Virginian News only dealt with news that might be of interest to the uppers—mostly politics and business. And what upper would care if some dockworker or prostitute had been injured?

Looking through the pages, she found a sidebar that listed the types of surgeries the company had performed at the hospital: liver transplant, heart transplant, attachment of a leg.

Shaking her head, she noted that at no time did the article mention where the transplanted organs and body parts came from.

She folded the newspaper into the same neat squares the doctor had put it into and tucked it beside her plate. She'd show the article to Mr. Holmes and get his take on it. Perhaps he'd be able to contact the reporter. From the slant of the article, she doubted the man would be willing to speak to her.

"Psst, Quillie!"

Quillian turned in her seat to find Ralph leaning around the door jamb, his face covered in raspberry jam and clotted cream.

"What have you gotten into, little man?" She pivoted in her chair to face the urchin, one knee curling up to accommodate.

The boy swiped a dusty sleeve over his face, which only served to smear more dirt. "Haven't got into anyfing. Missus Huddy gave me a treat for doing a good job pickin' beans in the garden this morning."

Smiling with a raised brow. "And she didn't give you a napkin?"

"That white fing?"

"Yes, you're supposed to use it to clean your face off."

"Oh." Ralph shrugged and sauntered into the room. "I didn't want to dirty it." He sat in the chair next to Quillian and swung his feet, hands clasped in his lap.

"Did you want to talk to me, Ralph?"

"Yes'm." He mumbled into his shirt and swung his legs harder, letting his heels smack into the rails between the chair legs.

Sighing, Quillian offered him the last of her sandwich, and it disappeared into his mouth.

"I know you and that feller been askin' questions."

Quillian straightened. "You do?" Good golly! Did Huddy?

He nodded. "One of me mates saw you down at the docks."

"I see." Stomach trembling, Quillian wondered exactly what Ralph's friend had seen, and who else he'd told. "Did he tell you anything else?"

Ralph nodded. "He thinks you need to go talk to his girl what works as a maid in a fancy townhouse in Olde Towne. The master is a fancy doctor at the Naval Hospital."

"Why should we go talk to her?"

"'cause she tol' him that funny stuff's been happening 'round there, and that the master's son's getting a fancy surgery that will make his arm work again."

"Do you know the master's name?"

"Nah. Jus' know what Hank told me." Ralph looked up at Quillian and grinned. "I can take you to talk to Hank, though. He might know. Or he can ask his girl."

Biting her lip, Quillian sucked in a sharp breath. Should she ask Mr. Holmes first? Would Hank be comfortable speaking to Mr. Holmes? Maybe it would be best if she sent a note requesting Mr. Holmes find the reporter, and she could go talk to Ralph's friend.

"Ralph! Quillian!" Huddy stood in the door, a thick slice of blueberry pie on a plate in her hands. "What are you two on about now? What if Dr. M walked in?"

Quillian jumped to her feet, Ralph jumping to his a moment later. "Sorry, Huddy. We were just talking."

"Hmph." Huddy set the plate on the table with a loud thunk. "Missy, you know better. Dr. M don't want you having staff conversations in the dining room. Better eat your pie and get on with your chores. Ralph, don't you have somewhere you need to be?"

"Yes'm."

"Oh, Ralph!" Quillian reached out and caught a corner of the boy's sleeve. "Come see me in the garden after you're done. We can talk again, okay? Where it's allowed." She winced inside. She hadn't meant it to sound so censuring.

Ralph glanced up at the thunderous expression on Huddy's face and gulped but nodded. "Sure, Quillie. I be there."

Then he took off like a cannon, his feet in his oversized boots slucking along the wooden floor of the hall.

"What exactly were you and Ralph talking about?" Huddy picked up the other dishes and wiped a damp cloth over the table.

Quillian sat at her place and picked up the dessert fork, noting that Huddy had set a large scoop of thick lemon curd on the plate with her pie. "Just about how we're supposed to act around here. Nothing bad."

Huddy snorted. "Lot of good it will do talking about how you should act when you're doing it where you shouldn't be."

"Sorry, Huddy, I hadn't thought about that. I just wanted to answer Ralph's questions." Quillian hated lying to Huddy. The woman had a knack for spotting lies, so she kept her eyes on her pie, forking up a bit of the blue-purple sweetness, dipping it though the lemon curd before tucking it between her lips. She hadn't thought she'd be getting the treat and wanted to make the most of it in case Huddy changed her mind about giving it to her.

"Well, the garden is a better place for those discussions. And don't let me catch you talking to Ralph in here again." With a quick swat of the rag at Quillian's arm, Huddy huffed out. "And make sure you get your chores done, too. Don't make me regret sneaking you that pie."

E. G. Gaddess

From the journal of G. J. Holmes

I wonder - sometimes - what brought my parents together. Had they met and fallen in love? Or had their marriage been arranged by their own parents? I only vaguely remember my grandparents, one set having died on a voyage to Africa, and the other having settled to the west on a business venture. Mother refuses to go visit for fear of the "savages."

I haven't the heart to tell her that the Indigenous Peoples are far more civilized than we are.

From the journal of G. J. Holmes

There are still parts of Father's house where I have never been. The maid's quarters, for instance. Though I suspect both Jacoby and Wilroy had an intimate knowledge of that space.

Other places in Father's house, like the library, are rooms that I know like my own bedroom – perhaps even better since Father threatened to turn my bedroom into a smoking room if I left.

I spent many a Saturday in the library, reading and discovering and avoiding Wilroy, whom I doubt even knows Father has a library. The books in the library hadn't cared that I was an invalid, that I couldn't run fast enough to avoid Wilroy's penchant for pinching.

Jacoby had known about the library, though. He'd been the one to pull my favorite books down from the higher shelves and place them on lower shelves so I could reach them.

23

The Hague housed the elite of the elite. Situated along the Elizabeth River, well away from the docks, the elegant homes—majestic brick and stone townhouses four stories and higher—had a beautiful view of the water and the water-wheeled gambling boats that traveled its length daily.

Greyson had the steamtaxi let him off at one end of the stone boardwalk that edged the lapping water; the regular steamtrams did not venture to The Hague and, at the moment, he could not afford one that did.

He was early, and wanted time to assess the situation before knocking on the front door of his parents' home. Dr. M's housekeeper, Huddy, had refused him entrance to Dr. M's home, citing that Miss Watson was busy with chores and Dr. M was away. He suspected the old woman had found out he'd taken Miss Watson to the docks.

Greyson couldn't help but dwell on Miss Watson. He wondered if she was truly working, or if she had gone with Dr. M, or if she was there, in the house, behind the drawn curtains, refusing to see him for reasons of her own. His performance at the docks had not been much to impress a young lady.

And why, he confronted himself, was he concerned with impressing this young lady in particular? Damn it all! Maybe his father could explain that to him. It was the kind of thing Jacoby had explained, before he died. Wilroy never picked up the slack in that area.

He kicked a pebble into the water, watching the ever-growing circles from its impact reach the fortified bulkhead. Gulls wheeled and called, diving to the water to skim its surface. Greyson watched them before turning back to the street. The white and grey birds gamboled in the air, spinning and diving and catching fish in their beaks. It looked a chaotic dance, choreographed so that none of the performers hit each other, but that the audience would watch in fear that they would.

A wide green lawn separated the bulkhead from the cobblestone street. A moment of nostalgia placed Greyson at a childhood picnic on the expanse. He saw himself throwing bits of bread to both birds and the adventurous squirrels that ventured from the trees at the park on the end of the street.

Those in The Hague still kept horses, though it was more status symbol than anything else. It announced to the world, or at least to Norfolk high-society, that you had enough money for a stable, and the servants to man it, to keep horses in town.

Midway up the street, a brown granite house loomed taller than the others, a deep ebony set of double doors centered in the façade. This was the grand home of Mr. and Mrs. Stanley Ignatius Holmes.

Greyson turned from the imposing monument and pondered the river again, still not ready to face his family. The ripples had stopped; the water's surface smooth once more. The Hague was protected from the currents and waves and occasional hurricane, a manmade inlet for the rich. That was the main reason his ancestor had bought the home here. His own father liked the grandeur, and it made his mother happy to have one of the most expensive houses in Norfolk.

Sighing, Greyson walked down the street. He used his cane, but it was more from habit than necessity today. He'd wanted to walk the whole way, but had thought better of it. Best to face his father looking fit and healthy, not pasty and sweaty. Father would likely think it was from the disease and lecture him again about a permanent solution to the problem.

Which was why Greyson thought his father might be able to provide him with answers or at least put him on the path to some answers. His father's solution was an operation where Greyson would get new body parts to replace the ones that were not functioning properly. He'd not thought much about it at the time, dismissing the plan only because his malfunctioning parts were internal and he wasn't sure the donor would survive the donation. He'd considered it one of his parents' hair-brained schemes that materialized out of nowhere.

But now...

Greyson checked his pocket watch. It was a quarter of three and he could stall no longer. Looking up, he stood before his father's house, the massive doors glossy in the sun. At one point, he'd considered this his home, but that had ended with a final argument that left his mother crying and his father throwing him out of the house.

The butler, Wallace, opened the door and stood at the top of the steps, looking down. The man had been ancient in Greyson's childhood, with his balding head and trimmed white muttonchops and beard, so how the man was still alive was a mystery. "Master Greyson? Your mother is awaiting you in the front parlor."

Greyson glanced down at his pocket watch then held it up to his ear, checking the steady ticks. It seemed to be functioning properly. He walked up the steps with purpose, dodging the hand that the butler held out when he reached the top. "I am not an invalid, Wallace. I do not need assistance up the stairs."

Wallace coughed and opened the door for him. Greyson frowned and stepped in, removing his hat and jacket.

The gray-haired butler took the hat and jacket, but did not take the extended cane.

"Wallace, I have already reminded you that I am not an invalid. Please take my cane."

Wallace took the cane, placing it next to the door to the parlor.

Greyson sighed and entered. There was not much use in fighting with a butler that was only doing as he'd been instructed.

"Greyson!" The white-haired woman on the settee rose with a flicker of fingers and hands before extending her arms out, crossing the room in tiny, jittery steps to envelope him in a hug and an overly strong scent of roses and musk. Her dusty pink dress was the height of fashion, and then some; layers of ruffled chiffon stuck out from the skirt, while a tight, darker pink corset pulled in her waist and caused everything above and below it to expand exponentially. "My dear boy, you should have come in sooner than now. I have been waiting. You made me send Wallace out after you."

Greyson looked down at his mother. "Your note said three. I did not want to be early and impose my presence on the household more than necessary."

Lady Gwendolyne Holmes frowned up at her son. "Your presence is always welcome here, you know that."

What Greyson knew was that his mother was lying, though whether to him or to herself, he was not sure. His father had been most explicit when throwing him from the premises.

"My apologies, Mother. I had not realized."

"Come and sit." She turned and walked back to the settee, using the same jittery steps as before. She sat, pink tufts poufing about her, and patted the seat beside her.

Greyson chose the chair across from the settee, ignoring his mother's moue of disapproval. "Thank you."

"Wallace will bring the tea. I hope you are hungry."

Greyson hadn't eaten since his attempt of rice-flour toast and apple butter at lunch, but his stomach was still tied in tight knots of tension. "I am sure I can manage something."

Lady Gwendolyne smiled and nodded. "How have you been, Greyson? Have you been keeping up with your regimen?"

"I am quite well, Mother, and keeping strict to my regimen."

She smiled and looked to the door.

Wallace entered with the tea tray laden with cookies and cakes and imported chocolate bon bons—his mother's favorite. The butler set the tray on the table and poured; he did not bother to ask Greyson what he wanted in his tea, simply added milk and sugar just as his mother took it.

Greyson hid his grimace behind a cough; he could not stand too-sweet tea, and he hated it with milk. According to Doctor Bhatnagar, it was the lactose in milk that caused some of his stomach cramps.

"Thank you, Wallace." Lady Gwendolyne smiled and the butler bowed, backing himself out the door without looking.

"Let us get some sustenance into us before your father arrives, shall we?" Lady Gwendolyne took a long drink of her tea, closing her eyes and sighing after. "He's been the morning with the solicitor about some financial matter. Likely be in a bear of a mood when he gets here."

Brilliant. Greyson took a quick sip of tea and held down the gag; it tasted like the sugar syrup for making sweet conserves. He made no complaint at the state of his tea. If father was going to be in a bad mood, he did not want his mother in one as well.

"How are you and Father doing?" Maybe if he kept talking, he wouldn't have to drink any more tea.

"We're doing well. I've missed you terribly, of course. And your father has kept himself busy with the company, as well as his investments and financials. This economy has him worried, though. He's been keeping much time with his solicitors of late."

Greyson nodded and fiddled with the cup in his hand. "Has Father been losing in his investments?"

His mother shrugged and waved a hand. "I have no idea. You know he never speaks to me regarding his money."

Sighing, Greyson raised the cup to his lips. Perhaps it was better to drink the tea, dash the consequences to his stomach. He swallowed and sighed.

"Um. I believe you have new neighbors?"

"New neighbors?" Lady Gwendolyne licked a sugar-coated finger. "You must mean the Dolans."

"Do they live in Number 127?"

"Yes." His mother frowned at him. "Why do you ask? The poor couple don't need any more trouble, dear. I think they've had quite enough already."

"Trouble? Mother, I have no intention of causing trouble. I just noticed them one day and am now making polite conversation."

"Hmmm." His mother's eyes narrowed. "Did you see them yesterday? When you came in a steamtaxi but didn't come to see me?"

He'd known he'd be caught, so why he was surprised at his mother's knowledge was unsettling. "Well, I realized that I'd be dropping in unannounced and thought I should request a visit instead."

Lady Gwendolyne pressed her lips into a tight thin line. She knew he was lying, but couldn't prove it aside from the crack in his voice. "I see. That is why you sent the note?"

"Of course." Greyson sipped his tea and picked up a cookie, stuffing it into his mouth before he said something else stupid and his mother caught onto him completely. If she did, she'd never answer his questions.

"Well," his mother relaxed her lips and leaned forward, nodding and whispering, "rumor is, Mrs. Dolan is a cripple."

Greyson raised his brows, his mouth still full of sugar and flour that was turning to a sweet paste that stuck his tongue to his palate.

"She had surgery not long ago, to fix a leg that wasn't working. It was shriveled, so I heard, and much weaker than her other leg. According to a very good source in their household, she did nothing but cry no matter how many trinkets her husband bought to cheer her up."

His mother's sources were always good, and quite accurate. He swallowed the pasty glop in his mouth and took a cleansing sip of tea, swishing it around before swallowing. "Do you know when she had the surgery?"

"Let me see." Lady Gwendolyne rearranged the bon bons on the silver platter, spacing them out so that they covered the flat bottom once more. "I believe it was just after you disappeared. They moved in the day after you left for that hotel after fighting with your father, and I can remember Millie having something to tell me the same day your father was upset because you had left the hotel and he didn't know where you were."

The front door opened and slammed. Lady Gwendolyne started in her chair, nearly spilling her tea. "Oh, dear. That does not sound promising."

Greyson sighed. Indeed, it did not. His questioning of his mother was over, though it had borne fruit. Mrs. Dolan's surgery was within the window of possibility. He would have to check his calendar in his room, but he was certain it was the day after Jezebelle's attack.

Father opened the door to the parlor and stalked inside, whipping the door closed behind him. "Bloody fools! Incompetent! Probably walking off with my hard-earned money. Damn solicitors. Damn them to hell!"

Sir Staley Holmes walked to the table and nodded to the tea tray before collapsing into the second chair that faced the settee.

Lady Gwendolyne poured milk and sugar into a cup then filled it with tea. Her hand shook when she handed the cup to her husband. "Not a good day, dear?"

"Bloody lousy day!" Sir Stanley drained the cup and handed it back to his wife, who refilled it and handed it back. "I never should have listened to those damn solicitors."

The parlor fell silent.

Greyson drank his tea.

Lady Gwendolyne took a bon bon, ate it all at once, and took another.

Sir Stanley rested back in his chair, eyes closed, breathing heavy. His face was red, though not from the sun. A vein pulsed at his temple and his nostrils flared with each intake of breath.

Greyson thought perhaps it would be better if he left. He set his cup on the saucer and the saucer on the tray and made ready to stand.

"So, Greyson. What brings you here? Are you in need of funds?" Sir Stanley opened his eyes and stared at his youngest son.

"No, sir. I just wanted to ask you some questions about your solution to my health problem."

Sir Stanley grunted. "No sense in even discussing it. I haven't the money to fund it now."

Lady Gwendolyne gasped around a coconut finger cake.

"Do not worry, dear." Sir Stanley waved a hand in his wife's direction. "You still have your shopping funds and such;

it is just the extra bits that will need to be curtailed in the near future."

Greyson bit back his snort. Though he was not interested in his father's solution, he did not like hearing his health described as an 'extra bit.'

Lady Gwendolyne relaxed and continued eating her cake.

"I am not looking for cost information, Father. I am looking for how you came upon the solution. Who may have mentioned it, that sort of thing." Greyson also waved a hand, like it was not all that important.

Sir Stanley pursed his lips at his son and frowned. "What are you about boy? You had no interest in my solution before. Why do you want to know more now?"

Greyson took up a strawberry cake and put it in his mouth, munching slowly while he thought. For some reason, likely his anger at his solicitor, Father was paying attention. He'd have to tread carefully so as not to arouse his suspicions. He swallowed the cake and washed it down with cold tea.

"I just thought, perhaps, I had been a bit hasty in completely disregarding what you suggested. I thought if I could obtain more information about such a procedure, it may not be so repulsive in the future, if my regimen begins to fail."

Sir Stanley harrumphed and shifted in his chair, draining his second cup of tea. Lady Gwendolyne refilled it when he held it out.

"Your regimen is still working?"

"Aye."

"Where are your quarters?"

"Not far from Brambleton."

"Working district?"

"Aye." Greyson did not want to give an exact address. If his father were to determine exactly where his room was...

"Wilroy said he was unable to find where you are staying."

"It is not an obvious establishment for renting a room." Greyson took another cake.

"You do not wish me to know where it is, do you?"

Greyson kept forgetting he'd gotten his intellect from one of his parents. "Not right now, sir, no."

Sir Stanley harrumphed again. "It is a safe building?"

Greyson thought of the guards and alarms that encircled Madame's brothel. "None safer in the district, sir."

"Well." Sir Stanley sipped his tea and rubbed his slightly protruding stomach. "If I recall, Lord Chambers mentioned something about such operations at last year's charity ball. You know," he waved a hand about his head, "the big one for the children's hospital. His wife hosts it each year as a fundraiser."

Greyson nodded but did not interrupt.

Sir Stanley frowned at the wall. "Seem to remember someone else there at the time. Someone in the know about such things. Likely one of them doctors that work at the hospital."

Lady Gwendolyne blinked. "Was it Dr. Frosher, dear?"

"No."

"Dr. Witherspoon?"

"No."

"Dr. Smithfield?"

"Smithfield?" Lord Stanley gaped at his wife. "Smithfield's into hogs, Madam."

"Not the elder. The junior; he's working some specialty at the hospital. Something to do with blood disease, if I remember correctly. It seems we humans share it with the pigs."

"Well, weren't him, then."

Greyson watched his parents, wondering that his mother could remember so many of the names of the doctors that worked at the charity hospital and that his father couldn't even remember who was responsible for coming up with the 'solution.'

"Perhaps it was Dr. Hershey? The female doctor?"

Sir Stanley snorted. "Think I'd remember that now, wouldn't I?"

"I suppose, dear." Lady Gwendolyne took up a sweet biscuit with bright red jam dotted on the top and examined it. "Do you remember if it was an old man or a young man?"

"Damned if I can." Sir Stanley sighed and shook his head. "My memory t'ain't what it used to be."

Greyson thought his father's memory was exactly as it used to be. "But you are certain that it was Lord Chambers that mentioned it first?"

Sir Stanley looked at Greyson. "As sure as I can be. Lord Chambers is the one that got me into the investment pool for the hospital wing where it's done."

Greyson nodded and took another cake, settling back into his chair, relaxing and sighing. That meant he couldn't be sure at all.

He was surprised, though, that he could relax. He'd expected Father to be angry at him, especially since Wilroy had been unable to locate him. Perhaps it had something to do with the economy and Father's financials; perhaps he was expending all his anger on the financials and couldn't spare any for Greyson.

"So, when are you coming home?" Lady Gwendolyne looked at her son with such a hopeful expression on her face Greyson found himself considering the proposition.

But the issue was not just his parents.

"Mother..." He sighed.

"Please, Greyson. I am sure you could follow your regimen much better here. Cook can..."

"No, Mother." Greyson leaned forward, stretching out one hand to take hers, gently. "I cannot. I find myself following my regimen much better on my own."

"Regimen, smegimen!"

Greyson winced and sucked in a quick breath.

"That regimen is doing nothing! Nothing, I say!" Sir Stanley rose from his seat, tea sloshing from the cup in his hand, the other hand waving wildly about his head. "Just some chinky charlatan taking all your money!"

Lady Gwendolyne grabbed a napkin from the tea tray and stooped to mop at the spilled tea.

"It is doing quite a bit, actually. It has been some time since I had a weak spell. And the establishment where I am staying has no qualms about providing me with special dishes no one else is eating." Greyson stood, his back straight, his head high. That meant he could look down at his father. "I have never felt healthier than I do right now. And I have no intention of stopping my regimen."

Sir Stanley's face grew darker, purple spreading from his chest up, across his cheeks and forehead.

Lady Gwendolyne stood, pulling the dirty napkin tight between her hands. "Stanley, remember your blood pressure."

"My blood pressure! I suppose there's a regimen for that, as well."

Greyson said nothing. In fact, there was a regimen for high blood pressure, but Sir Stanley had scoffed at it the first time he'd mentioned it.

"I have had a lovely tea, Mother." Greyson stepped to his mother, kissing her lightly on the cheek and gently pulling the dirty napkin from her fingers. He dropped it beside the tea tray and rested his hands on her shoulders. "Perhaps I can come again?"

"Of course, dear. Wilroy is usually out on Tuesdays and Thursdays."

Greyson nodded and hugged her, taking a deep breath of the powdery scent he always associated with the older woman. There was something different about it today. He didn't sneeze.

He turned to his father and held out one hand. Lord Stanley still had his teacup, now empty, in one tight hand and his other still in the air; he did not accept the offer of a handshake. Greyson dropped his own hand. "It has been good seeing you, Father. I hope you remain in good health.

Sir Stanley snorted and turned his back.

Greyson left with a single nod to his mother.

E. G. Gaddess

I know that Huddy came up from Carolinia. And I know her journey wasn't legal.

I don't know how Dr. M found her, though, or why he hired her to be his housekeeper. There's a lot I don't know about Huddy and Dr. M.

It never bothered me before.

But now, thinking about Ralph, and a lot of the other servants at Dr. M's, I can't help but wonder about them, too. Where did they come from? Some skitter and jump at the least little sound and seem to need to learn a lot about being a servant.

24

It was hours before Quillian got her chance to venture into the garden to look for Ralph. She'd been fretting about whether or not the rascal would show up, and it had distracted her from her own chores, and she'd kept spilling the bucket when scrubbing the surgery and mis-writing an entry while sorting the latest delivery from the apothecary. It had taken her better than an hour to neaten the log entries and recheck them against the medicine cabinet.

So now, she'd snuck off from her studies. If Dr. M surprised her with another quiz, she'd fail.

This was far more important, though. Were the stolen limbs being surgically attached to other people? Was the company that Mr. Holmes' father invested in somehow involved?

What would Mr. Holmes do if his father was involved? Would he still try to get to the bottom of it, or would he, like so many uppers, brush it away?

She wanted to believe that his sense of what's right would triumph over any feelings of class or family obligation. The strength of these feelings surprised her. Why did she care what Mr. Holmes did? Why did she care that he understand the plight of the lowers? And if she cared so much about what Mr.

Holmes did and thought, why wasn't she concerned that he lived at the brothel?

"Psst! Quillie!" Ralph hissed from behind a camellia bush, pushing his way through the thick leaves and drooping white flowers of the garden.

"Ralph. You remembered." Quillian pulled him from beneath the bush and dragged him to the worn wooden bench beside the apple tree. The apple blossoms were fragrant, in the heat of blooming, the small nubs that would be apples come the fall just forming behind the petals.

"I been under that bush waiting all afternoon. I thought you weren't coming." Ralph jerked his arm from her grasp and fell onto the bench.

"I had to finish my chores."

"You sure gots a lot of chores for a girl 'pprentice." Ralph dug in his pocket, pulling out a limp strand of licorice and biting off one end.

Quillian said nothing to his comment, but wrinkled her nose at the candy. "Must you eat that now?"

"I gotta eats it now. It's in pretty bad shape." He wagged the pathetic bit of treat in her face.

Swallowing hard, Quillian shifted out of scent range and plucked an apple blossom, holding it near her nose to ward off the offending aroma. "So, tell me about your friend Hank's girl and where she works."

Ralph shrugged, still chewing the piece of licorice. "She works at some fancy house 'cross the river; a blackie and a whitey house, so the kids a stripey. That's why they live in Portsmouth. The master's some big shot that imports from Carolinia. 'ccording to Hank, the kid has a problem with one of his arms. It's gimp or stumped or sumfing. Been that way since he was born." Ralph bit another piece of candy off, waving the rest of it in the air. He made his voice shrill and feminine. "Poor baby. It's just not fair."

"Have you been to this house?" Quillian lowered the petals. She should reprimand him about how he'd described the couple and their child, but that would make him clam up harder than a hermit crab.

"Nah. But Hank has, and I guess everyone fusses over the kid all the time. His girl's gots to run after 'im and get 'im whatever 'e wants if 'e can't reach it."

"It's a child who's getting the surgery?"

"Yup." Ralph nodded and tucked the last of the licorice away. "'ccording to Hank, he ain't much older'n me."

Quillian thought she was going to be sick. A child? If she was right, that meant another child was going to be attacked.

"Ralph, you're not going out tonight, are you?"

"Sure am. Ye wanna to talk to Hank, yeah?" Ralph stood up, looking for all the world like he was ready to run off that very second.

"Yes, but..." Quillian paused; how much should she tell the boy? "I suspect for this child to have his surgery, another child will be hurt. I'm afraid it might be you."

"You don' need to worry 'bout me, Quillie." Ralph puffed up his chest and stood tall. "I kin outrun every copper in Norfolk and I know all the 'iding places. I'll be okay."

"Ralph, please. I'd really like you to stay in the house tonight. It's dangerous. Truly." Quillian grabbed and hugged him, but Ralph squirmed his way out of her arms, scampering off to the back gate.

"I'll go talk to Hank righ' now and be back afore dusk. Maybe I'll bring 'im back with me, heh?" And he was gone before Quillian had even gained her feet.

He was quick, that was certain. But would he be quick enough?

From the journal of G. J. Holmes

I first met Dr. Bhatnagar before I left home for good. In fact, it was the regimen he provided me that instigated the argument that led to my departure.

Father doesn't believe in "herbal medicine." Personally, I think he just has too much invested in the scientific side of things that is all the current rage.

Mother just doesn't understand it.

Wilroy didn't care.

Jacoby had already passed away. According to Dr. Bhatnagar, he might have been able to help him recover. Unfortunately, I don't know enough about the disease Jacoby had, other than how he got it. It's not something anyone talks about now.

25

Greyson lay on his bed, face pale, sweat pooling at his temples, his stomach knotting in a roil of agony. It felt all the worse for it being so long since his last such spell.

Two months.

The two months since he'd left his father's house in The Hague and sought his own room where he could eat the foods of his regimen without someone berating him for wanting something different or sneaking 'good solid normal food stuff' onto his plate.

It was not just the milk in the tea. He had eaten cakes and cookies with his mother, forgetting for a moment in his desire to keep control of the conversation—and his father's temper—that he was not supposed to eat them. They had been rich, delectable in all truthfulness and he'd enjoyed every moment they'd spent on his tongue, but likely contained some of everything that he was not supposed to eat: rendered lard, wheat flour, more milk.

Greyson groaned and shifted on his bed.

At least he had the tincture from Doctor Bhatnagar and had made it up as soon as he'd returned and drank it. The tincture would help move the foul foods through his system, and the pain and discomfort would end.

Someone knocked at the door.

"Yes?" Greyson knew his voice was weak, but could not muster the energy to fake strength.

Madame opened the door. "Are you ill, Mr. Holmes? Cassie was shuttling linens between the upper and lower closets and heard you moaning."

"'tis but my stomach, Madame. I should not have eaten at tea with my mother."

Madame walked into the room, closing the door behind her. "Do you mean to say she had nothing made for you that fit with your regimen?"

Greyson shook his head and closed his eyes. A cramp rolled through him, moving upward from his groin. He lost his breath.

Cool fingers touched his forehead. "My goodness, you're burning up. I'll be right back."

His eyes still closed, Greyson heard the click of the door and the faint clack of heels and cane tip in the hall.

In what was likely only a few minutes later, but felt an interminable time, Madame returned with Dr. Brown and Mrs. Taggage. "Help him, doctor."

Dr. Brown was an older woman, her grayed hair thin to balding on the top of her head. She wore a dark grey wool skirt, white blouse and black corset; standard fare for a woman in the professional working class.

"Ah, Mr. Holmes. Where does it hurt?"

Greyson sighed. While Dr. Brown was supportive of his regimen, she did not truly understand his disease. "It is my stomach only. I ate some of the foods I am not supposed to eat at tea. I've taken a tincture to move it through my system. I will be fine by morning."

Dr. Brown turned to Madame, her thick brows meeting above her long thin nose.

"Make him comfortable, Doctor. Do something to help him." She propelled the doctor closer to the bed.

"Nothin's ailing 'im. Jus' needs to learn to stomach 'is food." Taggage sneered and clucked her tongue.

Rolling a bit to face the women, Greyson muffled a groan. "Madame, there is nothing she can do. I just need to wait for everything to clear my system and then I will be fine. I will also need to be extra vigilant with my regimen for a bit to compensate."

Rolling her eyes, Taggage spun in the door and marched off. "Waste a time with 'im, Madame. Waste a time."

Dr. Brown watched the woman leave then turned back to Greyson. "Would hot tea help to calm the cramping?"

Greyson closed his eyes. He really didn't know.

"That's what I give the girls when they cramp."

Opening his eyes, Greyson stared at the woman. Had she really just compared his condition with a female's monthly?

"I can fetch a small pot, just in case you'd like some." She patted his shoulder. "I might have a bit of tincture that helps constipation. What about that?"

Madame sighed and opened a window and a slight breeze entered, cooling the air.

"That does feel nice." Greyson tried to smile.

"Hmph. You may leave doctor." Madame sat in Greyson's side chair and the doctor opened the door. "Please instruct cook to take extra care in preparing Mr. Holmes' breakfast."

"Yes, Madame. The tea?"

"You may send someone with it."

Madame stood in the room, eyes closed, breathing deep. When she opened her eyes, she smiled down at Greyson.

He grimaced back.

"Is this the book you are reading?" Madame picked up a heavy tome from the table next to the chair.

"Yes." Greyson turned his face to the cool air.

"This marks your page?"

Greyson turned back. Madame was fingering the tasseled bookmark tucked between the pages.

"Yes."

"Shall I read to you for a bit? It may help take your mind off your discomfort."

"Yes, please." He blinked. Without his glasses, Madame was out of focus.

Madame opened the book and began to read at the top of the left page. Her voice was soft and steady. Though the book was scientific in nature—its focus was on the new mechanics of household automatons—she did not stumble over the odd words.

He watched her read for a while, focusing on the vague outline of jaw and lips form words. Mind wandering, he thought of Quillian, and how she'd asked questions when they'd gone to the docks, the way her jaw and lips had moved.

Greyson blinked and narrowed his eyes, concentrating his focus on Madame's face. The woman shared Quillian's profile: The same pointed jaw, the same full upper lip with a deep filtrum. Madame's attachment to Quillian was obvious to him now, and he felt a certain satisfaction at having figured it out.

He wondered if Quillian knew, or if the fact that she was the brothel-keeper's daughter was a secret from her as well. Pain rolled through him and he filed the question away, concentrating instead on keeping his moan low and controlled.

Greyson turned back to the window and closed his eyes. The fresh breeze bathed his face while the kindness of words bathed his mind.

Quillian's Log

The note from Mr. Holmes requesting an opportunity to take me for another "walk" surprised both me and Huddy - though Huddy was absolutely giddy with the notion that I have a suitor. I didn't have the heart to tell her it was anything different.

Although, when she pulled out the dress - pretty and lacy and far finer than anything I can remember ever wearing before - I rather wished I had a suitor.

I don't ever remember getting excited about getting dressed up. Huddy even used the hot iron to put little curls in the hairs around my face. I rather like how I looked - more grown up, maybe even pretty.

I'm not certain what's going on with me, but I am nervous about what Mr. Holmes will think of my dress. And my hair.

And whether or not he will also think I look more grown up - and pretty.

26

"You are certain Huddy approved our walk about town?" Greyson strolled next to Quillian, her right hand tucked securely into his elbow. She wore a fine dress today, pale green muslin with a darker green canvas corset trimmed with a same-colored satin and deep yellow lace. Her brown leather boots were heeled, giving her an additional couple of inches of height that he found disconcerting as it put her earlobes, on display beneath the corkscrew curls that framed her face, just below his lips when he turned his head.

A shuttered yellow parasol, something Greyson would never have considered the girl to own, dangled from her own elbow.

"Do you think I would be here, dressed as I am, if she had not? I never would have been able to leave the house without a third-degree questioning without telling her what I was up to."

"And she knows you are with me?"

"Indeed. Though I must confess, she insisted that I carry this parasol. It seems there is a metal point concealed in the tip that I can trigger with a push of a button."

Greyson stopped walking. "You are carrying a weapon?"

Quillian nodded, curls bouncing against her cheeks.

"What does Huddy think might happen?" Greyson looked around; could anyone hear their conversation?

Quillian only laughed and tugged him into movement. "Come along. We're supposed to be looking for Hank. Ralph told him to meet us here."

"Does Huddy know about that aspect of our walk?"

"Oh, heck, no. If I'd told her that, she'd have locked me in the attic. I just told her you'd asked me to take a stroll with you."

"That is all?"

"M-hm. That's all your note said. I had to show it to her, you know."

Greyson didn't believe her; she wouldn't look at him. "And how will Hank identify us?"

"I told Ralph I'd be carrying a yellow parasol from my elbow. He's supposed to be carrying a posey of daisies."

Sighing, he looked around the crowds near the grocer market. Permanent stalls sandwiched wagons, all selling fruits and vegetables and meats from nearby farms or from around the globe. Masses of people moved through the narrow passages and paths, carrying items bought in baskets and bags. Most were maids in black or gray uniforms, running chores for the household where they were employed. Others were cooks or chefs buying for restaurants or inns.

***

"Seen him yet?" Greyson wasn't even sure what a posey of daisies might look like.

"No." Quillian stamped her foot.

"Perhaps we should make a wider circuit?

Nodding, Quillian dragged him down a narrow alley, walled in by brick buildings.

"Isn't there another way-"

"This is faster. Come on."

Greyson allowed her to haul him into the foul-smelling space, wishing he'd brought one of his mother's hankies to place over his nose. "What is that stench?"

"Probably rotting food and piss." Quillian didn't even slow down, but plowed around the folks entering the market.

Swallowing his gag, Greyson kept his eyes firmly on the back of his companion's head.

"Eh, Gov, can ye spare a piece?" An old man with few teeth left in his head shuffled forward, limping against a gnarled, hand-made cane.

"Ignore him," hissed Quillian, speeding up as best she could, "giving him anything will be nothing but trouble."

"How so?" Greyson could not imagine a bit of money doing any harm to the man.

"Because then everyone will want something from you."

Shrugging at the man, he trotted behind Quillian, wincing when the man cuffed his shin with the cane. "What the...?"

"Come on." Quillian dragged on his arm, her short nails biting through his jacket and shirtsleeves. They were likely to leave a bruise.

"Ouch. Careful there." He loosened the clamped grasp of her fingers and she eased her grip, slowing her pell-mell barrage through the crowd.

They emerged from the alley onto a wider street lined with shops. Greyson could make out signs for an apothecary, a clockmaker, and a steamcar repair shop.

"My apologies."

The girl looked suitably chagrined, so he patted the fingers that had only just been torturing his arm.

She smiled at him and swung her parasol, looking about the crowd.

Greyson stiffened and straightened his shoulders, looking over the milling people.

Quillian snorted. "Now you're back to looking all formal and snobby. No one will believe you're working class like that."

Ignoring her, Greyson looked down the street. In the distance, the glitter of the Elizabeth River indicated the edge of downtown. In the other direction, black smoke from the city's steam generator spewed into the air. Run by coal brought by train from the mountains to the west, it was centrally located to pump steam throughout Norfolk via huge aboveground pipes.

"Ooh. I think that was him."

Greyson spun to watch Quillian sprint away. "Hey, wait for me."

He took off after her, tucking his cane under his arm to keep it out of the way.

She was fast; he had trouble keeping up. He'd known he was out of shape, not being that active before taking up his regimen due to always feeling ill, but he hadn't expected a girl to be that much faster, especially in heels.

Hell, she might be faster than Wilroy.

The young black man carrying a small tuft of white and yellow flowers looked up from where he was whispering to what looked like a woman in a ragged brown cloak, and noticed their approach. In an instant, he was off and running in the other direction. The woman spun around and disappeared into a shop.

Quillian followed Hank.

Greyson followed the woman. "Meet me back at the market!" He hoped Quillian heard him; she was half a block ahead of him by now, only her bonnet visible to him, closing on the hapless servant.

The shop was dark and the windows dusty, one broken with wood nailed over it. The door opened though, not even squeaking in protest. The interior was dark, only a single lamp in the far corner lit. A long counter, its colored front faded, ran down the right side. Tables and chairs, some broken, some merely lying on their sides, populated the left.

He walked through, looking neither right nor left. The only possible route the woman could have taken was through a door into the back rooms, or up the staircase to the second floor, also at the back. Since the staircase looked like it would collapse if a bee landed on it, Greyson deduced she'd gone through the door.

The first room through the door used to be an office, papers and ledgers strewn around the room. The door was open, and there was no place for anyone to hide.

There was a small storage room and a kitchen, both empty and decrepit.

At the end of the hall, a door stood open to another alley.

"Dash it all to Hades and back." Greyson pushed open the door and looked out. The cloaked figure was nowhere in sight.

He reentered the shop and walked back to the front, stopping to examine the office. Beneath the mess was a wide desk and office chair, still in good condition. The chair was free of debris, the desk littered with papers and a couple of open ledgers.

Greyson moved closer to the desk and chair, roving his eyes over the room. Something on a shelf caught his attention. It was a photo, the frame dusty, the glass cracked.

He recognized one of the two women staring back at the camera: Mrs. Taggage. She was younger in the image, but there was no mistaking the tufty hair and sharp nose. If that hadn't done it, the perpetual sneer would have.

Moving the papers on the desk, a ledger caught his attention. The writing, instead of being faded with age, was crisp and black. He sat in the chair and pulled the ledger closer, flipping through its pages. Most of the entries were recent, far more recent than the atmosphere of aged abandonment would have led him to expect.

The entries listed a column of various organs and limbs, whether from a male or female and their age, what he could only guess was the intended recipient, and a figure in the far-right column.

Damn.

From the journal of G. J. Holmes

It shouldn't surprise me. Never underestimate the lower classes.

And it makes sense, now that there are clues staring me in the face. Mrs. Taggage has access to the elite. After all, Madame's brothel caters to the best of the best. The woman's involvement might even be the reason she didn't want Quillian around the brothel; it brought Dr. M too close to Madame, too close to her.

I need more information, though, more proof. A ledger of entries and an abandoned photograph aren't enough to make a case.

27

Greyson espied Miss Watson waiting in front of the sugared ice vendor, a cup of the frozen sweet in her right hand, a spoon in her left. "Want some?" She held out the cup to an approaching Mr. Holmes.

He wiped a sweating brow. "No, thank you. I'm not sure what's in it."

"Frozen juice." She licked her spoon, her tongue already a deep pink from the fruit-flavored treat. "Maybe some sugar. I got the kind without milk in it."

He stared a moment, then looked to the vendor for a second spoon. "I guess a taste wouldn't hurt."

She grinned at him and held out the treat. "I lost Hank when he hit the river."

"He found a hiding spot?"

"Yeah—the river."

"The river?" Greyson's words garbled, his freezing tongue having trouble forming words.

"You really shouldn't take such a big mouthful." Quillian snickered at the young man, taking a dainty spoonful of her own.

Greyson swallowed and rubbed his tongue along the roof of his mouth to warm it up. "I didn't know."

"You've never had sugared ice before?"

He shook his head. "Not the kind of thing that gets served at my mother's table."

"Hank went into the river."

"He went into the river? You mean he jumped in? Or did someone push him?"

Quillian shrugged. "I don't really know. There was a crowd and all I heard was the splash near where he'd been last standing."

"Could he swim?" Greyson used his spoon to take a smaller bit of ice, careful to let it melt a little before putting it into his mouth.

"I don't know. He was gone when I got to the overlook."

"Hmm." He shifted the pilfered ledger under his arm. "I've found something, though."

"Really?" Quillian started walking, swaying through the crowd.

Greyson followed, keeping his eyes sharp for the woman who'd been talking to Hank. "I followed the woman."

"The woman? What woman?"

How had the girl missed seeing the woman? "The woman Hank was talking to when he took off. You didn't notice?"

"Oh. I missed that." Quillian looked up at him. Her cheeks flushed and damp tresses were rapidly losing their curl. She looked adorable.

Greyson frowned and took another spoonful of ice, steadying the cup in her hand. Miss Watson sucked in a breath; perhaps she didn't want him having any more? "She ducked into a shop along the street. She got away from me, but I found this." He lifted the ledger under his arm.

"A ledger?" She blinked at it then looked up at him.

"Aye. A new ledger, with new entries, hidden amongst several old ones from the closed shop."

"Closed shop?"

Greyson sighed and looked down at her. "The one the woman ducked into. It looked like a tavern or pub. Very run down now. Dirty."

"So, do you think it's been closed for a while?"

"Either that, or made to look so."

"Do you know the address?"

He stopped walking and swore.

Miss Watson laughed. "I take that as a no?"

"We should go back and get it." Greyson made to turn around but his companion placed her hand on his arm.

"Not yet. Let's visit the market a bit more before going back." Miss Watson tugged on his arm, careful not to grab him as hard as before, gripping just the fabric of his jacket.

He stopped and frowned. "Why?"

"I just chased someone into the river. It might not be a good idea to return so soon, especially in the same get up." She leaned close to whisper, and her scent filled his lungs. Drat, but what was wrong with him?

Nodding, Greyson shifted the ledger and resumed their stroll, looking for all the world like they had all day to get where they were going. "Point taken." He took up another spoon of ice. "This is very good you know. I must remember where the vendor is located."

"M-hm." Miss Watson's mouth was full of the ice again.

"I found something else, as well."

"Oh?"

Glancing around, he opened the ledger and showed the aging photograph, now pulled from its frame. "Recognize anyone?"

She stopped, letting a young man carrying crate of tomatoes bump into her, a half dozen of the fruit hitting the ground at their feet. "That's Taggage!"

"Indeed. That is who I thought it was as well." Greyson smiled at the young man and pulled a currency note from his pocket, handing it to him and nodding at the bounding red globes. "So sorry."

"No, I know it is. There are photos of her at that age at the brothel. It's her, no doubt about it." Miss Watson snatched up the photo, holding it close to check the details.

"You are certain?" Greyson had been going to show the photo to Madame and ask her opinion, but if Quillian was certain...

She handed the photograph back, her jaw clenched. "Check in the booze room. There is a photo of her and a young man over the bar."

"Booze room?" The pair walked again, dodging vendors and customers, the sugared ice nearly gone. Greyson dropped his spoon into a waste receptacle, leaving the last of it for his companion.

Shrugging, Miss Watson swallowed the last of the ice, tossing the cup and spoon away. "That's what it is. I've seen it on a couple of my visits to the brothel with Dr. M. It may be styled high end, but it's a place for the clients to drink."

"Why is her photo above the bar?"

"That's what she did before she came to work for Madame, I think."

"She worked in a booze room?"

Miss Watson snorted. "She managed a tavern. Maybe she and her husband even owned it. I think it went out of business when he died."

"She managed a tavern that went out of business? Like the one I found the ledger in? And her photo?"

Stomach knotting, the girl stared up at Greyson. "I guess it could be one and the same."

"And Hank took off when we saw him talking to her. I think that very odd, especially when he was going to meet with us." Greyson pressed his lips together. "I think we need to get back to Dr. M's house."

"To change and then come back to find out the address of the tavern?"

"No. I don't think we need that information now. I think we already know what we need about the tavern. Let's go." He grabbed her elbow and tugged her along.

"We could walk, you know. Dr. M's house isn't going anywhere."

From the Journal of G. J. Holmes

I sent Father a note. Not sure it was the best idea, but he's the only one I know to ask. The list in the ledger means that there has been far more victims than just those who've been treated by Dr. M. I really need to do some digging into who might be capable of performing the other surgeries.

I doubt there is any chance of finding Madame's missing girls alive.

28

He needed proof. He just couldn't find it in himself to go to Madame with his suspicions without proof. She seemed the type that wanted absolutes and not theories.

Taggage bustled down the hall, sneering in his direction when she passed, her arms full of fresh linens for the parlor tables. The brothel was preparing for its usual evening of steady business, and the parlor was the receiving room for the expected clients.

That's where the fancy liquors, wine and brandy were served while the gentleman, and the occasional gentlewoman, awaited their assigned courtesan. It was a high-end business; Madame provided nothing less than the best.

Greyson felt out of place, standing in the hall, loitering, waiting for a chance to see into what Quillian called the "booze room"—what was basically a fancy bar where those who had to wait longer for their fun could adjourn after their wait in the parlor and enjoy harder liquor, and maybe a little entertainment, either singing or music supplied by one of the girls not on the evenings work list.

Taggage jogged back up the hall, muttering under her breath about the waste of it all.

Backing into the wall, Greyson wished there were another spot where he could wait. Taggage had always made him uncomfortable; she didn't like him and had told Madame she was mad to let him stay here. Now, after this afternoon, and his new-found suspicions about the woman, it was even worse.

"Good evening, Greyson. Are you considering participating in the evenings activities?" Madame's cane ticked along the tiles, heralding her arrival as the grand hostess. She was decked out in a silk gown with deep purple insets and lace trim. Her corset was silver-grey, the buckles gleaming, the color matching her tall, ribboned boots.

"Aherm. Um, no, no, I'm not." Greyson wanted the floor to open up and swallow him whole. He felt like a child who'd been caught watching the neighbor's children playing with a new toy. One he didn't have but wanted.

"Were you waiting for me, then?" Madame stopped beside him, shifting her cane to keep her balance on her good leg.

"Not exactly." What could he say? He needed to say something to explain why he was waiting around in the hall for nothing. He cleared his throat again, finding it difficult to swallow; it was like lying to his mother. "Since you've been taking the time to educate me about the brothel business, I thought I might observe a bit this evening. If that's okay?"

Madame cocked her head to the side, long deep-red ringlets playing over pale bare shoulders. Unblinking, she regarded him a moment, and Greyson thought perhaps she could read his mind and know the truth in his lie.

"It is fine, Mr. Holmes. But I expect an explanation of your sudden interest in the brothel at some point."

"Yes, Madame." Greyson inclined his head, taking in a quick, calming breath.

"Is there any place in particular you would like to observer first?"

"Huh? Well, no..." Wait, what was he thinking? "Um, actually, yes. Could I sit in the bar area and observe the reactions of the men to the entertainment? I understand this is not offered in most brothels, except the new one downtown that advertizes as an entertainment venue."

Smirking, Madame shuffled past. "Of course, Mr. Holmes. Let me inform Taggage of your plans for the evening. Follow me."

Only a couple of girls were in the hall, both slated for entertainment in the booze room. One was to sing, and she trilled her voice up and down the scale in preparation, while the other played the piano. The pianist wriggled her finger and cracked her knuckles. Both wore demure gowns of fine quality in similar fabrics and colors, but not identical in cut. They smiled at Greyson when he passed, and the dark-haired piano player even winked at him.

He had no idea how to react to the display, so he bowed his head and refused to make eye contact, keeping close to Madame's skirts so as not to be waylaid.

They giggled when he'd passed, and Madame reprimanded them in a gentle tone. "Girls. Mind yourselves. Mr. Holmes is not a client, nor is he ever likely to be."

"Yes, Madame." The girls spoke in unison, keeping their voices moderate and sing song.

"Good luck tonight. Remember your stage presence. Keep your chins up and don't let anything your audience says bother you. Just keep to your performance. Johnson will be at the door in case anything gets out of hand."

"Yes, Madame."

"Come, Mr. Holmes, let's find you a good seat. Millicent and Amber are very good. I've got a line in to a fancy hotel in Boston that I'm hoping to get them to."

"A hotel in Boston?" What would a couple of whores do at a hotel in Boston? Prostitution was illegal up there, as well as most public consumption of alcohol.

"Yes. It is a grand business. They bring in entertainers from all over the world to perform for their guests. Last year, they brought an opera singer all the way from France."

Greyson still didn't understand.

Madame sighed. "This is their 'after' job, Mr. Holmes. They are hoping to become performers and earn their coin standing, or sitting, instead of lying down."

"Oh, oh." Greyson nodded, though he was still unsure of the significance of an 'after' job.

"Don't worry, Mr. Holmes, I'm certain you will come to a full understanding before you leave."

"I'm leaving?"

"Oh, no time soon, unless it is your desire. But I can't imagine you will want to live here long term."

"I...Yes, yes, of course."

"How about here?" Madame indicated a seat at the end of the long oak bar. It was a padded stool, its single leg of brass shined to within an inch of glowing.

"Yes, I think that will be perfect." From the stool, he could make out the photos hanging behind the bar, as well as hear the girls perform and watch Taggage. Greyson sat on the proffered seat, spinning it to face the room.

"Here, what's this?" Taggage emerged from a door behind the bar, carrying a wide tray of bottled beverages and a platter of tiny meat tarts.

"Mr. Holmes has requested the opportunity to observe this evening." Madame smiled at her second-in-command.

"What? In here?" Taggage dropped the tray to the counter, the bottles offering an ominous rattle.

"Yes, in here. Where else would he observe?" Madame tapped her cane against the wooden floor.

Taggage snorted. "From what I can tell, he really needs to observe what goes on upstairs."

Madame said nothing.

Greyson looked down, spinning the stool a little to use up a surge of nervous energy.

"Gor. Lighten up a little."

"There is no reason for a light demeanor this evening, Taggage. We still have not resolved the issue of the attacks and missing girls."

Setting the tray to one end of the bar—the far end away from where Greyson sat—Taggage started arranging the bottles and glasses on the shelves behind them. "Don't know why you're so hepped up about all that. Norfolk's a dangerous place. Should expect a little violence every now and then."

"These incidents were not a little violence, Taggage." Madame walked to the far end of the counter and chose a couple of the tarts, setting them on a small plate from a stack behind the counter, and taking them back for Greyson. "What are you drinking this evening, Mr. Holmes?"

"What? Drinking?"

Madame laughed. "You can't expect to observe unobtrusively without a glass in your hand. If you like, I can bring you a goblet of port from the parlor."

"Mm..." Greyson traced a line along the counter.

Taggage snorted. "He's probably never had even a taste of alcohol."

"I'll bring you a bit of sherry then. It's a fine vintage, and if no one sees it poured, they will never know what it is. You may nurse it all evening, if that is your desire, or move onto something stronger if you like it."

Madame shuffled toward the door. "Stay there, Mr. Holmes. I will be right back with your glass."

Sitting, watching Taggage work from the corner of his eye, Greyson considered the tarts. He couldn't eat them and was disappointed that Madame had forgotten.

"Here you are." Madame set the squat glass on the counter by his left hand. The older woman leaned close and whispered, her eyes darting to the pudgy form of the former barkeep. "And don't be afraid of the tarts. Those ones do not contain meat, only mushroom and parsnip, and the crusts are made of a flour that does not have wheat in them. I think cook used ground barley."

Surprised, Greyson grinned his thanks. His resentment at his issues evaporated for the moment, and he ate one of the tarts, enjoying the treat. The sherry, which he used to wash down the slightly dry tart, was sweet and burned a little going down.

"Not too much, Mr. Holmes. Sherry is made to be sipped, not chugged."

"My apologies." Greyson squelched an unexpected burp, flushing at the rude sound.

Madame laughed. "Enjoy your tarts and sherry, Mr. Holmes." She patted his shoulder and turned to leave. "I'm off to act as hostess. At breakfast, you may let me know what you think of the singing."

While Madame limped out of the room, Greyson wondered, not for the first time, about her injury. Had she been born with it? Or had she been in some accident?

Did her leg have something to do with her debt to Dr. M?

Taggage finished arranging the bar and sniffed, leaving out the door behind the bar. "Keep your fingers off the rest of them tarts. They're for the paying customers only."

Greyson ate the second tart, sipping the sherry after, enjoying the sweet burn now that he was ready for it.

With Taggage gone and the room to himself, he stood, stretching just in case someone was watching, and affected a nonchalant pace down the counter. He let his gaze run over the photos, noting that many were of famous members of the elite sitting at a bar, glasses raised.

There was none with Taggage in it, certainly not a copy of the one he'd found that afternoon. But there was a spot where a photo used to hang, a darker square of wallpaper announcing that something was missing from the wall.

In any other instance, Greyson would think nothing of it. But if the woman had been Taggage, there was no way she'd been unaware of who chased her earlier that day. And, if it had been the older woman, she knew he'd been inside the closed bar. She'd likely returned and discovered that he'd taken the ledger and photo.

And removed any further evidence to throw him off—or at least slow him down.

Quillian's Log

Sometimes, I have dream's I don't understand. I suppose that isn't anything odd.

But I suffer from a recurring dream, full of hazy and vague feelings rather than images.

I asked Huddy once, if she had "feeling" dreams, and she said yes, she did. They mostly were of her mother and brother, family she'd had to leave behind in Carolinia.

She'd asked me why I asked.

I'd found I couldn't answer her.

29

"Watson! Damn it, Watson!" Dr. M bellowed, snatching Quillian from a strange dream where she was stalked by a man with a windup in his back and a pistol for his hand. She'd fallen asleep in the library, sitting hunched in the window seat, drooling into one of her favorite books.

"Quillian!" Laced with desperation, Huddy's higher-pitched voice shook and cracked.

Leaping up, stumbling over cramped shins and toes that were asleep and prickling, Quillian tried to catch her breath and her bearings. She didn't need to be told there was an emergency. They wouldn't both be yelling for any other reason.

She crammed her feet into her boots, pulling the laces but not bothering to knot them. Grabbing open the door, she let it crash against the wall and close on its own, racing down the hall, pushing loosened curls out of her face as she went.

Stopping dead in the hall, she thought her heart would stop. What if it was Ralph? Is that why Huddy sounds so odd?

"I'm coming!" Picking up the pace, Quillian raced to the surgery.

Rounding the door, she stopped, gasping her breaths, staring at the surgical table. "It's not Ralph!"

"Of course, it's not Ralph. What are you on about? Get in here and help me!" Dr. M pressed against the wound at the boy's shoulder where his arm should be, trying to stem the flood of blood.

It might not be Ralph, but it was a boy, about Ralph's age, his skin melanin-filled a deep brown hue.

Quillian grabbed an apron while crossing the room and dipped her hands the scalding water and bleach mixture, then into a mixture of alcohol to rid them of any germs. "Got it!" She pressed her own hands into the wound, the blood-soaked cloth slipping a little in her lesser grip.

Dr. M moved away, dipping his hands back into the water and bleach, then the alcohol mix to clean them. "It's a bloody mess!"

The Constable stood to the side, watching, his face stoic, his fingers spinning an unlit tobacco pipe.

"He's bleeding too much." Quillian put a fresh cloth from the metal cart against the ragged wound, standing on tip-toe to gain leverage to press down harder.

"Huddy!" Dr. M bellowed loud enough to make Constable Dumphries wince.

Quillian heard the tap, shush, tap, shush of Huddy running from the kitchen. "Yes, sir? I've got the vats started on fer after."

"Dip your hands and take over from Watson. I need her to help me make adjustments to the mechanical."

Huddy dipped her hands and shook her head at the amount of blood soaking into the cloths. "Poor little bugger." Tears tracked down her cheeks, and she smeared them away with a raised shoulder, sniffing.

Constable Dumphries sneered and shuffled his feet, sighing and stretching his arms over his head.

Dr. M and Quillian met at the workbench, where the brass and tempered glass arm was laid out.

"It's too big." Quillian shook her head, sparing a glance at the slight figure on the table.

"It will have to do. We've no time to make one fresh. I've nothing fit for a child." Dr. M's hands shook.

Pulling the mechanical away from him, Quillian prepped the arm, dragging out the thin tubes that would be attached to the blood vessels in the arm's socket.

"Damn fools! Took it off too high." Dr. M snatched a shoulder cap of brass and leather from the shelf, matching it to the top of the brass armiture. "No time to weld things together, I'll have to use rivets and hope it holds."

Quillian was confused. She didn't know what Dr. M was muttering about. She didn't have time to consider it, though; the boy on the table started to moan.

"Give him more ether, Huddy, but be careful. He's too small for a full dose, it could kill him."

Huddy pulled the tube and horn down from above the table and fit it over the boy's mouth with one hand, smearing the glass with blood. The horn covered half his face, and she adjusted it so the ether wouldn't blow into his eyes. She turned the valve to let the gas out and the boy stopped moaning. "I can't get the bleedin' to stop."

"Damn it!" Dr. M applied a rivet to the shoulder cap, the snap of the riveter louder than Quillian ever remembered it.

Quillian winced, her fingers twitching on the arm. He'd almost caught them with the rivet. "I've got the tubes ready."

"Thank you, Watson." Dr. M. took a deep breath. "That will have to do. Let's get this on him.'

Nodding, Quillian picked up the arm, but ran into the back of Dr. M where he'd stopped only half-way to the boy.

"No." He whispered, the word ending in a soft moan. His shoulders trembled and he stooped over, his head hanging down, his hands braced against shaking legs.

Quillian peered around his hunched form. Huddy stroked the face of the boy, brushing his hair back from his face, letting her long fingers smooth the matted tendrils. She no longer tried to stop the bleeding at his arm. The bleeding had stopped on its own.

"What?" Quillian thought her heart might stop beating in her chest and struggled to take a breath.

Constable Dumphries stepped forward. "Dumb luck that, eh? Poor lad. Teach 'im a lesson, though, I reckon."

"Hefty lesson." Huddy spat the words under her breath and shot the policeman a scathing look.

"He's dead?" Quillian asked the question, even though she knew the answer. She didn't want the boy to be dead; he was so young, still a child. Just the age Quillian had been when she arrived to live at Dr. M's house.

She wanted—no needed—someone to say 'no'.

But Huddy nodded. Her cheeks were tracked with tears, blood smudged with the salty liquid where she'd used her fingers to wipe them away. "We'll have to see about finding his parents."

"No need for that, now." The Constable pulled a tin of tobacco from an inside pocket of his cloak. "He's an orphan, from Rutledge Home for Boys. Won't be missing the extra mouth to feed over there."

"There is no smoking in my surgery." Though Dr. M hadn't shifted position, he had straightened, and stood like a brass automaton before it was wound up.

"The boy's dead." The Constable waved a careless hand at the table and raised the pipe to his lips, the tin open, the contents spilling out and falling to the floor.

"This is still my surgery, and you will not taint it by smoking in it." Dr. M stalked forward, crossing the room in two strides and grabbing the tin from the startled constable and throwing it out the door into the hall. Dried tobacco flew across the floor. "This room must be kept impeccably clean at all times. Get out!"

The Constable removed the pipe from his lips. "Keep yer shirt on. I'm going. I'll be waitin' in yer study."

Dr. M turned, but did not look at the boy. His body shuddered, his shoulders curling down. "Huddy, make arrangements for his burial, please. See to it that it's done right. Whatever the cost, I'll pay it."

"Yes, sir." Huddy left the surgery, head down, her own form trembling.

Quillian stood with the mechanical arm in her hands. She didn't know where to put it. It couldn't go back in the cupboard, it had been adjusted to fit the smaller body and it didn't seem right to just leave it out on the cupboard, like a forgotten toy that no longer worked.

"Huddy was right. Poor little bugger." Dr. M pulled a clean white sheet from the stack kept ready on the shelf by the door, and spread it over the boy, tucking it gently around his body, like he was tucking him in for the night.

"Dr. M?"

"Put the arm away, Watson. In the cupboard will be fine. We'll deal with readjusting it later."

"Yes, sir."

Quillian turned back to the workbench and set the arm down, tucking the tubes back in the end to protect them, wrapping them in soft cotton strips to hold them in place. The cupboard shelves were sparse in places, where the sudden influx of patients had caused a backlog in Dr. M's creation of mechanical replacements. Closing the doors, she gripped the handles, shaking fingers trying to work the clasp that would lock them.

She didn't want to look at the white sheet on the table, knowing that little boy was underneath. Sucking in a shaky, wet breath, she squeezed her eyes tight. She didn't want to cry, not yet anyway. What would Dr. M think?

Cleaning the room as best she could, she avoided the cloth-covered table. She mopped the floor, sterilized the tools—barely keeping her fingers away from the steam—and put away the bleach-washed ether tube. Last, she turned off the globes, turning back for one last check.

She blinked away the tears, no longer able to keep them from falling. Flipping back one toggle, a single globe relit, bathing the room in soft golden tones.

She couldn't leave the boy alone in the dark.

E. G. Gaddess

From the journal of G. J. Holmes

I wonder if Taggage is correct, not in that I should observe the girls at work, but that I should at least be interested in that form of activity. It has been offered to me on several evenings since I moved into my room.

I had always considered it a reaction to Jacoby and Wilroy's shenanigans. After Jacoby's death, why would I be interested in such risky activity?

However, after meeting ~~Miss W~~ Quillian, and some of the thoughts I have about her, I am finding my interest piqued.

Though I do not think I would enjoy learning by observing, I rather think that is something I would prefer learning by doing.

30

Settled in his room for the evening, a pleasant buzz from the sherry relaxing him, someone knocked on Greyson's door. Sighing, he opened it, expecting another visitor encouraged by Mrs. Taggage.

"Sir." It was a maid; the girl curtseyed in her gray uniform. "Madame would like you to come to her study. There is something in the street she would like you to see."

Surprised, Greyson didn't answer for a moment. Clearing his throat, he found his voice. "I'll be right down."

The maid nodded and pivoted and Greyson closed the door. He slipped his shoes onto his feet and donned a vest over his shirt and trousers. After adjusting his spectacles, he left. Locking the door behind him, he slipped the door key into his vest pocket.

He used the back stairs to descend to the first level. The front stair was reserved for clients, especially during the busy periods, like this evening. Music and laughter filtered through the house, covering the guttural and earthy sounds heard on the working floor.

The main hall was empty, clients awaiting services were either in the downstairs parlor or listening to the performance in the bar. Their conversations, low and mumbled, leaked out the open door. Greyson wondered how many were waiting.

Taggage brushed past him from behind, a wide, white apron a stark contrast to the black of her dress. "Quit dawdlin' in the hall." She carried a bottle of port and another of wine and disappeared into the front parlor.

Greyson sighed and knocked on the door to Madame's private salon.

"Enter."

Opening the door, Greyson glanced around the room, expecting Madame to be sitting in her customary spot, the big leather chair by the fireplace or behind her desk.

Instead, she stood at the window, peering out into the street around a deep red brocade drape.

"Madame?"

"Come here, Mr. Holmes. I thought you might find this to be of interest."

Greyson marched across the room and pushed aside a drape, looking out into the dark. "What am I looking at?"

"Give it a moment."

A minute later, a slow-moving steamcar passed the house, the insignia on the side visible in the bright artificial gas streetlight. It belonged to his father.

"What?" Greyson leaned his cheek against the cool glass pane to watch the steamcar disappear down the street.

"It has gone past five times now."

"Five times?" He leaned back, fingers gripping the drape.

"Indeed." Madame turned to face him, both hands balanced atop her silver-tipped cane. "I think someone is looking for you."

"So, it appears."

"Do you want them to find you?"

Greyson sighed. If it was his father, in response to the note he'd left, yes; if it was Wilroy, no—never. "It depends."

"I can send a footman to flag it down. If it is not someone you want to see, I can have him ask if he is looking for the brothel."

"Very well. If it is my father, have him brought in. Anyone else, I do not want to see them."

"Your father?" Madame shifted on her cane, her eyes wide.

"I sent him a note this afternoon." Greyson shifted and lowered his eyes from her gaze,

"Very well." Madame reached for the yellow cord that would summon the footman. "Your father would be the only white-haired gentleman using that vehicle, yes?"

"Wilroy has brown hair, but he tends to use his automaton horse."

Someone knocked.

"Enter."

"Madame?" It was Johnson, a footman, dressed in a colorful uniform. He entered and stood at attention.

"There is a steamcar driving up and down the street, with the Holmes' family crest on the side. Please flag it down. If it is a white-haired gentleman, tell him to come in to speak to Mr. Holmes. If it is not, simply ask if they are looking for the brothel and let them know we are full up for the evening."

"Yes, Madame." Johnson clicked his heels together and spun out the door.

"Do you wish to speak with your father in private?" Madame stood at her desk, clearing papers away and setting them in drawers.

"No. I would like you to stay, please." Greyson faced the door, spine straight, head up. He smoothed his vest and adjusted his spectacles.

"Very well." Madame sat behind her desk, running her fingers through her hair in an attempt to tame the strands.

Soon enough, there was a commotion in the hall.

From the journal of G. J. Holmes

The brothel is amazingly quiet on the top floor. Madame and Mrs. Taggage maintain strict control over all who enter – employee and client alike.

Though I have never sought the services offered in a brothel myself, Wilroy often spoke about his forays into such establishments, and never did I hear him describe them like this one.

Madame offers a type of tearoom, only it isn't tea that is served, but cocktails and light refreshment. Perhaps, a men's club would be a better description, but I have never been in one of those, either.

One thing I do not understand, is how Madame chose Mrs. Taggage for her second-in-command. The woman is brusque to the point of being rude. From overheard mutterings, she thinks Madame is a bit prude in her service offerings, and often grumbles about how things will change when she is in charge.

I wonder when she thinks that will be?

E. G. Gaddess

I remember the day Madame brought me to meet Dr. M. I'm not sure why this memory surfaced, other than I thought about me being that age when I saw the dead boy on the surgery table.

Madame had carried a valise with her.

I hadn't realized at the time what was in it.

I only knew that we were going to an interview with a doctor. I thought it was for something that was wrong with me. I'd been having strange dreams - nightmares.

We sat, had tea - Huddy hadn't smiled at me then - and Dr. M had asked questions - lots of questions. Then he'd asked me to read from a book on his desk.

That is when he told Madame that he'd take me and Madame gave the valise to Huddy and looked down at me and told me to behave and do whatever Dr. M told me to do - and I'd be fine.

She'd promised that everything would be fine.

31

Despite the quiet hall, Quillian tiptoed. It wasn't a conscious decision, and though she knew she couldn't wake up the little boy, it just felt right.

Outside Dr. M's study, though, Quillian could hear shouting: Dr. M and Constable Dumphries. She paused outside the door, not bothering to tiptoe now. Nothing would be heard above the shouting inside.

"He was just a boy!" That was Dr. M's voice, raised as loud as Quillian had ever heard it.

"He was no one of consequence. No one will miss him. I told you." Constable Dumphries didn't shout. He sounded more like someone discussing the weather than the death of an innocent child.

"You lied to me!"

What? Quillian leaned an ear to the door, straining to hear the constable's words.

"Don't be daft. You knew what was going on."

"Not until Dr. Bergeron came to see me with his patient." Something—a decanter?—clanked against a solid surface.

"Oh, come now, doctor. No one will ever believe that."

"I never would have agreed to the mechanicals if I'd known." Dr. M's words slurred.

"So, ye're backin' out now, eh?"

"I will not be a part of this."

"And how do ye suppose to get yerself out of it?"

Dr. M snorted. "I'm not in it. And I do not have to help you." There was another clink of glass and slosh of liquid.

"Yer getting drunk."

"Yes."

"You cannot be drunk when the Mitchum boy arrives for his surgery."

"I'm not doing it. Get Dr. Bergeron, like you've been doing."

"He can't. You know he can't. Not anymore. Not since he flubbed the last one." Constable Dumphries' voice rose, its timber getting higher. "His concentration's shot."

"You can't make me do it."

"You are correct there, doctor. But you will have had this boy in your surgery die for naught?"

A glass hit a surface hard, followed by the tinkling sound of glass shards hitting the floor. "I will do it tomorrow."

"You cannot do it tomorrow."

"The arm is on ice?"

"Yes."

More sloshing liquid. "Then what is the problem?"

"Lady Caine is expecting a new hand tomorrow."

Heavy breathing. Whispered cursing. Another clink of glass. "Great bloody hell. What are you doing?"

The faint bell to the kitchen echoed up the hall and the tap, shush, tap, shush that approached meant Huddy was responding. "Just the boy. I'll only do the boy."

The constable laughed; Quillian thought it sounded like the monkeys in the menagerie, the ones that seemed to shriek, choking on a banana.

"Oh, you will do them, all of them. You have no choice, doctor. You won't let someone die. Not when you can prevent it."

Quillian backed away, once again on her tippiest toes. She needed to get away. She needed to not be seen or heard.

Shaking her head, she slunk through the shadows she never noticed before, hugging close to the wall. She didn't want to understand the overheard conversation; didn't want to believe what she had heard.

The tap, shush, tap, shush of Huddy's gait got louder. Quillian spun around and sprinted up the stairs, away from the shadows, retreating to her small attic bedroom.

Patch was nestled in the rumpled quilt; the globe at the head of her bed lit and casting a soft glow about the room. It made for a cozy tableau. It was hard to imagine, seeing the warm scene, feeling the calm essence of the retreat, that a dead boy lay downstairs and a policeman spoke of another surgery on the morrow—like it had been scheduled in a physician's office.

Quillian stared at the cat, the hum of its mechanical bits a reassuring thrum in the otherwise still room.

She couldn't help but think of the boy downstairs, still laid out on the surgery table. There was no way she was going to fall asleep, no matter the quiet and rest that beckoned. She dropped her bloody apron in the brass hamper and checked over her dress. It, too, was stained, the red turning a rusted brown.

She pulled it off over her head and removed a clean one from her armoire. Retrieving a fresh corset and solid walking boots at the same time.

She needed to get out of the house. She needed to speak to Mr. Holmes.

She needed to tell him about the boy, both the one downstairs and the one in Portsmouth—'Mitchum' Constable Dumphries had said. It was too late to help the boy, but they could help the next victim. Because some high-faluting lady expected to get a new hand tomorrow. Which could only mean that tonight, if she understood what Constable Dumphries had been forcing Dr. M to do, someone else was going to lose hers.

It would likely be a prostitute. A lady wouldn't want a true working woman's hand, with calluses and scars and weathered skin. No, a lady would want a fine hand, with soft skin.

And that meant it had to come from someone who took pride in their looks, who relied on those looks.

A lady would also want someone healthy, someone without disease.

And the best bet for all of that was one of Madame's girls.

32

Groaning, Greyson took a deep breath, preparing to meet whoever had been stalking the street in front of the brothel. The commotion in the hall got closer, grew louder, and he tensed.

"Where is my son?" The bellow was enough to make Greyson flinch and cringe. He almost wished it had been Wilroy.

"He's this way, sir." The footman's voice was strangled, like he was trying to keep his laughter in, and two sets of footsteps approached the closed door.

Taking another breath, Greyson straightened, braced his cane to the floor, and faced the door.

"A brothel! You are living in a brothel?" Sir Stanley barged into the parlor like a bull in a barn, hat and coat still on and cane in hand, his mouth agape. His hair stuck out from beneath his hat, his oversized sideburns askew, like he'd been pulling on one side while the other rested in a palm and flattened. "Do you know what will happen if I am seen exiting this place?"

Greyson couldn't hide his snicker. "There are benefits, Father."

"Indeed!?" His father threw his jacket over the back of an armchair and removed his hat. "Your mother will have my hide and make a chair of it."

"Most importantly," Greyson felt it necessary to explain, "is that few would guess I am living here. And I will explain to Mother for you if it comes to that."

"Oh, God! You're not...working...here are you?" The man's face, red when he'd walked in, turned pale to nearly transparent.

Raising his brows, Greyson watched his father. "Define 'working'."

Sir Stanley collapsed into the armchair, his limbs spread out, his head shaking back and forth.

"Your son has not been entertaining clients, Sir Holmes, though he has been asked to perform certain tasks for me in exchange for a reasonable discount on his rental rate." Madame's voice censured Greyson.

Greyson sighed. "Rest easy, Father. I have only been making inquiries for Madame."

"What sort of inquiries?" Color crept back into Sir Stanley's cheeks.

"Regarding injuries to some of her employees. Also, there are three who have disappeared entirely."

Sir Stanley snorted. "Is that why you came by the house asking questions?"

He offered his father a brief nod.

The older man sighed and rubbed his forehead, then scrubbed at his eyes. "Your mother made a list of all the doctors that were at the fête."

"A list?" Greyson paused mid-sit in the armchair nearest his father, within an arm's reach, and straightened at his father's casual comment.

"Let me see. Where did I put it?" His father rummaged through his pockets, pulling out a sheet of pale pink parchment. "Here."

Greyson took the paper. More than twenty names were written on the page, all in his mother's short, flourished hand.

"What sort of injuries are you talking about?" Sir Stanley drummed his fingers along the arms of the chair.

"Limbs—arms, hands—were taken. We are not certain of the ones who disappeared." Madame spoke from behind her desk.

"Good God!" Sir Stanley lunged forward in the chair. "Do you think the missing girls were fatally harmed?"

"It is the conclusion I have reached so far, yes." Greyson scanned the names and sat down. There were only a few he recognized.

"So, you are probably looking for a surgeon?"

"Most like, yes." Madame spoke again, twirling a mechanical quill between her red-tipped fingers.

"Oh, Father. My apologies. To you as well, Madame. Father, this is Madame, my landlady and employer. Madame, this is my father, Sir Stanley Holmes."

"How do you do?" Madame nodded from her chair.

"Same to you." Sir Stanley did not rise, either. He snapped his fingers at Greyson. "Give me that list back."

Blinking at the brusque demand, Greyson handed over the list.

His father dug through his pockets again then placed the retrieved reading monocle over one eye. "Might I borrow your mechanical quill, Madame?"

Madame raised her brows, but silently handed over the brass contraption in her hand.

Sir Stanley placed a tick next to a name, then next to another, and another. He handed the list back to Greyson, and the mechanized quill back to Madame. "There. Seven who are surgeons now, and one who served as a surgeon in the last war with Carolinia, but no longer practices such."

Greyson read over the indicated names. None were names he recognized. "Mother said you had invested in an enterprise with Dr. Bergeron."

"Yes. It failed, I believe."

"You believe?"

"He's disappeared. No one has seen him for better than a week. We were supposed to meet for lunch today—my treat mind you—but he never showed. I am certain it was because he owes money to his investors, one of whom is me." Sir Stanley shifted and sniffed. "Probably suicide."

"I was not aware that a body had been found." Madame rose from the desk and walked to the front, using her cane only the slightest bit.

"Oh, nothing's been found. But I can imagine him doing something like that. Emotional man was Bergeron. Obsessed with curing his daughter of some ailment his wife died of. Some blood disorder, I think. Got all distraught and weepy every time he mentioned it."

"Murder." Greyson folded the list and placed it in his vest pocket next to his room key.

"Why would someone murder his wife? I told you, she died of some illness."

"Not the wife, Bergeron. Because he botched the venture. Told someone about it that he shouldn't have. I believe he was involved in a limb-stealing business. Was responsible for securing the stolen limb to its new owner."

Sir Stanley sat quiet in his chair, one finger tracing back and forth over his cheek.

Madame stood and walked to the fireplace; Greyson suspected she wanted warmth from the flames for her bad leg.

"I suppose that is a possibility." Sir Stanley fixed his gaze on his son.

Greyson shifted under the directness.

The older man sighed. "Is that why you left me a note of warning?"

He nodded.

"Wilroy was determined to blame you for your mother's bout of tears this afternoon."

"I am sorry. She overreacted to my concern when she told me that you were in business with Dr. Bergeron."

Sir Stanley waved a hand. "Wilroy blames you for everything. Think nothing of his tirades. I'm about to throw him out of the house, as well. He upsets your mother far more than you or Jacoby did combined."

"I have no more rooms to let." Madame spoke again. Her face was pale and just a bit perspired. Her hands squeezed the handle of her cane.

Snorting, Sir Stanley stood and retrieved his hat and jacket. "I'm surprised he's not here as a client."

"I assured your son that I would refuse his brother service here when he decided to let the room."

Greyson stood, taking up his father's hat and holding it out to him.

"Good move." Sir Stanley donned his hat and nodded to Greyson. "I will be home for tea tomorrow at three. Wilroy will be at his club; he plays poker on Thursdays."

Greyson followed his father to the front door, walking with him all the way out to the steamcar. "You would like me to come?"

"Yes." Sir Stanley turned to his son, taking his arm in a warm grip. He leaned forward, whispering. "I have some papers from Bergeron's venture that I can give you. Perhaps they will help in your inquiries. And cook found a place that sells rice flour. She's been experimenting with tea cakes."

From the Journal of G. J. Holmes

My perception of my father has completely changed and I do not know what to make of it. It is like reality has shifted and I am lost among the new landscape.

"Cook has been experimenting with rice flour."

I cannot fathom why, of a sudden, this has changed. Did father or mother notice how healthy I was at tea and recognized the benefits of my regimen? Did they decide to make such concessions in order that I might visit more often?

I am afraid I will never know the answer, as I am too afraid to ever ask.

Quillian's Log

I'm remembering things I never knew I'd forgotten.

Life at the brothel. Madame teaching me to read and do sums. Singing me to sleep. Tucking me in.

Life when I was little, before I understood what went on at the brothel, what the girls did there.

I remember that I loved that house.

My room was on the top floor, but not the attic. Madame's rooms were next to mine. There was a door between our rooms, so I could get to her whenever I wanted.

My room had a big bed with long curtains around it and I could pretend it was a fairy world where I was a princess and I defended it from all invaders.

Well, all but one invader.

It's still murky and only a half memory. But I remember when I was attacked.

33

It was dark in the garden, but Quillian did not need light. She knew her way around it as well as she knew her bedroom. Reaching the back gate, she lifted the latch, sucking in a sharp breath when the hinges creaked.

Only after she heard no sounds of investigation or inquiry, did she decide it was safe to close it and leave.

She was not so familiar with the alley as the garden. She crept along, windows leaking light through open drapes, so she could see her way, and once she reached the main street, gas globes shed enough wavering beams to rival daylight.

The wide pipe that provided steam to this area of the city was in good repair, the copper solid and cleaned and well-oiled, not a spot of verdigris. Relief valves stuck up from the top at regular intervals, but no steam leaked out. They were closed tight, the steam inside pushing along with a steady, rumbling shush.

Madame's establishment was three blocks down and five over—though it seemed a world away. Quillian took a direct route, keeping to the main streets, well into the artificial light. She did not want to risk meeting a ruffian in a dark alley. She didn't have a mini-cannon for protection and she was no good with a knife, even though Huddy insisted she carry one in an inside sheath in her boot.

The streets were mostly deserted, the only traffic, those of the upper crust leaving the high-end parties early. In another hour or two, the streets would clog with steamcars and carriages pulled by automaton horses, the elite making their way home just before dawn.

Mechanical horses clopped down the middle of the street, pulling a police wagon behind. Dirty hands jerked at the barred windows and curses flew between them. A policeman hanging on the back struck the windows with a billy club and the fingers disappeared, but the cursing only increased.

Quillian didn't look too closely at the wagons. She didn't want to see the faces of those inside, sneering at her, spitting black chaw between rotted teeth. She'd asked Dr. M about them once. Asked him why they were in the wagon and what the words were that they shouted.

He'd only pursed his lips and sighed, stating something about the ridicule of the mayor.

Quillian waited for the wagon to pass and crossed the street, running to reach the other side before another mechanical horse or steamtruck came along. Not everyone stopped for a person in the street, especially at night.

Madame's home was grand; the wide front porch of the discrete establishment fronted Granby Street with wide doors of dark polished oak and brass. The gingerbread trim was painted a muted purple, similar to the muted greens and deep blues of the other houses along the street. Unless you knew what went on inside, you certainly couldn't tell from the exterior, except that the steps leading to the doors were wide, perfect for ladies in heels and long gowns to traverse without tripping, and a shallow arc cut into the walk in front, so a vehicle could pull out of the road a bit when picking up or dropping off one of the girls.

There was a carriage in the short, curved drive, the automaton horses pawing the matched cobbles with their iron hooves. Quillian couldn't chance being seen—word could get back to Dr. M, or worse, Huddy—so she did not bother even passing by the front, instead walking at a brisk pace down the dim alley behind.

The steam pipe that led into Madame's house was painted brown, made of iron instead of shiny copper, but like the ones in the alley behind Dr. M's home, it was well kept. Farther down the alley, obscured by dark shadows, the rush of steam venting from a piece not so well maintained hissed into the dark.

As a child, Quillian had thought it a great writhing snake waiting to strike. And though it was not a monster, one still had to be careful in the lower neighborhoods; not everyone paid to keep their pipes in order, and a blowout was known to take a man's head off or cook him through.

The back door to the brothel was smaller, though a bright gas globe hung above it, casting a golden round of light on the ground, with a shiny brass number and knocker on the door. The brass ring hung lower than on most doors. Quillian reached out and pulled the heavy clapper, letting it fall against the door. She heard scuffling feet inside, moving toward her.

She made sure to stand under the globe, removing the cap that hid her hair and lifting her face so the person inside would be able to see her clearly through the peephole. She knew what was expected.

"Lawd a mercy! Miss Quillian. What'r you doin' here?" Taggage stood in the open door, one hand on her hip, her eyes wide and her mouth open. Heavy make-up accentuated the older woman's wrinkles, her deep-red lip tint smearing into the skin around her mouth. Her hair, naturally white and ashy brown, was dyed a strawberry blonde color and curled into fat ringlets.

"I need to see Mr. Holmes. It is most urgent." Quillian didn't step forward; Madame's second-in-command hadn't invited her inside yet and being pushy could get her thrown out.

"Now you see here, Mr. Holmes 'as retired fer the evenin'. I ain't getting' 'im outta 'is bed fer you."

"Who is it, Taggage?"

Madame.

Quillian took a deep breath and straightened her spine. "It's Quillian, Madame."

"Quillian! Let her in Taggage. Let her in!" Madame's distinctive gait—step, tink, shush—started down the hall.

Stepping around Taggage and through the door she'd sworn never to cross of her own free will, Quillian took a breath and tried to keep her eyes on Madame, dressed in her usual black, but with hints of bright purple lace at her plunging neckline and petticoat trim.

Taggage tsked and closed the door behind her. "Most people would be abed by now."

Quillian didn't bother to respond. Taggage knew it was lie. The woman was fully aware that most people in Norfolk were certainly not in bed yet, well, not in bed *asleep*, anyway.

"I'm sorry for disturbing you so late in the evening, Madame, but I must see Mr. Holmes, immediately." Quillian clutched her hat in her hands, feeling very much like an errand boy.

Madame stared a moment, standing in the center of the main hall, one hand gripping the top of her cane. Gas light flickered from the wall sconces, fluttering over her features. Though Madame's hair was also red, unlike Taggage, it was her natural color, and in the flickering light, Quillian made out a dusting of silver strands at her temples.

"Cecily! Please fetch Mr. Holmes." Madame took a wider stance, moving her good leg out, and placing her other hand atop the first, the cane centered in front of her.

"Aye, Madame. Right away, Madame." Cecily, a slender blonde in a black maid's uniform, dipped a low curtsey and rushed up the stairs.

Taggage tsked but said nothing.

"What is it, Quillian?" Madame's make-up was lighter than Taggage's, and the slight crow's feet at the corners of her eyes crinkled in a frown.

Quillian thought a moment. What would happen if she told Madame? After all, she knew Madame always took care of her girls.

"Are any of the girls out tonight?"

"Why, yes." Madame laughed low in her throat. "There are two out for the evening. It was slow tonight. And I've been a bit more discriminating in our customers of late. Only long-term clients; ones I trust." Madame grimaced and shifted on her cane. "Why do you ask?"

"Bring them back. Now!" Quillian bit her lip. "Someone—a lady—is looking for a hand."

Taggage snorted and waved a hand at Quillian. "The chits comin' up with even weirder tales than when she was a babe!"

Quillian closed her eyes and sighed. Maybe Mr. Holmes would be able-

"Johnson, Ferby." Madame addressed two liveried men that stood at attention in the hall, her voice a knife cutting through the air. "Each of you, fetch two others and retrieve Magda and Florence. Immediately!"

Gasping, Quillian popped her eyes open.

The footmen nodded, the moves sharp, respectful, then ran down the hall, calling to the other footmen.

"And take weapons with you! Don't be afraid to use them if you are challenged."

"Madame?" Taggage looked shocked, one spotted hand placed over her heart. "We've never-"

Madame held up a hand to stop the woman's chatter and turned back to Quillian. "What did you hear, Quillian? What has happened?"

"Shouldn't we wait for Mr. Holmes?" Quillian wasn't certain she could get through her story twice.

"I am here." Mr. Holmes descended the stairs, his shirt misbuttoned and his dark hair standing on end. He rubbed his hands over his face, squinting without his spectacles. "I apologize for my appearance. I assumed it was urgent?"

Quillian nodded. "Lady—I think the last name is Caine— will be at Dr. M's tomorrow expecting to receive a new hand."

Taggage clucked and rocked back on her heels. "So…the old madman is preselling his mechanicals now is he?"

"Not a mechanical hand. A real hand. Which means that tonight, someone will be losing theirs."

"Good God!" Mr. Holmes staggered backward. "It is as I suspected!"

"Such a story." Taggage laughed it off, waving her hands about her head, her jowls jiggling.

"See to the maids, Taggage. I want the gentlemen in residence tonight to leave once they have received the services they have paid for. Admit no one else; we are shut down for the rest of the evening."

Taggage sniffed but moved obediently down the hall, slowly and muttering beneath her breath.

"Mr. Holmes?" Quillian sounded breathless. "What do you mean, as you suspected?"

"Someone has been stealing human parts for those in the upper classes."

"What?" It was Quillian's turn to stagger. Sure, she had thought...but she had hoped it was just the wild imagination from her childhood returning to haunt her.

"Let us adjourn to the parlor." Madame led the short way down the hall to a room on the right, her cane thudding heavy on the floor, following by the shush of her bad foot. Flipping a switch just inside the door flooded the room with gas light from a dozen small globes suspended from the ceiling, brass tubes connecting them in an elaborate, decorative crisscross.

The room was just as Quillian remembered, even down to the small replica of Madame's chair that sat in the corner. On that chair, Quillian had sat in the corner as a child, studying or reading, while Madame conducted her business.

This evening, a porcelain doll sat in the chair, its pale cheeks painted peach beneath the strawberry blonde curls held back on the sides by pale green ribbon that matched the sheen of its dress.

Quillian looked away from the doll and blinked. She sat on a settee, Madame in her usual chair—the largest in the room—and Mr. Holmes sat in another across from the settee.

"Quillian, tell us everything."

"Quickly, though. There may not be much time." Mr. Holmes sat forward in his chair, resting his elbows on his knees, his hands clasped in front of him. He reminded Quillian of an overeager student.

"A young boy was brought in with a missing arm. Just a child really, only a dozen years old, perhaps not even ten, yet. Dr. M was so upset. The boy was bleeding too much. And then, he said something odd, under his breath really. I don't think I was meant to hear it anyway." Quillian licked her lips and looked at the overlarge seascape painting above the fireplace. "He said 'Damn fools. Cut it off too high'."

Mr. Holmes frowned and sat back. "What does that mean?"

Quillian sighed. "Someone cut the arm off, it was too precise for anything else. The cut was up on the actual shoulder, so it severed a main artery. The mechanical arm we had was too large for the boy; it took too long to prep it."

Quillian looked at Madame. Madame was watching Quillian, her hands clutching her skirts. "And then?"

"The boy died. He'd lost too much blood, I think. Or maybe Huddy gave him too much ether by mistake. It is so easy to do with children.

Madame closed her eyes and turned her head. "Poor thing."

Mr. Holmes was leaning forward again. "So, you already had a mechanical arm ready?"

Quillian swallowed and nodded. "When all this started, when these patients started coming in, Dr. M decided to keep something of everything we had ready and prepped."

"Why are you here? Why not tell the authorities?" Mr. Holmes reared up in his chair, arms in the air.

"That boy was brought in by Constable Dumphries. They've all been brought in by Constable Dumphries. Every last one of them. And he's the one that threatened Dr. M. He said Dr. M wouldn't let someone die, no matter what. He didn't have it in him."

"Hmm." Mr. Holmes collapsed back in his chair, a frown settling over his darkening features.

Madame turned back. "It was Constable Dumphries who brought in the boy this evening? And he threatened Dr. M?"

Quillian nodded. "I overheard Dr. M and the Constable talking—or rather Dr. M was yelling and the Constable talking—in Dr. M's study after the boy died and I'd finished cleaning the surgery. Dr. M was angry and told the Constable that he wasn't going to help him. The constable laughed. And Dr. M was drinking, already half-drunk I suspect. And then, Constable Dumphries told him about Lady Caine expecting a hand tomorrow. He said Dr. M would do it because he wouldn't let someone die."

"And you know nothing of what he meant?" Mr. Holmes stood over Quillian.

"Mr. Holmes!" Madame stood as well, and took a quick step forward, stumbling a little without the cane. She inserted herself between Quillian and Mr. Holmes. "You will do well to watch yourself!"

Mr. Holmes stepped back.

Madame turned to Quillian, her voice softer. "Quillian, what else do you know?"

"Nothing really." Quillian licked dry lips. "Just...there was once...a surgeon brought someone in-" She checked the time on the large water clock on the mantle, trying to count the days backward," the day before yesterday. Dr. Bergeron, I think his name was. Something had gone wrong. Dr. M had to replace a replacement or something. I wasn't allowed near the surgery. I thought it was a mechanical replacement, like what Dr. M normally does, but..."

"But?" Mr. Holmes leaned over Quillian.

"And Dr. M was off to see Dr. Bergeron, without even eating a proper breakfast. Dr. M always eats his breakfast."

"Impossible." Mr. Holmes flipped his hand through the air.

"That Dr. M always eats breakfast? It is the most important meal of the day."

"No, about Dr. Bergeron. He's dead."

Quillian jumped to her feet. "He was alive when he was at the surgery."

"Mr. Holmes, you only suspect that Dr. Bergeron is dead because your father said he was missing. Perhaps he is missing because he is hiding out, possibly with Dr. M."

Mr. Holmes frowned, two fingers playing with his bottom lip. "I could be wrong. It is difficult for me to believe that someone would stand up lunch with my father."

"Is your father really that powerful?" Quillian sat, clasping her hands.

"I always thought so." Mr. Holmes dropped his hands to his narrow hips and turned back to face her, pressing forward. "And you never really suspected anything about Dr. M and his surgery?"

"Mr. Holmes, I warned you." Madame stared at the young man, who lowered his gaze and backed up under the pierce of hers.

"What if it wasn't supposed to be mechanical? What if...what if it was supposed to be a real limb? Dr. Bergeron was scared afterward that his patient would be upset because it wasn't what it was supposed to be." This wasn't exactly what Huddy had said, but Quillian was smart enough to figure out what was meant.

"Bloody hell!" Mr. Holmes pressed his palms over his face.

"'tis not true."

Quillian made to stand. She hadn't really expected anyone to believe her, but she'd thought they'd listen a little more.

"Please Quillian, stay." Madame placed a hand on Quillian's arm and Quillian flinched. Madame immediately released it. "I do not mean your story to be a lie, but Mr. Holmes' conclusion."

"My conclusion? How do you know my conclusion?" Mr. Holmes squinted at the older woman.

"You do not appreciate Dr. M's abilities."

"I think them unnecessary."

Madame shrugged and looked to Quillian. "Mr. Holmes thinks that Dr. M is in on this scheme." She turned to the young man, shaking her head. "He is not."

Mr. Holmes sighed and began to pace. "You do not think he was aware that the emergency of this evening was related to his earlier surgeries? If Quillian is correct, and this surgeon brought someone to him who'd had a real limb attached, do you honestly think he wouldn't make a connection?"

"I refuse to believe he would knowingly participate in such a scheme. He has no need."

"This country is in the midst of an economic crisis, Madame. Neo-Virginia is on the brink of war, either with the United Briton States or Carolinia, if not both. The Free Trade agreements are breaking down; we are no longer able to import resources at a cost that allows us to sell our manufactured goods at a profit. Most folks are scrambling for money."

"I doubt Dr. M has any financial worries to trouble him."

Mr. Holmes opened his mouth to speak, but was cut off by a commotion in the hall. Someone was weeping and someone was shushing them and someone was demanding to see Madame right away.

Taggage opened the parlor door, rushing in, her cheeks pink and her hair falling out of its contrived ringlets. One of the footmen sent out to fetch the girls home followed her, his livery jacket torn, a bruise deepening on his chin. "Madame!"

"What is it, Ferby?"

A young girl followed him, limping, her eyes red, her dress torn and dirty.

"What happened?" Madame immediately went to the girl, her cane rapping fast on the wood floor, wrapping her arms around the pale, weeping blonde. "Was it your gentleman? What happened? Who did this?"

"Weren't her gentleman, Madame. Were a band of blackguards. Tried to cut 'er they did."

The girl's wail cut through the room and she sobbed into Madame's shoulder, shaking.

Quillian sank back against the cushions; her hands shook, so she hid them in her skirts.

"Are you alright? Are you hurt? Taggage, don't just stand there. Fetch Dr. Brown at once." Madame ran her hands over the girl's arms and tilted her face up so she could see her face.

"There ain't nothing wrong with the girl-"

"Fetch Dr. Brown!" Madame's voice boomed.

"Yes, ma'am." Taggage sneered, then spun on her heel and left the room.

"Timmy and Brucie went after 'em, t'see if they could catch 'em."

"Very good. Please watch for them. I want to see them immediately when they return. Also look out for Johnson and whoever he took with him."

Ferby nodded and left.

"You called me, Madame?" Dr. Brown's cheeks were flushed and a few long bits of grey hair stood straight up from the tight braid she's put the rest of it in. Her robe hung open, the tie trailing behind, showing the prim nightdress beneath.

"Yes, Dr. Brown. Magda has had quite a scare this evening and was nearly injured quite severely. Please examine her and provide her with a sleeping aid. I am sure she will need it."

"Yes, Madame."

"Cecily? Are you there?"

"Yes, Madame." The blonde maid showed herself in the open door. She still wore the black and gray uniform of the household staff.

"Accompany Magda and Dr. Brown, please. See that Magda makes it safely to her bed and stay with her until she falls asleep."

"Yes, Madame." Cecily curtseyed and wrapped an arm around the crying girl, leading her out of the parlor behind Dr. Brown.

Madame closed the door and stood, clutching the knob for a moment. "This is turning into a nightmare."

"Indeed." Mr. Holmes stood next to the fireplace.

"You do not seem upset, sir." Quillian was near to tears.

"It is best to keep one's head in such circumstances. To become upset muddles one's thinking and makes it difficult to see the resolution."

Quillian looked to Madame. She had turned from the door and was once more facing the room. Her eyes were wet, her kohl smearing.

The woman sniffed and dabbed a stark white handkerchief against her nose, before blowing gustily into the piece of cloth. "Oh, Lord, what are we to do?"

"Go to the police, of course." Mr. Holmes seemed surprised at Madame's question.

"Have you not been listening?" Quillian stood and stomped her foot. "Constable Dumphries is likely in on it."

"Oh, I highly doubt that."

"Why not?"

"Why, this matter is too complex for him to be a part of it. At least, not a big part of it; certainly not the mastermind behind the scheme."

"You think the lower classes are less intelligent than the upper classes?" Quillian was angry at the man. He stood there like he had written the encyclopedia, eyes wide and mouth agape.

"They are less schooled, therefore-"

"Ugh!" Quillian threw her hands in the air and turned away. She stabbed a finger at Madame. "I cannot believe you are letting him live here!"

Madame shrugged. "He is paying rent and helping me." She tottered on her feet.

Quillian frowned a moment until she realized that Madame's cane was lying on the floor at her feet. She darted forward, grabbed up the cane and held it out to Madame, waiting for the woman to take it.

"Thank you, Quillian."

Quillian nodded and scurried back to the settee.

Someone knocked on the door.

Madame used her cane to move to her chair, sinking gracefully into the cushion and discretely stretching out her bad leg. "Enter."

Quillian frowned again, ignoring the opening of the door and the footman that entered. She had not known Madame to have quite so much trouble with her leg in the past.

"Madame." It was a footman. He bowed in Madame's direction.

"Were you able to catch them, Bruce?" Madame leaned against the back of the chair and closed her eyes.

"Almost, Madame. But they's had a steamcar waiting. It had a big brass trunk on the back with steam comin' out. Just like afore."

"Steam?" Mr. Holmes frowned from his place by the fireplace, flipping one hand in the air. "That is ridiculous. You must have followed the wrong men."

Bruce flushed. "We followed the right ones, I tell ye. And there was steam or smoke coming out the trunk."

"It was ice vapor." Quillian rolled her eyes and shook her head at Mr. Holmes. "There was likely ice in the trunk, very cold ice, to keep the hand 'fresh' until it could be attached to its new owner. The ice was warming too quickly to turn to water, so it turned directly to vapor."

"Did you get close enough to recognize them, Bruce?" Madame still had her eyes closed, and Quillian wondered if she was in pain. The woman was pale and her breathing just a bit ragged.

"No, Madame. But it wasn't a fancy steamcar. It was painted all black and didn't have any light globes."

"Thank you, Bruce. Please make sure the perimeter is secure."

"Yes, Madame. Oh, and Johnson returned with Florence without incident. Theys is safely inside."

Madame nodded and Bruce backed out the door.

Quillian's Log

I've never liked Taggage. She used to come with Madame on her visits. Like a companion or something. For some reason, Madame stopped bringing her a couple of years ago.

I don't like how she looks at me, her lips curling in a sneer. I know she thinks I'm worthless. She used to snort when Dr. M would explain how good I was doing at my studies, even though Madame would nod and smile.

Funny, that I remember those smiles now. I guess I forgot, because I always paid more attention to where Taggage was and what Taggage was doing.

I'm beginning to wonder if I was always more afraid of Taggage than I was of Madame.

34

The room fell quiet, the silence heavy and labored.

Mr. Holmes still stood by the fireplace, Madame still leaned back in her chair with her eyes closed, and Quillian sat on the settee, watching Madame. The woman was even paler now and dark circles rimmed her eyes.

Quillian thought she looked old. She could see the fine wrinkles at her eyes and around her mouth, the thinning of her lips and the slack flesh along her jaw line.

It made Quillian's insides twist, though she didn't know why. She couldn't dwell on her stomach, though. There were far more important issues to think upon first.

Taggage returned, wiping her hands in an apron tied haphazard around her green satin gown, scowling. The woman addressed Quillian. "You stayin' the night?"

"No." Quillian stood, her stomach roiling. "I will return to Dr. M's."

"No." Madame's eyes snapped open and she sat up, reached out one hand to Quillian. "It is far too dangerous to walk the streets at night."

"Nonsense, Madame." Taggage sniffed from the doorway. "Who'd be wantin' a hand like hers?"

Quillian looked at her hands. They were not soft and delicate, like the girls that lived and worked at the brothel.

Her nails were rough and bitten off, her fingers calloused and thin, the skin browned by the sun. She couldn't find fault in Taggage's statement.

"I should go home."

"I agree." Mr. Holmes rested against the mantle, leaning one elbow against it and resting his chin in his hand. "It may be suspicious if she is not there in the morning."

"Nonsense, I will send a footman-"

"I will not stay here." Quillian stood in front of Madame's chair, staring down at her.

"Very well, I will send a footman with you." Madame made to stand up.

Taggage stepped forward, leaning toward Madame, shaking her head. "Madame, the footmen's all busy, securing the house from intrusion—at your orders. There ain't none to spare."

"I will be fine." Quillian lifted her chin. "Those men are long gone by now. They won't dare take a chance at anyone else. They'd be fools if they did. Besides, I have my knife." Quillian lifted the hem of her skirt and twisted her calf to show Madame the silver hilt poking up from the shaft of her brown working boot.

"I do not like it. I wish you would stay here." Madame shifted, her hand inching ahead, like she wanted to extend it and touch Quillian, but it clutched in her skirts instead.

"I will not stay here."

Madame closed her eyes and nodded, and collapsed back against her chair once more. "Please be careful, Quillian. I do not know what I would do if anything happened to you."

Quillian blinked and swallowed. She wanted to lean down and hug Madame, but she resisted. Why would she want to do that? Instead, she nodded to Mr. Holmes and brushed past Taggage, heading for the back door. "Best come lock up behind me."

The sound that came from Taggage was much like the sound Patch made when encountering another cat in the garden and sought to warn it off his territory. It was not a pleasant sound, but rough and mangled, like it got caught in Taggage's throat halfway out.

On the back step, Quillian looked around, listening to the rough shove of the lock ramming back into place. The alley was still dim and the main street bright, the light squeezing between the houses to flood the alley in stripes of gold on the dark gray-brown cobbles. There was still a rush of leaking steam farther down the alley, and someone—a drunk most like—sang off tune even farther away. Quillian recognized the tune and was quite happy that the singer slurred the words.

The parties were letting out. The hiss and grind of steamcars wound down the alley from the street, and the steady, metallic clop of metal hooves on stone reverberated.

It was dangerous to walk the main street when it was packed. An impatient driver was known to take to the sidewalks to bypass traffic, never mind if a pedestrian was already using it. And an automaton horse couldn't actually see you to avoid a collision—it depended solely on its rider or driver. Heaven help you if they were drunk or didn't care.

Deciding to take an alternate route home, Quillian backtracked down the alley, stooping to avoid the steam, and made to turn through a footpath between the row houses behind Madame's establishment. It was a darker road, but it was shorter, shorter still if she ran.

But someone was in the way and she crashed into the solid body, the impact knocking the breath from her lungs and making her clutch at his shirt to keep from falling to the ground. He was dressed in black, his face covered by a mask, and a long, slightly curved knife glinted in the gaslight.

Screaming, Quillian kicked at the man's shins and turned to run back to Madame's.

But another man, also in black, blocked her way back and grabbed her, wrapping his arms around her middle. A third wrestled with her left arm, pulling it out, stretching it, pulling back her sleeve to expose her wrist.

Quillian kept screaming; her voice grew hoarse. Surely someone would hear? She reached down with her right hand, finger curving around the hilt of her own weapon. She pulled the dagger out, arcing it high and hard toward the man that held her.

He squealed and his grip loosened but didn't let go. The noise from the street grew louder, the steam and dust made its way down the alley, muffling and obscuring everything.

Quillian gasped, unable to scream anymore. There was pain at her left wrist, followed by intense cold. Cold like when she'd been digging too long through Huddy's ice box looking for the frozen treats the housekeeper always hid at the bottom. Cold like in the winter, when she'd been outside too long and could no longer feel her fingers and toes, and then they'd prickle so bad she'd cry when she finally got into the warmth.

But she knew there would be no prickle felt in that hand ever again—at least not by her.

Dizzy, the gas globes spun around her head, speeding up so that they looked like a single, fuzzy halo in the black sky. Images flashed before her eyes: Madame smiling down, Huddy swiping over the breakfast table, Dr. M and his monocle in the lab, Mr. Holmes peering at her over his spectacles, a dark figure looming, its face unrecognized.

Blinking the memories away, Quillian looked to her left hand, but it was gone, and blood—lots of blood—drained down onto the sidewalk, trickling around the cobbles in little red rills.

She staggered forward, toward a band of light that cut across the alley, dropping her dagger. Beyond that stripe was another, and then another, leading to Madame's back door. She made it to one, then another, then fell to her knees, the cobbles digging through her skirts to the flesh.

Someone screamed again and Quillian wished they would just shut up so she could think what to do. She buried the stub of her wrist into her skirts, pressed it in as far as she could to stem the bleeding.

And then the screaming stopped and the world went black.

35

"Open the dashed door!" Greyson wanted to strike at Taggage.

The woman fumbled in her skirts for the key to the back entry.

Quillian's screams stopped.

His heart stopped beating right along with it.

He'd heard her from his room and flung open the window, straining to see her in the darkness. But it had all been black. He'd heard the scuffle of heavy, running feet and the roar of rushing steam as a steamcar accelerated down the cobbles.

Running down the hall and stairs, jumping the final five steps to the bottom, he'd been hollering the entire way.

Taggage had tumbled into the hall from the accountant's office, a bottle of sherry in one hand. Madame had come hobbling from the front parlor, pale.

And now, he had to wait, hand already pulling on the knob, while a doddering old woman searched for keys she'd had in her hand only moments before.

"Here!" Madame, half-collapsed against a wall, her cane lying on the floor by her feet, threw a metal ring at him. "It's the large key with the red ribbon wound in its head."

Greyson caught the jangling bits of metal and shoved Taggage aside, ramming the key into the lock and turning it furiously. The door was heavy and creaked when he pulled it open, leaning back to make his body weight open it faster.

A body lay in a pool of light, the short curls escaped from a brown cap, a red river seeping away from its twisted skirts.

"No. No. No." He turned the body, stroking back the blood-soaked tresses, running a finger along a cool, pale cheek. "Call for a doctor!"

"Madame, I don't think—argh—aaah." The second-in-command's scream stopped.

"I've called for my car." Madame tottered with her cane, her hair disheveled, her breathing escaping in little pants. "It'll be faster to take her to Dr. M."

"Dr. M?"

"He's the best for this. Trust me." The older woman collapsed to the cobbles, crawling to the girl he cradled in his arms. "Oh, god. They took my baby's hand."

Madame put on hand over her mouth, stifling the choking gag that erupted. Breathing in deep, she lifted the black silk of her skirt and tore at her petticoats, taking a large swathe of the white cotton to wrap around the still-bleeding stump of Quillian's wrist. The white cotton turned red, and the older woman wrapped more cotton around it.

"She's so cold." Greyson hugged the limp form to his chest, willing the heat from his own body to seep into it.

Sniffing, Madame bowed her head, her hands clutching the cotton to the wound. "I knew she shouldn't have left. Why did I let her leave?"

Anguish cut through Greyson. He'd said she should go, that it would be safe. "I don't understand why they were here."

"We probably never will." Madame's voice was low, the rasp even more pronounced.

Gas lights from the front of a steamcar cut down the alley.

"Ferby is here with the car. Get her in and to Dr. M. He'll know what to do."

Standing, staggering under the dead weight, Greyson quick-marched to the car. The footman at the wheel was already out with the back door open, ready to help get Quillian into the conveyance. Struggling, they managed, Greyson climbing into the back, keeping her injured arm elevated, with pressure on the severed end.

"Madame?" The footman called out. "Ain't you coming?"

"No. Go. Get her to Dr. M's. I'll come along as I can."

Nodding, the footman slammed the door shut and pushed a lever. "Hold on back there."

Greyson tightened his grip and Quillian groaned. It was the loveliest sound he'd ever heard. "Hang in there, Quillian. We're getting you to help. Just hang on."

Steam hissed through copper tubes and the vehicle surged backward, weaving a bit over the cobbles. At the end of the alley, the driver spun the rudder, and the steamcar swung to one side, shuddering when the brakes were applied. Another lever, and the car shot forward, the rumble of pulsing steam echoing beneath the floorboards.

Quillian's Log

It's funny how your mind works, how your heart works. How when you think you are dying, they work together, reminding you of your life – good and bad.

I saw Madame, a much younger Madame, smiling at me, hugging me, kissing me – and I wasn't afraid of her. She wasn't limping and she wasn't wearing black.

There was a smiling man, too. And he hugged me and Madame. And he used Madame's cane.

I recognized him, but I don't remember his name.

Their faces darted around in my head, scenes scurrying back and forth, like they were frantic for me to remember even more.

Maybe they were.

36

The cold of the metal surgery table seeped into Quillian's back. She knew it was Dr. M's surgery table, or one very much like it, as she'd laid out on it once to take a nap in the midst of cleaning.

Only once though. Huddy had found her and scolded her into next month. She'd been warned never to do it again or Dr. M would know all about it.

Quillian sighed. The fuzzy memory was interlaced with images of Madame and Huddy, the brothel and Taggage, Mr. Holmes and Dr. M—and a man she couldn't name.

She winced and moved her head to the side. She was undressed, but she couldn't remember undressing. The flat metal pressed against her bare skin, a cotton sheet covering her front, skin to cloth. She shivered, an eruption of goose flesh down her arms and across her hands—no make that hand.

Her left hand was numb.

Her left hand was gone.

She opened her eyes, blinking.

The room was out of focus and the bright orb above the table made it worse. She had to squint so it would not hurt, and that made everything blurry.

"Madame?"

Why was she asking for Madame? She didn't want Madame, did she?

"It's okay, Watson. Just relax." Dr. M paced around the table, his arms darting out to grab instruments. "Madame's waiting outside with Mr. Holmes. Huddy's giving her something now to keep her calm."

Quillian's hand was still numb. She made to flex her fingers and felt pain—a mind-numbing pain—shoot up her arm.

She gasped. Her whole body flinched, jerking, sliding on the table.

"Don't move, Watson. Please. You'll start it bleeding again."

Quillian shifted her right hand, feeling for her left one.

"Please, Quillian. Don't move." Dr. M stood above her, one hand resting lightly on her right arm, stilling its movement. His left hand moved up, pulled the tube and horn down, and he used his thumb to flip the toggle.

Gas rushed, filling the tube, and the coolness of the ether caressed Quillian's cheek.

Dr. M placed the horn over her mouth. "Breathe in Quillian. Slowly, evenly. Breathe in. You know the drill."

Quillian took in a slow breath, keeping her gaze on Dr. M's pale, sweaty face. She could taste the ether in her mouth: tinny, metallic. She had not known it to have a taste. It was not something she had ever dared to play with.

"Breathe deep, chile." Huddy came into view, and stood beside the table, holding the tube to her face. Huddy's face was striped with wet tracks and her eyes were red. She swept the hair back from Quillian's forehead, traced her cheek with one finger.

Quillian filled her lungs with the gas, her eyes started to itch and her legs got heavy. Blinking, she tried to stay awake. She needed to help Dr. M. He couldn't do a surgery alone.

Dr. M moved back into her line of vision. He held a contraption in his hand, but Quillian couldn't make out what it was. He set it on the table to her left and fiddled with it, pulling tubes and adjusting joints.

Just before she let the ether take her under, Dr. M looked up at her, and she thought she saw a tear track down his cheek, too.

Quillian's Log

I don't remember much about that night.

I had to be told how Greyson heard my screams and ran for the back door, how he and Madame had struggled with the lock and ran outside, only for Madame fall with her bad leg. I was told how Taggage tried to keep her back, told her it wasn't safe, but that Madame threw the woman back.

Taggage, I'm told, required ten stitches in her head where it hit the bombe chest in the hall.

Mr. Holmes told me how he'd picked me up, blood streaming from my arm, and carried me to the steamcar to take me to Dr. M.

I sort of remember what happened at Dr. M's but I don't, not really. It's all blurry, like I watched it happen to someone else.

I wish it had happened to someone else.

From the journal of G. J. Holmes

I never would have believed Dr. M's housekeeper could ever be so rude. One would think I had done the unimaginable when calling upon Quillian. I only wanted to know how her recovery was going, if she was well, if there was anything the poor girl needed.

But there was the housekeeper, standing in the door like a Doberman, snarling and baring its teeth in warning.

I was tempted to remind the woman that I had been the one to save Quillian, and had I not acted immediately upon hearing the strange noises from the alley, she surely would have died.

But I did not. I stayed the gentleman and bowed, asking her to relay my regrets and my sincere desire that Quillian recover quickly and completely from her ordeal.

Blasted woman!

37

The sun bore through Quillian's eyelids and into her eyes. She opened them and blinked, squinting when the glare was full in them.

Turning her head away, she saw the brown and faded teal of her room. She lay in her bed, her quilt and blanket tucked around her, Patch snuggled against her stomach, purring.

She scratched the cat with her right hand, just under the chin, where the calico liked it best. Patch opened her eyes and blinked, her pink tongue darting out once to lick at her lips before she yawned and closed her eyes again, succumbing to the scratching.

Quillian sighed. They would be looking for her soon. She had never slept in so late before. She was usually up long before dawn. Who had cleaned the surgery last? Was it ready for an emergency?

She wondered what had happened that no one had come to wake her. No one had yet yelled her down the stairs. Was Dr. M ill?

Stretching her legs and toes, she reached her arm over her head. The movement displaced Patch and the calico mewed her displeasure, but resettled easily enough.

Quillian reached to pat the cat, to rewind his mechanicals, and that is when she saw her left hand.

Only, it was not *her* hand. It was brass cogs and wooden pegs, with tubes stretched down the back that disappeared beneath a leather cuff mid-forearm. The fingers were long and tapered, made of metal, without even the facsimile of nails.

Oh.

On instinct, her nerves flexed the fingers and a dull ache throbbed its way up her arm. It wasn't a sharp pain, and Quillian realized that her hand was mostly healed. She had lost track of several days, if not a full week or two.

Quillian dropped back against her pillows, memories crowding into her mind. She didn't really want to remember, but knew she had to.

She also had to get up and see what was going on. Though she remembered a lot, there were gaps that she wanted filled. Like who had brought her to Dr. M's? Constable Dumphries? She had not seen him during the attack, but that meant nothing really. She had not seen much of anything but her arm with the blood running out the end, the slats of light on the cobbles, the men in black that held her. Had she really stabbed one of them? Surely the Constable would not let himself be seen by any of the victims? He could not be a simpleton, no matter Mr. Holmes' opinion.

Quillian sat up and picked up the calico, cuddling her a moment before standing and placing her back amongst the blankets. Patch rolled over, curled her good legs in, and left the mechanical ones stretched out. Quillian wound the key that stuck up from the cat's back and it whirred.

Standing only in her shift, Quillian stared at the reflected hand in her mirror. She had to think to make it move, concentrate on what she wanted the hand to do. She flexed the fingers, watching them straighten and curl, the tubes along the back bending with the movement. Her arm hurt, the pain—sharper now—shot up from the leather cuff, all the way to her shoulder before fanning out and dissipating.

She sighed and rubbed her shoulder. Careful of the mechanical hand, she got dressed, rebuttoning her dress when she realized she'd missed buttons. Her left fingers reacted so much slower than those on her right. The hand was heavier, too, and her arm was tired after just the movement from dressing.

Arranging a crocheted shawl around her shoulders, she fashioned a makeshift sling with it, so it was not obvious it was holding her arm up.

"Coming, Patch?"

The cat stretched and watched her through the slits of her eyes, before it stood and stretched some more. After a moment, it jumped from the bed and wound itself around her ankles, the tip of its tail in the shape of a crook, stuck out from the back end of the mechanical casing.

"Let's get going then. I think I'm hungry."

Quillian patted at her hair but did not stop to brush it out. It felt thick and oily; brushing would only make it worse. She really needed a bath, but knew she couldn't take one for a couple of days—not until her body finished healing and accepted the mechanical hand. Perhaps she would be able to convince Huddy to brush out her hair later, and wash it at the sink.

The quiet of the upper story surprised Quillian. If her hand had been taken just last night, then today was Thursday, and the cleaners should be in working on the second and third stories.

It only confirmed that she'd been asleep longer than that.

On the second story landing she heard voices from the first floor coming from Dr. M's study. She thought she made out Madame's, and maybe Mr. Holmes' voice, too.

She adjusted her shawl, making sure no glint of brass could be seen, and opened the study door. She did not bother knocking.

"Quillian!" Madame's voice cut across the others' and Quillian jumped at its intensity. Before she could back away, Madame had crossed the room and crushed her to her chest. Madame did not seem to be of any mind to let her go.

"Watson, you should be in bed, resting." Though there was a note of censure in Dr. M's voice, it was not overly so, and he sounded happy.

"I'm not tired." And it was true. Her arm ached from the weight of the hand and there was a little pain at her wrist, but she was not tired.

"Nonsense, you need to rest, your hand-"

"It's doing fine. It's just a little heavy."

"Quillian." Madame picked up her cane, dropped in her haste, then engulfed Quillian in her arms again, pulling her close and burying her nose in Quillian's hair. "Oh, Baby. I am so sorry."

Baby? As soon as the word was spoken, more memories rushed at her—early memories, the same memories that had rushed at her when she thought she was dying. Quillian blinked them away, her lids wiping away a sudden blur.

Did she dare ask about the man?

Madame squeezed her ever tighter, and Quillian decided to wait. She was not up to dealing with an angry Madame. Though, there was something she really did need to ask.

"How long has it been since I lost my hand?" She swallowed and took in a long breath. "...since my hand was...taken?"

Mr. Holmes answered first. "Three days. Today is Saturday."

Quillian nodded, satisfied.

Nodding, Dr. M poured a measure of amber liquid into a glass on his desk and downed it in one go, rapping the surface of the desk with the glass when he was done. "Anyone else need a bit?"

"No, thank you." Mr. Holmes watched Dr. M from across the room, standing behind one of the leather armchairs.

"Oh, God! Why didn't I see it earlier?" Dr. M poured himself another measure.

"See what?" Mr. Holmes crossed his arms over the back of the chair.

"The scheme. The plot. The danger. That it was all a lie." Dr. M took another drink, slamming the glass on the desk once more.

"Calm down." Madame turned, but didn't let go of Quillian. "His accomplice was in my employ, and I had no idea what she was up to either. And now she's gone and we have no idea how to find her. Took some of my silver serving pieces, too."

Dr. M snorted and sloshed the last of the liquid onto his desktop.

Mr. Holmes sighed and dropped his head. "How much have you had to drink, Dr. M?"

"Not enough." Dr. M held up the carafe. It was empty. "Huddy!"

"I think you've had enough." The censure in the young man's voice was tempered by dash of pity.

Dr. M made a rude hand gesture with one finger, directing it at Mr. Holmes. "You're a bit commandeering for such a young man."

"Perhaps I take after my father. He is a commandeering sort of man. He's Gentry." But Mr. Holmes did not seem in the least offended by the gesture.

Dr. M snorted and poured the last of the liquid from the carafe directly into his mouth. "So's mine. Ah." He threw the carafe into the fireplace, shards of glass splintering into the room.

"Sir?" Quillian's voice was muffled where her face was pressed to Madame's shoulder.

"Yes, Watson?"

"Thank you for the hand."

"Don't be thanking me. You shouldn't be thanking me." Dr. M leaned back in his chair, his head lolled to one side. "You should be blaming me. I didn't see it."

"So, you keep saying." Mr. Holmes stepped forward, avoiding the glass on the rug. "But you don't say what you didn't see."

"That they weren't accidents. That there weren't any fights. Everything was so clean. They had someone else doing the nob surgeries. Dr. Bergeron. Good man, I thought. Used to be anyway." Dr. M groaned and slumped forward. "If I'd seen it sooner, maybe I could have stopped it."

"Sir-" Mr. Holmes frowned.

Dr. M barked out a laugh and wagged his finger. "Dumphries thinks I'm in too deep to get out."

"Are you?"

Dr. M shrugged. "All I've done is the surgeries on the mechanicals. And the one Bergeron brought me. Said it was an accident. That the man had cut off his hand in some mechanical toy he was making. Thought there was something funny about his hand—that it didn't quite match—but I've known Bergeron for years. I didn't doubt his story. Until..."

"Until?" Mr. Holmes sat in the chair and crossed his legs, his hands steepled at his lap.

"Until the boy. The story didn't make sense. The accident and all. The arm was too clean cut. Poor lad. Probably easy to hold him down and stop his struggles."

"Did you contact the authorities?"

Snorting, Dr. M banged his glass on the table. "What authority should I contact? My district constable?" He chortled and it turned into a wet cough.

Mr. Holmes sighed. "You could always contact the magistrate directly."

Dr. M laughed, the sound hollow and devoid of joy. "Magistrate Wallace will not accept a meeting with me."

Mr. Holmes frowned. "Why not? Magistrate Wallace is a-"

Dr. M wagged another finger at Mr. Holmes. "Do not tell me what Magistrate Wallace is or is not. I know Magistrate Wallace and nothing will change my opinion of him. He's a-"

"Remember, Quillian is in the room." Madame's spoke coolly.

Dr. M stopped his tirade and banged his glass again. "Huddy!"

"Since you did not contact the authorities, I doubt you will be able to get out."

"What do you mean?" Quillian pushed away from Madame. "Why can't he get out? What can't he get out of?"

Huddy bustled into the room, a new flagon of port in her hands. She set the flagon on the corner of his desk. She patted Quillian on the shoulder, nodded at Madame, and left.

"Oh, Watson. I should have recognized that those surgeries, those emergencies, were planned. Long before I did. By the time I realized, it was too late. I should have put a cannon shot through Constable Dumphries." Dr. M poured a drink from the new flagon. "He'll be coming down with me, though. I keep records."

"Records?" Mr. Holmes straightened from the chair. "What kind of records?"

"Who was brought in, best I can figure out. I never really got a name. What I used to replace the missing limb. What Dumphries told me—when he arrived with his 'emergency' patient. Dates, times." Dr. M waved his glass in the air.

"May I examine them?"

"Certainly." Dr. M stood. "Let us adjourn to my study."

Mr. Holmes frowned and looked about the room. "What is this?"

"My public study—the one most people see." Dr. M pierced Mr. Holmes with a look through his magnifying monocle. "D'you honestly think I'd let just anyone into where I keep my private possessions?"

Quillian's Log

Taking things for granted. Seems to be a theme for me of late.

I've always assumed I'd have my hands, my full mobility. I've always assumed I'd finish my training. That one day, I'd have my own workshop and surgery.

And now, my hand is gone. My future - the one I was so sure of - is vanished.

Other things that I've always "known", like my relationship with Madame and what my life was like at the brothel, I'm starting to doubt.

I think when all this is over, I'll have to ask her about that.

I need to know a little more than that she's my mother.

38

Dr. M's private study was locked. It always was. Dr. M pulled a single brass key on a ring from an inner pocket of his jacket.

No one else had a key; there was only the hidden spare in the cracked vase that Quillian wasn't supposed to know about.

Quillian had been invited into the study for her test and quizzes. The walls were covered in dull grey metal, the rivets holding it together in a pattern reminiscent of the tufting buttons on the chesterfield in the library. The wide desk in the center, inlaid with leather, the big leather-padded desk chair behind it, the two side chairs that flanked it on this side.

The room had no windows. Four gas globes hung from the ceiling.

"Good God!" Mr. Holmes stood just in the door, staring openmouthed at the wall behind Dr. M's desk.

Or rather, at the array of weapons displayed on the wall.

Quillian was familiar with the shoulder-cannon that held center stage. She even knew where the cannons and tinder for it were locked away.

Besides the shoulder-cannon, a large Indian scimitar rested on brackets above, long-barreled pistols—a pair, one on top of the other, pointing in different directions—was on the right, and a small, experimental mini-cannon, with an automatic tinder, was mounted on the left. Several small ornamental daggers filled in the bare spaces.

"What is all that for?" Mr. Holmes dragged his eyes away from the weapons and looked at the rest of the room.

Dr. M squinted up at the display and pointed. "The one in the middle's for saving stray cats."

Quillian snickered. She tried to cover the sound with her hand, but knew she'd been unsuccessful when two pairs of eyes rested on her. "Sorry."

"The rest, well..." Dr. M cleared his throat. "The pistols were a gift. As was the sword. The other mini-cannon was an early invention of mine. Had trouble making it work. Then, I decided it wasn't worth it to try to finish it."

"Why not? If we go to war-"

"We could kill so many more of the enemy, eh?"

Mr. Holmes pressed his lips together.

"Have a seat." Dr. M waved to one of the side chairs. "I'll get my ledger."

Quillian knew Dr. M kept his ledger—and his ammunition and tinders—in a safe installed beneath his desk. The safe kept up one side of the desk. It had a combination lock on the front, the dial made of brass with black numbers.

Dr. M nearly fell over opening the safe, but he managed it and dragged the heavy leather-bound volume out and dropped it on his desk. "Here we go."

Mr. Holmes made to stand but Dr. M waved him down in his chair.

Quillian sat in the other chair, tucked her flesh and blood hand into the mechanical one, trying to ignore the cool of the brass. The mechanical hand flexed, squeezing the flesh one hard enough that it hurt.

She concentrated on relaxing the mechanical digits, and wriggled her real fingers to help loosen the grip.

Slowly, the mechanical hand responded and the pain in the flesh one lessened. She removed her hand, used it to grasp around the fingers of the mechanical. She usually held her hands the other way, left outside the right, but decided she would have to learn new habits. Either that, or risk breaking her remaining good hand.

"It's all here." Dr. M opened the ledger, ran his fingers over the pages. He turned the ledger toward Mr. Holmes. "Take a look."

Mr. Holmes leaned forward in the chair and pulled the ledger toward him. His eyes scanned the page, flipped to the next, and continued to scan.

"All of these are mechanical attachments?"

"Yes."

Mr. Holmes turned back a page. "At the beginning, they were quite far apart. Once every other week or so?"

Dr. M leaned back in his chair, his eyes closed, the lid behind the monocle exaggerated in its magnification. He nodded.

"Then they got more frequent. Once a week, or even more frequent?"

Dr. M nodded again.

"And you never questioned that?"

Dr. M opened his eyes to slits. "'course I did. Dumphries said it was due to the rising violence. The conflicts have been all over the papers, why would I doubt him? He was a lawman, after all. Said Bergeron had recommended me. Bergeron was a well-respected physician, as well as a close friend. Why would I have asked too many questions? Especially with a patient in dire need of my services at the door?"

Mr. Holmes nodded and went back to perusing the ledger.

Dr. M closed his eyes again, his head lolled to the side and he snorted.

Quillian knew he was falling asleep.

"Where is the-" Mr. Holmes cut off when he saw Dr. M.

"Where is the what?" Quillian asked.

"The entry for the other surgery." Mr. Holmes frowned at the ledger. "I see no mention of it in here."

"It will be on a separate tab. That is for the mechanicals only." Quillian stood and stepped to the desk and the ledger. She turned the ledger toward her with the brass hand, fingered the manila tabs with her right, then pointed to one. "It will be here."

Mr. Holmes opened the ledger to the new tab and read the single entry.

"There is only the one?"

"Dr. M only deals with mechanicals. He never performed a traditional surgery after university." She nodded at his contraptions.

"Why is that?"

"I have no idea." Quillian turned and stepped back to her chair, flopping down hard to the seat. "He stops talking when I ask about it."

Mr. Holmes frowned down at the entry.

"Then why do this one?"

"I think because the boy was dying. He had no choice. And Dr. Bergeron was a friend. An old friend from what I gather. He visited on occasion, coming to dinner or for a late drink."

"You saw him on these visits?"

"At dinner, yes."

"But not for the late-night drinks?"

"No. I am usually studying by then. In my room. But I have heard him."

"Heard him?" Mr. Holmes looked up from the ledger.

"Sound carries quite well up the main stair from the entry."

Mr. Holmes stared a moment then returned to the ledger, flipping the pages back to the mechanical entries.

"I am surprised that Dr. M did not discern that these might be connected."

"There are many articles in the newspaper about the hooligan gangs and all the mayhem they have been creating. I thought it was simply due to that. Why would he think any different?"

He sighed. "I still do not understand why he did not contact Magistrate Wallace."

"They do not get along. I believe it is a difference of politics. Any time Magistrate Wallace is quoted in the Neo-Virginian News discussing politics, Dr. M denounces it all."

They turned at a knock at the study door. It was opened by Huddy, who leaned in, not even looking around the room.

Dr. M started in his chair and blinked.

"Constable Dumphries is here, sir. Says he's got yer client in a steamcar outside, waiting."

"Client?" Mr. Holmes sat up in his chair.

"That would be Lady Caine." Dr. M stood and swayed behind his desk.

Huddy huffed. "Yer in no state to be performing surgery."

"Certainly not." Dr. M closed his eyes and rubbed at the one without the monocle.

39

They met Constable Dumphries in the entry. The policeman stood just inside the door, his hands behind him, looking at a portrait of a young Lincoln that hung opposite a long mirror.

Quillian could see the back of the constable's head and the bald patch there, the skin made red by the sun.

Madame stood in the door to Dr. M's office. She leaned heavy on her cane, one hand braced against the jamb, her face still wan.

"Huddy." Quillian turned to the housekeeper and whispered. "Could you bring tea? I know it is early, but I think Madame could use a strong, hot cup."

"Aye. I think I'll make a pot of coffee, as well. I think the doctor could use a strong, hot cup of that."

"Thank you, Huddy."

"Have a bit of company, eh, doctor? Think that's wise under the circumstances?"

"Circumstances?" Dr. M blinked and swayed.

"You have a surgery today, remember?"

Dr. M stared at the Constable. "I agreed to no surgery."

"You have no choice, sir. Remember?"

"No. I don't remember. I always have a choice."

"Look, you and your girl need to get ready fer a surgery. Yer patient is waitin' outside in my steamcar."

"My 'girl' needs to rest." Dr. M fixed his monocle on the constable.

Constable Dumphries snorted. "Why should the chit be restin'? Have her get the surgery ready. I told you, Lady Caine is waitin'" The Constable shot a glance at Mr. Holmes and Madame, obviously thinking that Dr. M would make them leave at the mention of the name.

"Watson is in no state to be prepping a surgery. I told you, she needs to rest. She needs to recover from her own surgery." Dr. M stalked into the office, brushing past Madame, stopping behind his desk. He poured a measure of amber liquid into his empty glass.

Madame followed, limping even with her cane.

Dr. M watched her walk, his hand tightening on his glass, before he downed the liquid.

"Where were you Wednesday night, Constable Dumphries?" Mr. Holmes spoke low. He crossed his arms and frowned at the policeman.

"Look here, I'm the law. I don't need to be answerin' any of yer questions." Constable Humphries strode into the room. "Dr. M-"

"I'm afraid you do, Constable Dumphries. I also want to know where you were Wednesday." Dr. M stared at the policeman.

Constable Dumphries snorted. "I was makin' me usual rounds. Lookin' fer trouble to break up after the nobs get out from their high-falutin' parties."

"Where in particular?" Dr. M took an unsteady step closer to the constable, who took his own step back.

"Along Church Street—toward downtown. My usual place."

Dr. M sighed and leaned back against his desk.

"Near the intersection with Brambleton? Isn't that near the Lower District?" Mr. Holmes looked at Constable Dumphries over his spectacles.

The constable nodded. "Yeah. I believe it is. What of it?"

"It is in that area that one of Madame's girls was attacked that night. Someone tried to cut off her hand." Mr. Holmes stepped into the room, his arms still crossed over her chest.

Quillian couldn't help it. She flexed her left hand in the shawl. Entering the room, she avoided the constable, stopping next to Madame.

Madame reached out with her free hand, grasping Quillian's left arm at the elbow.

Quillian flinched. The arm was tender and sore from the extra weight.

Madame released her grip and shifted away.

But Quillian shifted closer, reached over with her right hand to hold Madame's.

Madame looked at her, eyes widening. The woman pulled her closer, let go of her hand and reached her arm around her, pulling her to her side.

Shivering, Quillian allowed Madame to hug her close, even resting her own head on the woman's shoulder.

Madame held her even tighter. Quillian could feel the woman's tears on her own cheek.

For some reason Quillian could not ascertain, she was loathe to pull away. Instead, she leaned deeper into her shoulder, sighed against the soft cotton of Madame's blouse.

Madame stroked her back, whispering into her ear. "I am so sorry, Baby. I am so sorry."

She sniffed and looked back to the men.

Constable Dumphries stood between the men, looking just a bit like a squirrel caught between two stray dogs.

"Just what are ye suggestin'?"

"That you knew about the attack. That you were, in fact, in on the attack itself." Mr. Holmes' voice could have formed icicles.

"I'm the law!" The Constable spat the words out.

Mr. Holmes pulled his handkerchief from his front pocket and used it to wipe spittle from his cheek.

"It is rather strange that you always knew what type of mechanical would be necessary." Dr. M took a step toward the Constable. "I should have questioned you about it long before now."

"Yer too far in to get out now." The Constable smirked at Dr. M.

"Actually, that may not be true, but you, sir, have crossed the line." Mr. Holmes also took a step toward the constable. "From what Dr. M told me, things started going wrong of late. Your surgeon nearly lost one of your clients, and you needed Dr. M to set it right. Dr. Bergeron was a highly accredited surgeon in Norfolk. No one would suspect him of participating in such a scheme. But he wasn't good enough. He wasn't able to attach one of the stolen limbs. You had him bring the patient here. You thought to coerce Dr. M into helping you."

"Aye. Made it easier, it did. Just the one doctor involved then. Instead of one fer the mechanical and one fer the transplant." The constable rounded on Dr. M again. "An' like I said, yer too far in te get out now."

"Perhaps he doesn't need to get out." Mr. Holmes stepped forward, hands in his trouser pockets. "Dr. M has been keeping records."

"What?"

Mr. Holmes smiled. "I've seen these records. He's also got notes on every other surgery he's done. All the ones you brought to him as emergencies. Ones you told him were accidents, from fights at the docks."

"And just what de ye suppose yer goin' te do with those?"

Mr. Holmes quirked a brow. "I have connections in high society. I'm sure I can use those connections to figure out just who in society were your clients."

Constable Dumphries laughed. "And what good de ye think that will do? Ye think they'll talk to ye? They know better. Ye think the law'll do anything? I am the law." The Constable barked a laugh. "Those records mean nothin'."

"Perhaps not alone. But I also have access to a second set of records. Ones that indicate names and money paid for nonmechanical limbs."

Constable Dumphries swallowed and stepped back from Mr. Holmes, only to brush up against a teetering Dr. M.

Madame backed away from Quillian and turned to the men. A micro-cannon—the new, single-use kind with the tinder installed inside the barrel with the ball—was pointed directly at the constable. Madame held it straight out, one hand still on her cane, keeping her steady on her feet.

Constable Dumphries tried to duck away, but Dr. M pushed him forward.

The muzzle touched his chest and the man shuddered and turned his head away, his face pale, the skin almost transparent. He swallowed hard. "What ye think yer doin'?"

"Payback."

"Payback?"

"Yes." Madame raised her chin. "You took from me—from my girls—so I will take from you."

"Ye...ye can't do that!"

"Why not? Three of my girls are presumed dead; two injured. You took their lives and limbs away from them. Why can't I take your life in retribution?"

"Ye won't get away wi' it!"

Madame smirked. "You are not the only one that has favors that can be recalled."

"They were jus' whores! Lower than low."

"And you are just a low-life law officer with no regard for anyone but yourself. You think the upper class is nothing. You think the lower class is nothing. I have news for you. You are the one who is nothing!"

The bullet careened into the crown molding.

The constable pissed his pants and fainted. No one moved to catch him, and he hit the floor hard.

Dr. M held Madame's hand high, directing the micro-cannon toward the ceiling.

"We cannot let him die here, Maryam. That would be letting those who benefited from this scheme get away with their part. I will make sure it is in the papers, and that Constable Dumphries is charged in court."

Dr. M let go of her hand and turned to the now groaning constable.

"You made a fatal error, Constable Dumphries. Your last command to your thugs was your downfall. You see, when they didn't get the hand from the girl they were supposed to, they got desperate and took a hand from someone else." The doctor glanced to Quillian. "They took the hand of someone important to me, and for that, I will go to goal, even to death, with you if it means you pay."

E. G. Gaddess

Quillian's Log

Constable Dumphries is in gaol awaiting trial. Mr. Holmes isn't sure he'll be convicted. We still aren't sure who in high society was involved. No one is talking, even when it is Dr. M asking the questions.

Taggage is gone, no one can find her. Madame and Dr. M both sent men to find her, but they haven't yet.

Magistrate Wallace is not helping; he's not putting any police on the investigation and everything the papers put out about it makes it look like it was nothing.

My hand is working better all the time. My nerves are learning how to make it work. I've had to rethink my choice of career. There is no way I will be able to perform surgery on people. I won't have sufficient fine motor control in my left hand.

So, I'm reconsidering.

What will I do now?

From the journal of G. J. Holmes

I am finding it difficult to put recent events from the forefront of my mind. I have not had this problem before, and I do not understand why I am having it now. Surely, it cannot be due to my regimen?

Perhaps, it is due to the violent nature of recent events, and that I held Quillian in my arms while she bled in the alley from her wounded arm. "Wounded". What a term I use for having one's hand cut clean off. But, I know not what other term to use.

It is strange, though. I close my eyes and see her pale face, the blood running through the cobbles, her red hair matted with sweat and dirt. And I cannot sleep. I shall ask Doctor Bhatnagar if he has a tincture I might use to relieve my mind. I fear if I do not, I will never be able to concentrate on the business of finding the mastermind behind the scheme.

40

Greyson lounged in his darkened room, thinking about Miss Quillian Watson—again. When he'd seen her in the street, bleeding from the loss of one hand, he'd thought his heart would stop beating in his chest.

He'd never felt that before.

So, he pondered it.

"Mr. Holmes?" A soft knock accompanied the female voice.

Greyson roused from his bed, straightened the blanket and quilt, and fluffed the pillow. He sat in the chair near the window, steepling his fingers, his elbows resting on his knees.

"Enter."

The door opened and a young woman peeked around the oak-stained panels. She held out a small cream envelop. "Good evening, sir. Miss Emily wanted me to give you this. It came a little while ago, but everyone else is busy and couldn't deliver it to you."

Miss Emily, one of the older prostitutes who'd been studying numbers, had been promoted to second-in-command for the interim. And though Miss Emily has a line on a management position at a company along the Western Borders, she's staying on for a bit as a favor.

Greyson smiled at the girl; she was sixteen at most, and new to the brothel. Miss Emily was more astute than Taggage; the younger second-in-command honored his polite refusals at having a girl keep him company.

"You may give Miss Emily my thanks." He took the envelope, glancing at the rough scrawl of his first name on the outside: Father.

The girl cocked her head to the side, batting long, sootened lashes, her soft blonde curls brushing a bare shoulder above a pale pink satin corset and cream bustled skirt. "Are you certain, you don't want company?"

"Most certain." Though Greyson knew that Madame took excellent care of the health and well-being of her girls, it was well-known to him that the men of the world were not so careful.

Greyson was taking no chances. He already had one disease—the one he was born with—and he needed no others to make life worse. Besides, he rather thought Quillian would take offense if she ever found out.

The girl looked at him, batting eyes of a deep clear blue. "You are alone here too much, I think."

Greyson thought of Quillian's troubled gray eyes and sighed. "I like being alone."

The girl nodded and retreated, closing the door behind her.

Greyson relaxed back against the chair, looking out the window at the darkening sky. It looked like rain; dark clouds gathered on the horizon and the tops of the trees swayed from a still-silent wind.

And he thought of Quillian again. What was she doing? Was she still in pain? Had she finished healing from the surgery?

It bothered Greyson that he did not know. It bothered him even more that not knowing bothered him so much. He had completed the task set forth by Madame and the man responsible for the disappearance of three of her girls and the maiming of another two was in prison, awaiting trial. Although, the woman who helped—at least they all suspected she had and her runoff seemed to confirm it—was still at large.

Not that he expected much from the trial or the search. He suspected that Constable Dumphries and Mrs. Taggage had not been alone in this scheme. The elite of Norfolk had been benefiting from it; ergo, someone in the elite had to be involved. The elite did not mix with the working class—at least not when it came to surgery and doctors—unless someone from the elite was in charge. It was all a matter of trust.

And the member of the gentried elite—or an upper as Quillian would call them—at the head of it was surely someone with connections to the lower class, perhaps a merchant or business man with money that could span the layers of society.

Greyson sighed again. He wanted to find this person and put a permanent stop to the mess. Constable Dumphries would be easily replaced, as would Mrs. Taggage, and most likely by someone a bit more cunning.

But to continue his investigation meant he would have to go home. For yet another visit.

Dash it all.

This was becoming the norm instead of the exception. He was seeing more of his parents living outside their home than when he lived in it.

He opened the envelope, unfolding the short note inside.

Bergeron was found in the river this morning. Near the high bridge to P-town. Chambers is the one who got me to invest. Drop by and we will talk.

Greyson reached for paper and mechanical quill. Though he no longer had to make sure he'd be welcome before he arrived, it was common courtesy to let them know he was coming.

And if all went well, he just might be bringing a companion along for this meeting.

41

Quillian lay in her bed, her quilt pulled up to her chin, her feet sticking out the bottom, wool socks keeping her toes snug. The lamp was unlit, the curtains pulled tight against the light. She sniffed and wiped her good hand over her eyes. She couldn't tell if she was still crying, or if it was just the tears that refused to dry.

Her arm throbbed, the mechanical fingers jerking every time she moved the fingers of her natural hand. Each spasm sent pain shooting up her arm to her shoulder.

Patch mewed from the hall, the closed door preventing the calico from joining her on the bed. Huddy had closed it when she's ushered Quillian up the stairs and under the blankets.

Sighing, Quillian turned over to her back and stared at the slanted ceiling, listening to the shush of the pendulum clock. The cat scratched at the door, crying louder. She knew Quillian was inside and alone.

Sitting up, Quillian swung her feet over the side. The splay of light that crept beneath the door was broken by the flailing paw trying to gain entry.

"Give me a mo', Patch."

Standing, Quillian took inventory of her body. Everything felt good, except for the left hand. It was heavy, so she held it in her other hand and walked to the door.

Once the heavy oak was cracked open, the cat streaked inside, jumping and landing on the center of the warm blankets, curling into a purring bundle of unconcern.

As far as Patch was concerned, nothing had changed.

Quillian stood by the door, mechanical hand propped to her chest. Maybe the cat was right. What had really changed? Sure, she had a different hand, but things could have been worse. She could have died.

She thought of Greyson and the sketchy memories of his blue eyes staring at her, his arms tight around her, his ragged voice in her ear commanding her to *hold on, we're almost there.*

And he'd been to see her today and been turned away.

Not that it was her decision. She'd already been hidden away up here when he'd called. But Huddy had answered the insistent gong of the door chime, and her sharp voice explaining how Quillian was not entertaining visitors had shot all the way up the stairs. She'd never heard the housekeeper speak that loud except when reprimanding someone.

She couldn't imagine the ever-proper Mr. Holmes being reprimanded for anything.

Pursing her lips, Quillian took a deep breath and held up her mechanical limb, without propping it up. Her shoulder protested; it was much heavier than her muscles were used to, but it was manageable. Maybe she could work on something lighter for the future. Something that helped her hide tricks up her sleeve.

E. G. Gaddess

She smiled at the picture forming in her head.

It would be something far better than what she had now.

42

"You were unable to find out anything more about Quillian?" Madame sat at the head of the table once more, knife and fork poised above her steak. There were usually additional guests at dinner, but this evening it was simply he and Madame. Greyson wondered if it had been arranged so that the two of them could safely discuss Quillian, or if this privacy had been simply a product of the additional security measures Madame had set in place.

"No, Madame, I'm sorry. Huddy turned me away at the door. Said Dr. M was away and Qui—Miss Watson was still recovering. By that, I can only assume her to mean that the young lady was resting." Greyson's dinner consisted of wilted greens and lentils made especially for him by Madame's cook.

"That is odd." Madame rested her knife on her plate and tapped her fork against the table. "The doctor never travels. Or at least, hasn't for a good many years. I wonder where he went?"

"Perhaps he went nowhere, and Huddy was lying?" Greyson took a sip of water. "I cannot imagine she is overly fond of me right now. After all, I am the one who got Qui-Miss Watson into this mess."

Madame snickered. "You may as well call her Quillian in front of me, Mr. Holmes. I am aware of your, shall we call it, budding friendship?."

Greyson's cheeks flushed with heat, but said nothing and stuffed a large slice of sauced mushroom into his mouth, chewing furiously.

"I approve of that, by the by. And I am more than certain you are in Huddy's good graces. After all, you are the one who heard Quillian's screams and ran to investigate. If you had not found her so quickly, she likely would have lost a great deal more blood. Mr. Holmes, you saved her life. I know that. Huddy knows that. Dr. M knows that. We are all grateful."

Greyson nodded and ate his lentils, though it was hard to swallow them down remembering Quillian's limp form and spilled blood.

They ate in silence for long minutes—or rather, moved the food around on their plates and made a facsimile of eating.

Finally, Madame cleared her throat, and waved her fork at Greyson's plate. She had resumed cutting her steak. "Are they enjoyable? Your lentils?"

"Yes. Though it is a bit of an acquired taste. I have heard that the East Indians use many spices when they cook them. I think I may set about acquiring some for your cook."

"Feel free. Perhaps, once you have done so, I will try them." Madame placed a thick piece of steak in her mouth.

Greyson tried not to think about how much he missed eating meat. Though the mushrooms were hearty and meaty, they were nothing compared to the steak his father had his cook prepare, all marbled fat and garlic and pepper.

"What else have you learned? I understand you received a message by street urchin today."

Greyson sighed. "Dr. Bergeron is dead. Someone found him floating in the river. A man named Chambers is the one that involved him with the man. I'm to drop in and we will discuss it more."

"Chambers? Did he give you a first name?"

Greyson shrugged. "No. Just had Chambers in the note. I know the family is high-strung society. I think old man Chambers was a doctor at one time. They do a lot for the Children's Hospital. Lady Chambers is an official Daughter, I think. Probably where he got the idea for my treatment. I have often suspected that they perform many experimental procedures there." He rested his fork and sat back.

"Do you think...?" The woman licked her lips.

Greyson looked at Madame.

The woman stopped eating with a bit of food half-way to her mouth. She set the morsel down on her plate and leaned forward. "If they are performing experimental procedures, perhaps they performed an operation to attach a new limb there."

Greyson nodded. "The doctors are always looking for ways to make money for the charity work they do. And their equipment would be adequate. No one would question patients coming and going. It is a hospital, after all."

Madame tapped her fingers. "One might question adult patients. The hospital specializes in childhood diseases."

Frowning, Greyson swallowed a bit of greens. "Wasn't the patient that died, the one that sent Quillian running here to speak with me, a child? A young boy?"

Madame nodded; she'd finally placed the bit of steak in her mouth.

"Did Dr. M say anything about being asked to do the attachment surgery? For the real limb?"

Madame swallowed. "Yes, but the boy never came to him. Constable Dumphries only brought Lady Caine for her new hand." Madame set her own fork and knife on her plate and leaned back in her chair, staring at Greyson.

"I wonder who performed that surgery?" Something niggled at the back of his mind, something he needed to remember. He'd have to go back over his notes.

"I think you've found a question that needs an answer."

"Indeed." Greyson resumed eating, his mind not on the food, but on who he might ask about a recent surgery on a young boy about twelve.

43

Greyson sat on the settee across from Quillian, who sat in the armchair usually reserved for Dr. M, while Huddy made a cacophony in the kitchen, clanking the kettle, cracking spoons and platters, and slamming pots.

"I wanted to know how you were doing." Greyson decided to jump into the conversation without bothering with the pleasantries. All that noise suggested that the housekeeper did not like him visiting. It might be best not to overstay.

Quillian flexed her new mechanical hand. "It is getting better. Not so much lag between when I decide I want it to do something and when it does it. I still have to think, though. It's not quite automatic yet."

Greyson nodded.

"Good thing it's not my leg. I'd really be in trouble then, eh?" Quillian let out a sound that only seemed a laugh, the mechanical fingers twitching, the flesh ones curling into their palm.

He smiled but couldn't laugh.

Quillian looked to the door. Huddy was still making loud tea.

"I get the feeling she's hoping I leave before she gets here with the tray."

Quillian shrugged. "Well, I'm happy for the company. Huddy wants me to stay in bed all day resting. It's just my hand. The rest of me is fine."

She rolled her eyes and Greyson couldn't help the half-laugh that escaped, but it felt wrong to laugh at an event so serious and traumatic.

"And I'm out of books to read." Quillian pouted and batted her lashes at him.

Greyson had to smile at that. "You like to read?" Quillian's eye batting didn't irk him the way the young prostitute's had at the brothel.

"Love it." The redhead grinned, and her eyes crinkled at the corners. She leaned forward, as if sharing a secret. "I have a whole stash of penny novels hidden in my room. I daren't let Dr. M know I like to read them. He'd be mortified, lecture me to no end, and confiscate them."

Greyson laughed and tried not to stare at the dimple that appeared in her left cheek when she grinned; Madame had that same dimple on the rare occasion he'd seen her with that same expression.

They fell into silence again and Huddy arrived with the tea, huffing, her face pink. "Well, here you go." She dropped the tray on the table so that tea sloshed out the spout.

"Thank you, Huddy. I am enjoying my company, you know."

Huddy sniffed and left, strutting through the parlor door with her nose in the air.

"Do you want me to pour?" Greyson reached a hand for the pot.

"Oh, no. Let me! I can practice with my new hand. I won't feel so embarrassed in front of you." Quillian sat at the edge of her chair and leaned forward, slowly reaching out with her mechanical hand to grasp the tea pot's handle. The fingers wrapped around it in jerky increments.

She winced when the weight of the pot stressed her wrist, and Greyson's stomach tightened. He restrained himself from grabbing the pot.

Slowly, Quillian moved the pot over the cups, the tip of her tongue visible between her lips. Frowning, she tipped the pot, holding the cup with her other hand, managing to spill only a little of the dark liquid.

Grinning, Quillian set the pot back on the tray with a bit less care than when she'd picked it up and offered the plate of tea sandwiches. "Not bad, huh?"

"Not bad at all." Greyson looked over the tray, but did not choose a sandwich.

Quillian took a sandwich for herself and set the plate back down, clinking it loudly on tray.

"Still a little jerky, though." She glanced at his empty hands. "Aren't you hungry?"

"Remember my special diet; I can't eat wheat flour."

Quillian raised a brow. "I sent Huddy off to Quan Lo's for rice flour."

Greyson stared.

"The bread is denser and takes more yeast to make it rise, but it is not too bad. Huddy hasn't complained too much about using it." Quillian took another bite of sandwich.

Glancing to the plate, Greyson examined the sandwiches. "Huddy made the sandwiches with rice flour bread?"

"Aye."

"Thank you. I have issues with milk, too." He tipped his plain cup of tea in her direction but picked up a sandwich. "It is best if I only eat and drink what is on my regimen."

Quillian stayed silent, sipping her own tea, laced with milk and sugar.

Greyson sighed; he did miss milk and a little sugar. Doctor Bhatnagar had suggested he try amygdalate in his tea, but it was made from almonds and imparted a nutty flavor to his tea that he did not like. It was fine for cereal, or even coffee, but not tea. And coconut milk added flavor that was fine with coffee, but not tea. It was the same for cashew milk.

"Have you heard anything about the constable? Mrs. Taggage?" Quillian took another sandwich.

Shaking his head, Greyson swallowed his tea. "No. I've seen nothing in the papers, nor have I learned anything from my inquiries." He bit into the sandwich.

"They won't get away with it, will they?" Her mechanical hand flexed on her lap and she winced.

"Not likely." Greyson leaned forward, studying the replacement appendage. "Whoever was at the head of the scheme will make certain that Constable Dumphries takes the full brunt from it. If Taggage were here, she'd go down without assistance from him, either."

"You think someone else is behind the scheme?" Quillian's mechanical fingers jerked and she spilled her tea. "Damn!"

"Do you think either of them intelligent enough for it?" Greyson restrained himself from jumping up to help the girl; he suspected she would not appreciate it.

Quillian set her cup down and stared at the tea tray, frowning.

"Though many from the lower classes are exceptionally bright, I do not believe that Constable Dumphries is one of them. However, he had enough brains to pull off his end of the bargain, and keep Dr. M ignorant of what was really going on. I cannot think him a complete ninny."

Greyson grimaced; he was pissing her off again. He had not thought of that. Dr. M was a doctor, a very bright, innovative gentleman to be certain. For a man like that to be fooled by a lowly constable meant that the constable in question could not have been completely unintelligent.

"On the other hand," Quillian continued, "I cannot imagine him coming up with this scheme. I doubt he has the connections to convince anyone in the upper class to participate in it. Not one of Norfolk's uppers would give him the time of day."

"True." Greyson sighed. "I did not. I also doubt they had the connections needed with the elite. Someone needed to find buyers for the stolen limbs. No one in the elite would listen to Dumphries or Taggage."

Quillian sipped her tea, slowly lowering the cup back to the saucer. "What about Dr. Bergeron?"

"Dr. Bergeron is dead."

"What?" Quillian dumped her cup of tea on her skirt. "Damn!"

"What? What's wrong?" Huddy rushed into the room, kitchen knife in hand.

"Nothing, Huddy." Quillian blotted at the spilled tea without looking up.

Greyson swallowed and shifted back in his chair, bracing himself against the arms.

Quillian looked up. "Huddy, what are you doing with that knife?"

Huddy brought the knife down to her side, covering it with her skirts. "Nothin'. Just had it in me hand."

Quillian sighed. "Huddy, Mr. Holmes is being a perfect gentleman. You have nothing to worry about."

Huddy snorted but spun on her heel and left.

"Huddy?"

The cook spun back.

"Do we have any fruit?"

"Fruit?" Huddy placed her hands on her hips, the knife pointed back and away.

"Yes, fruit. Mr. Holmes is on a strict diet regimen for his health issues. I would like to offer him something in addition to the sandwiches."

"Is something wrong with the sandwiches?" Huddy stepped forward, concern lighting her features. "I made 'em with the special flour."

Greyson shifted forward. "Nothing is wrong with the sandwiches. And I am very appreciative that you went to the trouble to make them with the rice flour so I could enjoy them. Please, it is fine Quillian. The sandwiches are more than enough. Certainly more than I expected."

"No, it is not. Mr. Holmes has an ailment, Huddy. Please, bring a tray of fruit."

"Hmph." Huddy stared at Greyson, making him squirm in his seat. "Can ye eat cheese?"

"No. I also have an ailment that stops me from eating dairy products in high quantities."

Huddy snorted and pivoted to the door. "I'll see what I can do."

Greyson watched the woman stalk away, the knife still glinting in her hand. He turned to Quillian. "Are you certain she won't poison the fruit?"

Quillian snickered and ate a sandwich.

"I see nothing amusing about the possibility that I might have been skewered."

She shrugged and sighed. "The tea. I swear I'm laughing at the tea. I'm afraid I keep making messes."

"I'm sure your hand will keep working better."

Licking her lips, she nodded and peeked at him. "You said that Dr. Bergeron is dead?"

"Aye. My father sent a note that he was found floating in the river early yesterday. Sorry, I didn't get to tell you that bit." He really needed to stop getting side-tracked when speaking with Quillian. Such distraction could mess up the investigation.

"Oh, dear." Quillian's right hand tightened to a fist in her skirts. "Do you think it was Taggage? I think she's more than capable of such a thing."

Greyson had not considered that Taggage might have taken it upon herself to kill the doctor. "Do you think Dr. Bergeron would have known Taggage or the constable outside of this scheme?"

"Maybe he was a client at the brothel?"

"From what I understand, Dr. Bergeron preferred the company of men after his wife died."

"Oh. Oh." Quillian almost upended her teacup.

"What?" Greyson leaned forward, hand outstretched to catch the cup if necessary.

"That might explain why Dr. M helped him."

"What do you mean?"

"Dr. M also prefers the company of men."

"Oh." Greyson leaned back and considered the tea tray. That would explain a lot about Dr. M's involvement in the matter, and why he might have turned a blind eye to some of his suspicions.

"He was never a client at the brothel, either." Quillian snickered and kicked his shin, a gentle tap with the toe of her boot.

Client of the brothel.

So much suddenly made sense to Greyson and his stomach sunk through the floor and into the cellar.

Investments.

"Quillian, do you still have the Neo-Virginian News with the photo of my father in it?"

44

Greyson sighed. His parents' home loomed before him once more, the manicured lawn and freshly scrubbed bricks, a façade to intimidate. This revisit to his mother for tea was far sooner than he'd planned. And it was Wednesday—which meant Wilroy was likely to be at home.

He shook his head while ascending the steps. It did not help that he was not expected.

The brass knocker gleamed in the sun, the ring held in the mouth of a lion, its mane a riotous knot of curls. He pulled the ring up and let it fall, and again.

He waited.

The white lace curtain of the side lite fluttered and there was a scramble of feet behind the double doors. Greyson imagined Wallace scuttling around to prepare Lady Gwendolyne for her son's visit.

The door opened, showing Wilroy's scowl and chipped front tooth. He'd chipped the tooth in a brawl at a pub on his first day of legal drinking.

"What do you want?"

"To speak with Mother."

Wilroy stepped outside, pulling the door not-quite-closed behind him. "Mother doesn't want to speak with you."

"She did the last time I called."

Wilroy's brows arched. "When did you come visit?"

"And Father. At tea."

"It's past tea."

"I know. I'm not here for tea. I simply want to speak with Mother." Greyson gripped the handle of his cane. He wanted to swat Wilroy up the side of his head, but resisted the urge. It would not accomplish anything but alarm his mother, and she wouldn't be able to speak of anything but her poor, bleeding Wilroy.

"What do you want to speak to her about?"

"My subject of conversation with Mother is none of your concern."

Wilroy pulled the door all the way closed and crossed his arms over his chest, leaning back against the door. He drew himself up, looking down his long, battered nose. "Then I won't let you in."

Greyson closed his eyes and rubbed them with two fingers. Though he'd never gotten on with Wilroy, this was getting ridiculous. The woman was his mother, for God's sake, he ought to be able to see her.

"Wilroy-"

The doors parted and Wallace swept them wide.

Wilroy staggered back, only a quick grab of the door jamb kept him from landing on his posterior in the entry.

"Master Greyson, Lady Gwendolyne awaits in the front parlor."

Wilroy straightened and pulled down on his purple vest. "I'm not letting him in."

Wallace stared at the man, his mouth tightening. "Lady Gwendolyne has approved his presence."

Wilroy sneered at Greyson, but pushed his way past Wallace.

"Sir." Wallace half-bowed, crossing his eyes when the surly young man had passed.

Greyson smiled at the butler, whispering a hurried 'thank you'. He entered the house and looked around. It was the same as before, not that he had expected any big changes. But if Father's finances were as bad as he'd indicated, he wouldn't put it past the man to start selling stuff off.

"Very good, sir." He accepted Greyson's hat, coat, and even his cane, bowing him into the parlor.

"Greyson!" Lady Gwendolyne reclined on the settee, adorned in peach satin and yellow tulle.

"Good evening, Mother. You are looking well today."

"Was I looking not well last time?" The lady rose, graceful, until she walked forward, the mincing steps making her gown's flounces bounce. She held her cheek out for a kiss.

Greyson obliged, his mother's cheek dry and powdered beneath his lips. "Not at all. It was just a casual observation."

"Would you like a refreshment?" His mother smiled up at him, hands clasped at her bosom.

"No, thank you. I've just had tea." It was only a little fib. Tea and sandwiches with Quillian had been over an hour ago.

His mother moued her disappointment.

"I will not object if you request something for yourself."

His mother hopped and clapped her fingers then reached to pull the cord to summon a servant. "Wilroy found me a new chocolatier and I'm dying to try her confections."

"Mum?" A maid, olive-skinned and ebony-haired, dressed in black from head to toe, stepped into the open door.

"Yes, Margia. I would like a tray of tea and those lovely chocolates Wilroy brought me."

"Yes, mum." The maid curtseyed and backed out.

Lady Gwendolyne jittered to the settee and flopped down on it. "So, Greyson. I hadn't expected another visit so soon."

Greyson looked at his mother. While he had gotten his intelligence from his father, he rather thought he inherited his gift of observation from his mother. "I have a couple more questions I wanted to ask you."

"About the surgery Stanley wanted you to have?"

"No. Not exactly." Greyson rubbed his hands together and leaned forward in his chair. "I was wondering if you knew a Dr. Bergeron."

"The one found dead in the river?"

Greyson blinked. He hadn't expected his mother to pay attention to such things. "Yes."

"Dreadful, isn't it? It was in the Gazette this morning." The woman fluttered her hands around her head. "The paper said it wasn't suicide, but one has to wonder, what with everyone's financials as they are. I do wonder how they determine that sort of thing."

"Indeed. Were you acquainted with him?"

"Oh, no." Lady Gwendolyne shook her head, stiff white ringlets bouncing against her cheeks. "Though I think your father had business with him. His death upset Stanley this morning."

"Yes, I'm sure it did."

The maid entered with the tray and Greyson smiled at the girl.

She didn't smile back, but placed the tray on the table and poured two cups of tea, adding milk and sugar to Lady Gwendolyne's.

"Mmmm." Greyson's mother had already chosen a chocolate and looked near to swooning with it in her mouth.

Once the maid had left, Greyson resumed the conversation. "You said Father was upset?"

"Oh, yes." Lady Gwendolyne drank some tea and chose another chocolate from the serving plate. "He was upset enough to curse his breakfast."

"I see." Greyson extended a hand to clasp his mother's, stopping her mid-reach for another bon bon. "Do you know what business Father had with him?"

Lady Gwendolyne stared back at him, only glancing once to his restraining fingers. "No, dear, I don't. Though I suspect it was some type of investment. Once your Father finished swearing at his kippers, he went off on how all of his investments are failing."

Greyson closed his eyes and let his head drop, drawing his hand back to his lap. "Damn."

"Greyson James!"

"What? Sorry, Mother. Should have used 'dash.'"

Lady Gwendolyne's pursed her lips. "You didn't learn such language in this house."

Greyson didn't point out that he'd learned just such language, and worse, from his father in this very house.

"My apologies, again."

"I should think so."

"It's just..." Greyson pondered how much to tell his mother. "I suspect that some of Dr. Bergeron's business dealings were not entirely legal."

"Do you think that's why he's dead?"

"Most like."

"Oh, dear. Do you think Stanley's in danger?" His mother grabbed his arms, her fingers biting into the flesh, cutting off the blood flow.

Greyson thought a moment, working his mothers clasp loose of him. Was his father in danger? Would his father have invested in a scheme to swap body parts for mechanical replacements? Could whoever had been in charge of the scheme go after his father? "I don't know. I suppose it depends on how deep Father was into the business. How much he knew about what was going on. What he could tell the authorities."

Lady Gwendolyne blinked her eyes; Greyson thought he could see tears gathering in them.

"Mother, do you suppose it was Dr. Bergeron who suggested surgery for me?"

His mother shrugged, releasing her hold on him. She stuffed one more chocolate into her mouth, another waiting in her hand.

Greyson sighed. "Might I leave a note for Father? Explaining some of my suspicions?" Leaving messages for his father was turning into a habit.

She nodded and pointed with a chocolate-smeared finger to the small escritoire in the corner.

Lifting the cover, Greyson found neat stacks of scented paper, and both black and red ink pots. Choosing a wide nib, he wrote a quick note to Sir Stanley, explaining his doubts about the validity of Dr. Bergeron's business, and that making it known he was an investor might be detrimental to his health.

He waved the note dry, folded it precisely, and closed the ink pot.

"Shall I ask Wallace to give it to him?"

Lady Gwendolyne nodded. Tears tracked down her cheeks, leaving lines of unpowdered skin.

"Don't worry too much, Mother. I'm sure Father will be fine. It is only a suspicion I have, hardly fact."

She nodded and sniffed, swallowing the sweets in her mouth. "You'd best be going dear, before Wilroy sees me crying. He's sure to blame you."

"Yes, Mother." He pulled the cord and Wallace appeared. The butler must have been waiting in the hall. "I'll need my things, please."

"Yes, sir." Wallace bowed and left.

Greyson stooped to kiss his mother, patting her on the shoulder. "No need for tears, yet." He offered his handkerchief.

She took it and wiped her eyes and nose. "Of course." She squeezed his hand. "Do be careful, Greyson. I don't want anything dire happening to you, either."

"I shall strive to remain healthy."

Wallace brought his things, holding his jacket out for him to thread his arms through.

"Wallace, please make sure my father gets this." Greyson held out the note. "It is for him only."

"Certainly, sir."

"Thank you." Greyson took his hat and cane and left, grimacing once he'd reached the front step and the wide doors closed behind him. He hadn't gotten around to asking his mother if she knew Dr. M.

Quillian's Log

So, Greyson solved it - though I am taking part of the credit. I certainly helped him. I'm thinking about my future, and I've decided I would like Greyson to be part of it. A big part if I have any say.

And I've been considering a new line of work. Something Greyson and I could do together. I think we make a very good team.

And there are lots of plots and schemes out there that take advantage of the lowers.

Someone needs to put a stop to it.

45

Quillian blinked at Ralph and the young man that stood behind him. "This is Hank?"

"Yes'm. It surely is." Ralph's smile split his face.

The young man, his black curls glinting, nodded and gripped his cap tight.

"But I thought..."

"I can swim, miss. Ever since I was little. When that bloke hit me in the head and pushed me in, I jes' played dead when I hit the water and let meself sink."

Shifting to one end of the garden bench, Quillian patted the seat next to her, though Ralph had to elbow his friend so that he'd sit. "Do you know the man who pushed you?"

"No'm. But he wore a policeman's uniform."

Constable Dumphries. Who else could it have been?

"And the woman you were talking to?"

"I don't know her name, jes' that she were older and dyed her hair. She was wantin' to know what I was doin' in the market. I tol' her I was fetching something for my girl, and showed her the flowers. I don' think she believed me, and when I saw yer yellow thingy, I jes' ran."

Quillian nodded. She believed the young man. She would have panicked, too, if she were in the same situation.

"Can you tell me anything about your girl's master? Did the little boy have his surgery?"

"Yes'm, he did. That's one reason I thought to ask Ralph to bring me here. I thought you needed to know." The twisted cap would never fit right on Hank's head again.

Watching Ralph hunt with Patch, Quillian took a deep breath. "Hank, do you think…?" She couldn't voice the question, her stomach knotted to tight and her throat constricted with it.

"Yes'm, I think Ralph was supposed to donate his arm. The woman was asking about where to find Ralph. That she'd seen us together in the market and had a job for 'im."

Quillian shot her gaze to the young man's face. His warm brown gaze was trained on the younger boy.

Hank faced her, his eyes wet. "He don' know, but he's me half bruvver."

Nodding, Quillian sighed and turned back to watch Ralph and Patch. This whole mess was getting more complicated all the time.

"Do you know where he had the surgery done?" It hadn't been here, by Dr. M. And from the accounts in the paper, Dr. Bergeron had already been deceased. Had Constable Dumphries been able to drag another doctor into his scheme?

"Don' know that. But I overheared the master talking to Mr. Chambers, whats wife runs the big fundraiser ever' year for the kiddy hospital." Hank flapped his cap to straighten out the wrinkles. "Mr. Chambers came 'round quite a bit afore the surgery. Kept looking at me girl, too, looking her over like 'e was buying a dog or a horse."

"Oh, Hank, where is she now?"

"At the house, taking care of the kid. But she's staying right there, all the time. Master won't let her go out without two or three men with her."

So, it seemed the master of the house suspected something, too. Or he knew the whole of it. And yet, he had let some other child suffer? Quillian sucked in a breath. Would she sacrifice a stranger for someone she loved?

Turning to Hank, she grabbed his hand in her right one, squeezing to keep his attention. "Make certain she does just that, Hank. And if you can, convince her to leave that employ. There's nothing that would stop Mr. Chambers from forcing her employer to let her out alone just so he can have his thugs get to her. He's got something to use against him now." That's what Constable Dumphries had tried to do with Dr. M. "Go, now. Both of you get out of town if you can." Quillian waved him to the gate.

"If I leave, can I take Ralphie wit' me?"

Quillian glanced at the younger boy, half-way up the apple tree. "I'll have him ready to go when you get back."

From the journal of G. J. Holmes

My relationship with my father has always been tenuous. I fear I was a great disappointment for him after Jacoby and Wilroy, both strapping lads that could sport about with the best of the best.

My ailments were always a sore spot for him, one he rarely mentioned when other men were about, and fussed at my mother whenever she fussed over me.

He used to tell her she would turn me into a girl one day.

46

Greyson sat in the chair in his room, the lamp positioned just so behind his chair so that the light fell to illuminate the book on his lap. It was a political pamphlet extolling the benefit of allowing Neo-Virginian's to purchase slaves from Carolinia as indentured servants.

Usually, the plight of Carolinia's slave population was of great interest to Greyson, and this pamphlet was new, providing fresh propaganda for an upcoming vote to Neo-Virginia's laws, but he could not concentrate on the words.

His father had responded to his note. It was unexpected, this adult back and forth with his parent. For the first time, he felt his father was seeing him as someone other than a disabled, disappointing son.

The note stated Father had information that could assist in Greyson's inquiries. That was not unexpected. But his offer to share that information? Father would be very interested in bringing about the downfall of those he perceived to be responsible for the failure of one of his investments. Greyson just hadn't thought his father would actually involve him.

Something hit his windowpane.

Greyson looked to the window, black from the night outside, framed by simple blue curtains. Was a storm coming, bringing hail or hard rain? Listening, he heard nothing, so he went back to his book.

There was another ping against the pane.

Frowning, Greyson rose from the chair and approached the window. Four stories below, standing in a circle of light from a gas lamp, stood Quillian. She must have caught sight of him in the window, because she waved with her good hand and motioned for him to come down, then stepped back into the alley's shadows.

Why was Quillian here?

Greyson didn't dwell on the question. Before it had fully formed in his brain, he'd grabbed his shoes and shoved his feet inside, picked up his room key and left, locking the door behind him. No one else was in the uppermost hall. The next floor down—the private rooms for the working girls—was quiet as Greyson passed by the back stair. The next floor was the working floor, and muffled laughter and grunts still echoed. Greyson was careful passing this floor; he wanted none of Madame's clients to see him, and possibly recognize him. He was getting along with his parents and wanted to do nothing that might change that.

On the main floor, where the entertainment parlor and bar were housed, as well as the offices of Miss Emily, Dr. Brown and the head footmen, laughter drifted from the front. Greyson looked left, then took a breath, and looked left again. There was nothing to his right, but the back door, which he needed to get through to meet with Quillian outside.

The door was flanked by two doormen, but not yet barricaded for the night, which meant there were still clients in residence. Greyson did not want to be locked out, but he did not want anyone to know he was going out. He supposed it couldn't hurt to let the doormen know—if he was nonchalant about it, maybe they wouldn't think it odd or unplanned, and simply let Madame know he was out when it was time.

Nodding, smiling, Greyson glided past the doormen, meeting the gaze of the one to his left and opened the doors. The two men asked no questions, but nodded back.

Once outside, Greyson let out a pent-up breath and looked around for Quillian.

"Qui-Miss Watson?" He called out, but did not yell. Madame's outdoor guards were on high alert for any unusual sound and he did not relish being mistaken for a thug and thrown to the ground for a beating.

When there was no answer, Greyson took another step down the back stairs, keeping well into the light shed by the lamps. "Miss Watson? Where are you? Why are you here?"

Greyson moved no farther than the bottom step, his stomach tightening in nerves. He was certain it had been Quillian. The lamp light had glittered on auburn curls and the female figure had kept her left hand close to their body, throwing the pebbles with their right hand.

"Miss Watson, if you do not answer, I am going back inside." Anger sharpened his tone and his voice rose.

"I'm right here. Sorry, someone came along and I had to hide." Quillian's freckled face peeked out from a hoary bush.

"Miss Watson! What are you doing here?" Greyson advanced toward her, crossing the alley to join her at the bush.

"You might as well call me Quillian. And you really ought to let me call you by your first name as well, Greyson."

Greyson sighed. "Fine." He put as much sarcasm in his voice as he could manage. He did not really want her to know how much he'd been wanting the privilege of using her given name—and of hearing his from her.

"Good. I have news, and I thought you might want to know."

"Indeed. Tell me."

Quillian stepped into the alley, her glance darting left and right. "Promise you won't tell Huddy I was here?"

"Like the woman would listen to me anyway. She's most like to stab first, ask questions later."

"She's not that bad, Greyson."

Greyson shivered. He quite enjoyed hearing his name on her lips. "What is the news?"

"Well, I had a visitor today. Hank came back from the dead."

"Hank? What, Ralph's friend that went belly up in the river."

Quillian nodded. "Seems a policeman—or a man wearing a policeman's uniform anyway—bashed his head and shoved him in the river."

"Constable Dumphries."

"That's what I think, too. Anyway, seems Hank can swim, and played dead so he could get away."

"I see." Greyson paced across the narrow alley and back. "How do we know he's telling the truth?"

"We don't. Except my gut says he is. And the boy, in Portsmouth, that needed a new arm?" Quillian stood close and Greyson almost forgot what they were talking about. "He got it."

"He got it?" Greyson blinked and concentrated. "But where was the surgery done? Dr. Bergeron was already dead."

Smirking, Quillian leaned even closer. "It seems Mr. Chambers, whose wife does the fundraising for the children's hospital, has been frequenting the boy's house."

"Chambers." Greyson's stomach cramped. He knew that name.

"What?" Quillian clutched his arm.

"My father mentioned that name. Damn." Jerking away, Greyson stalked the alley.

"Anyway, there's more."

"More?" Greyson whirled to face her.

She nodded. "Hank says he's Ralph's half-brother. And that's why he wanted to talk to us. He thought Ralph might be in trouble. A donor, so to speak. And it seems that Mr. Chambers has been sizing up his girl, too."

"So, it's still not over."

"Doesn't seem that way."

"Damn. I need to think." He'd gotten nothing from his father so far about the business. Should he go back and ask in person? It would be late, but the footman on watch would let him in, wake Wallace, and Wallace would wake his father. Wilroy was likely at a gaming hall or brothel—nowhere near the house. "Let's go."

Greyson grabbed Quillian's good hand and tugged her along the alley.

"Go where? Greyson, it's too late to go anywhere." She resisted his tugging. "Besides, I have more to tell you."

"Talk while we walk."

"I told you, it's too late to go anywhere."

"We're going to my father. We need to ask him questions about Chambers."

"Can we at least ask Madame about using her steamcar?"

Greyson stopped his head long rush and turned to look down at Quillian. "Yes. I guess that would be a good idea."

"She might even want to come along."

The thought of talking both Quillian and Madame to his father's house was the most ridiculous thing he'd ever heard. He grinned. "Let's do it."

Rounding about, he dashed back to the service door of the brothel and bounded up the steps, shoving the door open. Quillian followed, though just a bit slower and protective of her left hand.

Once inside, Greyson sprinted to Madame's private parlor, pounding on the door for entry.

The door opened to reveal a wide-eyed Madame. "What on Earth?"

"We need your car, Madame. I need to speak to my father right away."

"Of course, Mr. Holmes. But who are we?" Madame stepped back into the room to tug the cord that would summon a footman.

"Quillian and I."

"Quillian? Is she here?" Madame leaned forward, peering out into the hall.

"Yes, Madame, I am."

"Quillian!" Grinning, the woman swept out and wrapped her arms around the girl.

Quillian reciprocated with a one-arm hug, her left hand still clutched tight to her side.

"Oh, Baby! How are you doing?" Madame let go and stepped back, cupping Quillian's cheeks with both hands.

"Better." Quillian flushed, but offered a small smile.

"Madame," Greyson thought it best to remind her of his urgency, "I really need to get to my father."

Panic flooded his system. What if his father had read his note and started to ask questions? Dr. Bergeron hadn't committed suicide. Would whoever killed him make an attempt on Sir Stanley if they thought he had figured too much out?

"Calm yourself, Greyson." Madame released Quillian's visage and raised her voice. "Johnson, are you coming?"

"Yes, Madame." The footman's voice was muffled from down the hall.

"Please prep the car. We're going for a drive."

"Yes, Madame."

47

The Hague was quiet, quite normal for the gentrified community when approaching midnight. The gas globes emitted their light in wide safe circles on the empty street. Madame's steamcar stopped in front of number 131 and Greyson hopped out, barely remembering to act the gentleman and hold the door open for Quillian and Madame.

"Go ahead. I've got this." Johnson jogged around the back and grabbed the door, letting Greyson sprint off up the steps to clang the knocker against the door.

"He's worried." Madame stood, gripping the top of the door until her cane was secure in the cobles.

"I think he's scared that his father asked questions." Quillian agreed, gripping Madame's arm, not certain if it was to steady the older woman or to soothe her own nerves.

She was going to meet Greyson's parents. What if they didn't like her? Did it matter?

Johnson closed the car door and offered Madame his arm to ascend the steps. Quillian trailed, her eyes on Greyson.

The young man stood before the wide doors, dropping the doorknocker, only to pick it back up again and again. His feet tapped the stop step, and his unused hand drummed against his thigh. He wore no jacket, only his shirt, and his suspenders fell about his hips.

Quillian had never seen him so disheveled.

The door opened and Greyson started back. "Wilroy? Why aren't you at your club?"

"What are you doing here?"

"I've come to see Father." Greyson ducked under his brother's arm and darted into the house. "Father!"

"What the-?" Wilroy would have slammed the door but Johnson got there first, wedging himself in.

"It's bloody important we see the guvnor." The footman stared at Wilroy.

"He's busy."

"Busy?" Greyson rounded on his brother. "At this hour? What do you mean busy?"

The elder Holmes was well known for an early night after his glass of port and Cuban cigar.

"He has a business visitor." Wilroy crossed his arms over his puffed-out chest.

"Indeed?" Greyson spun in the hall, marching down its length to burst through a door on the right. "Father, I need to speak with you-"

His words cut off and Quillian heard a deep silence, followed by a blast of sound. Greyson was thrown back from the door to collide with the wall across from it, knocking a mirror to the floor to shatter into shards.

Someone screamed on an upper floor, and thudding footfalls reverberated on the floors.

"Damn." Wilroy dropped his crossed arms and ran for the front of the house, scrambling out the doors and away into the dark.

Quillian ignored him and rushed to Greyson, who still crouched on the floor.

Johnson grabbed someone running from the room, tackling him to the floor and sitting on him.

"Let me go. You do not know who you are dealing with!"

Helping Greyson regain his feet, Quillian looked at the man struggling on the floor. He was dressed in a fine tuxedo, his top hat rolled off his head to show a head of thinning gray hair.

"But I do." Madame stepped forward, setting the tip of her cane against the man's forehead, pressing his skull to the floor. "Montgomery Chambers."

"What the bloody hell?" Sir Stanley staggered in the door frame. "What is going on?"

"I'm not certain, Father." Greyson stood on his own and faced his sire. "I came to speak with you and Wilroy was home and when I opened the door..." He waved a hand at the debris.

"Stanley?" A querulous voice called from above. "Stanley, are you alright?"

"Come down, Gwen. Come down." Sir Stanley leaned against the wall, his own suit rumpled and askew. Then he whispered. "Someone tried to shoot me."

"What?" Greyson stepped to his father and wrapped his arms around him.

Sir Stanley patted his son's back. "If I'd drunk my port like usual, probably would have succeeded."

"Why didn't you drink your port?"

"Your high blood pressure regimen. The regimen you recommended to me....it recommended cutting back on alcohol."

Greyson released his father and took a step back just as his mother came tittering down the hall, all pale pink nightgown and negligee. The older woman fell into her husband's arms, weeping.

Quillian stared at the man trapped on the floor. She recognized him, having seen his image in many nightmares. In that instant, she knew why he'd been an inhabitant of those dark dreams. In that instant, she knew a lot she hadn't known, hadn't remembered.

Johnson looked up from his seated position on the man's chest. "Shall I summon the police?"

"No." Madame tapped her cane on the man's forehead, making him wince and suck in a breath. "I dare say the police would only let him go. I'm sure he has them deep in his pockets."

"You have no idea." The man spat the words out, glaring up at them. "I own them. Every last one."

"Do you?" Magistrate Wallace asked the question from the still-open front door. Dr. M stood beside him, dressed neatly in a grey suit, his hair brushed, his magnifying monocle nowhere on his face. "I think I'd like to know more about that, Mr. Chambers."

"Magistrate Wallace!" The man scurried to flip over, Madame allowing this by raising her cane from where it held him down and nodding at Johnson to let him up. "Have these people arrested for assault!"

"In their own home?" The Magistrate raised his brows and looked to Sir Stanley. "Sir Stanley, what would you prefer?"

"I would prefer this man hanged. He tried to kill me." Sir Stanley shushed his wife and propelled her into Greyson's embrace. "Come see my favorite chair. The whole back's been blasted apart."

The Magistrate strode forward, glancing into the decimated room. "Chambers?"

"Well, I...I..."

"Hmmm?' Magistrate Wallace turned to Madame. "And you, madam, what would you have me do?"

Madame's jaw clenched and her nostrils flared.

"You can't ask her, Wallace. She's nothing but a dirty whore."

"Be mindful, Chambers. Madame's establishment pays her taxes on time, which is more than I can say about yours."

Montgomery Chambers swallowed hard and his glance darted from one person to another. Dr. M remained behind him, near the door, making flight impossible.

"You, girl. I haven't done you any harm." The man jabbed a finger in her Quillian's direction.

"You haven't?" Quillian's voice was soft and her gaze fixed on the stuttering man. "Have you forgotten what you did? I haven't. Not anymore." Her voice cracked.

Madame gasped and lurched when her cane slid on the tile. "Quillian, no." She reached for the girl, fingers clutching her right shirtsleeve.

"And now, I have this," Quillian raised her mechanical arm, "thanks to you. What more do you think I'll let you take from me? Not my mother," she motioned to Madame, who paled at the identifying word, "not my employer," she motioned to Dr. M, who nodded at her, "and certainly not my friend." Lastly, Quillian jerked her head toward Greyson, who struggled to keep his mother in an upright position.

"You've taken an awful lot from me, probably even more than I know. I shan't let you take anything more." Quillian raised Madame's mini-cannon and leveled it at Montgomery Chambers, her mechanical fingers jerking in response to her natural fingers curling around the handle and trigger. "You can either start talking, or I'll put cannon shot through your brain, just as you tried to do to Sir Stanley. And I won't even bother trying to make it look like suicide."

"Talk, why would I talk? Go ahead and put a hole in my head." The man tossed his head, sticking his chin toward the ceiling. "No way I'm going to gaol. The only person that could identify me is dead."

So, Taggage was gone for good. And Constable Dumphries had never met with him. They could get him for what he'd done here—but what had he done? A good solicitor would probably get him off in a misunderstanding argument.

Quillian tightened her fingers on the mini-cannon, squinting to keep her focus on the horrible man in front of her. She wanted to put a hole in his head—no, she wanted to blow it clean off. But she couldn't.

She lowered the weapon and sobbed.

Greyson released his mother back to his father and stepped forward, pulling Quillian to him and holding her to his chest. Magistrate Wallace unwrapped her fingers from the mini-cannon and pulled it out of her grasp.

Montgomery Chambers snickered.

Magistrate Wallace, brown eyes narrowed in an ever-reddening pale freckled face, raised the mini-cannon and shot him through the temple.

Quillian's Log

I'd never met Magistrate Wallace before, not even seen a photo of him in the newspaper. Dr. M always kept them away. I'd never understood why, and now, well...maybe it makes sense.

To him anyway.

Just months ago, I didn't remember my mother. But now, after memories erupting and blooming in my brain, I know it's Madame.

But this...

It is a sudden jolt to watch a man shoot someone in the head, and be told that he is your father.

E. G. Gaddess

www.ingramcontent.com/pod-product-compliance
Lightning Source LLC
Chambersburg PA
CBHW070427170726
48291CB00002B/390